MURPHY'S FAULT

MURPHY'S FAULT

A MYSTERY

Steven Womack

St. Martin's Press
New York

Although the city of New Orleans is a real city, all of the characters and events in this story are fictitious and bear no resemblance to any actual happenings or to any real persons, whether living or dead.

Library of Congress Cataloging-in-Publication Data

Womack, Steven.
   Murphy's fault / Steven Womack.
      p.   cm.
   "A Thomas Dunne book."
   ISBN 0-312-03896-8
   I. Title.
PS3573.0576M87   1990
813'.54—dc20   89-27138
                                                             CIP

10 9 8 7 6 5 4 3 2

This book is for two women who have graced my life:

Ethel Hawkins Womack, my grandmother, a truly grand lady. I've tried to learn her lessons well, but I'm still working on that patience stuff. . . .

Cathy Yarbrough, who continues to love and laugh with me, through the good stuff and the bad. All writers should fall in love with a psychologist. . . .

Man is conceived in sin and born in corruption, and he passeth from the stink of the didie to the stench of the shroud. . . .

—Robert Penn Warren

Acknowledgments

Bear with me, please, while I remember some people who have been important in this process.

I'm deeply indebted to my editor, Ruth Cavin, and to Tom Dunne, both at St. Martin's Press, for their support, encouragement, and guidance.

Same goes for Bob Robison. We've had some interesting times together. No doubt the future will hold more of them.

My thanks also to Jeris Bragan, Woody Eargle, and Bill Eliott for their inspiration and support and guidance. They're all talented writers whose work will someday, I hope, get them Executive Clemency.

And to all my film writing buddies at Tennessee State University, thanks for keeping me sane and interested and still passionate about the art of storytelling. Especially dear to me are Barbara Holder, Jan Parrish Hendon, Bill Stewart, Anne Taylor, and Stephen Schaller.

Some twelve years ago, when I was struggling with the first draft of this book, Melanie Redler quite literally kept me from starving. That time still lives fondly in my memory, and I owe her a lot.

MURPHY'S FAULT

One

It was all that sonofabitch Murphy's fault.

This all really started—if you go back long enough—nearly ten years ago. Back about the time I first met him. Murphy was the mayor's executive assistant then. Murphy and the mayor were both tied in with the Old Man, by virtue of the Old Man bankrolling the mayor in his bid for office. Murphy managed the successful campaign and, after the election, became the mayor's right-hand man.

There was a longshoremen's strike that summer that paralyzed the city. It went on for weeks. When the Port of New Orleans shuts down, people hurt bad. The shipping companies were losing money like crazy; the city was losing port taxes and fees; all kinds of people were out of work; there were riots down by the docks.

Things were very tense.

At the Old Man's suggestion, the mayor finally decided he'd had enough. He told Murphy to settle the strike one way or another, using any means necessary. Just get the damn thing over with. In an uncharacteristic display of intestinal fortitude, Murphy went down to the docks personally, where the longshoremen had set up picket lines and barricades. It must have been funny to see Murphy, even then an enormously fat man who appeared to be in the grip of a terminal heat rash, walk up to the union representative, with his gangster bodyguards surrounding him, and tell him the strike was over.

"You're finished," Murphy was supposed to have told the man. "It's time to sit down and get this settled."

Murphy was aided by the squad of helmeted, riot-squad police behind him who were just itching for a chance to break some heads. The union representative, seeing that he was outnumbered and outgunned, decided to acquiesce to Murphy's suggestion. Then Murphy went before the bargaining representatives of the shipping companies and told them that if they didn't reach an agreement with the strikers, he was going to call off the police. By the time the governor could get the National Guard down there, Murphy warned, there wouldn't be enough of the docks left to roast a hot dog over.

Management agreed to sit down with the strikers. Within a week, the port was back in operation.

Murphy pulled it off in high style. The mayor, the Old Man, even the governor, congratulated him for settling the strike. The mayor and the council decided to throw a huge celebration in one of the most expensive restaurants in town. Everyone who was anyone was there.

It turned out to be the social event of the season for the overfed politicos. The union boys and the company boys were there as well, all slapping each other on the back and congratulating each other. Now they could return to the serious business of getting rich off their customers, the union members, the city. Whatever it took.

The party went on all night. I've seen the pictures and even the Old Man, who never drinks or goes to parties, had a drink in his hand, a cutie under his arm, and a smile on his face. The mayor was there, with the Old Man on his right and Murphy on his left, toasting each other over their victory.

It was plush and expensive. It would have been a grand event, except for the one big mistake the V.I.P.s made: they charged it all off to the city.

The newspapers had a field day with that one. TAXPAYERS PAY FOR HONCHO'S PARTY, the headlines read. $12,500 FOR MAYOR'S GOOD TIME! Overnight, a couple of small-time city hall reporters became avenging angels.

I was a newspaperman myself back then, only for a different newspaper. We didn't print that story. I knew about it. Hell, everybody did. But we didn't print it because we knew the Old Man would blow a cork over it. After all, he signed our checks.

Well, kind of. In fact, the Old Man had never met any of us. He'd bought the paper on a fluke a few years earlier because he got tired of what the regular newspapers were saying about him. He never even bothered to drop by to visit his latest acquisition. I can't blame him; it wasn't much of a newspaper.

The Old Man was out for blood. He just plain didn't like what the other newspapers said about him and his buddies. He decided to hit back.

Sally Bateman, who back then had the title Business Manager to go with her secretary's salary, took his call.

"Christ almighty," she said to me, since I was the only reporter who'd bothered to show up on time that morning. "Get over there fast."

I crossed the street to the Old Man's bank and took the elevator up to his suite of offices on the twentieth floor. Madge Kelly, the receptionist who's been there since day one, asked me who I was.

"I'm from the newspaper," I said, half scared to death.

"Get on in there," she ordered. "He's been waiting for

you. Go down the corridor, make a right, then another right. His office is at the end."

"Yes, ma'am," I said.

"By the way," she added, "if you want to come out with your jaw in one piece, you'd better put out that cigarette. Mr. Jennings doesn't allow smoking."

"Oh, I didn't know."

"Yeah, well," she snapped. "You do now."

I walked down the corridor, past the framed pictures, citations, paintings, autographs. There was even a citation from Harry Truman, thanking Mr. Jennings for his contribution to the war effort. I'd always heard the Old Man made a fortune off the war.

In spite of my nervousness, I found myself fascinated by this place that reeked of power. It was my first inside look at how shakers and movers really work; I've been enamored of the process ever since.

"I'm from the paper, Mr. Jennings," I said, stepping through the open door of his office. "You wanted to see me?"

An acrid taste came into my mouth. My hands were cold and sweaty and I could feel my toes curling up in my cheap, scuffed shoes. I was only twenty-five years old at the time, and not that far out of college. I was in way over my head.

"Sit down," he yelled, in what I would learn over the years was his normal speaking voice. "Listen!"

He proceeded to bellow and stamp and pace the thick carpet behind his huge desk, which was cluttered with stacks of papers and files and what to me looked like junk.

His eyes rolled and the shocks of white hair that seemed to sprout from his head like an uncontrollable growth shook. He told me what sons of bitches those reporters were and how they were using this as an excuse to embarrass him and his friends, after all he'd done for this city.

"If it was up to me," he yelled, "they'd all rot in hell!"

I sat and made notes and nodded my head. Midway through the tirade, I noticed the framed cartoon hung on the wall behind his desk. The same drawing hangs there still today. It was of a comical little character with a fierce scowl on his face and a menacing fist raised. Under the drawing, in bold 72-point type, hung the caption SUE THE BASTARDS!

It was then, I think, that I got my first indication of what working for the Old Man was going to be like.

He told me what he wanted me to do. Write an editorial, he said, an editorial that would blast all those idiots to the nether regions, make them look like fools, shut them up for good.

"We'll run it on the front page," he yelled. "In a box. And we'll have extra copies printed and give them away free on the street."

I was not inclined to do this. I've never been very fond of politicians anyway, especially ones who bill the public for parties that the public hasn't been invited to. On the other hand, this was my first decent job. I'd just gotten married the year before, a marriage that's long since fallen by the wayside, and I really couldn't afford to be out on the streets again.

So I did it. I pulled down my pants, bent over, and spread my legs.

And I wrote the best damn piece of propaganda this town had seen in a long time. A Bourbon Street hooker couldn't have pulled it off better.

All the bigwigs, I wrote, had put in long, hard, overtime hours without pay trying to settle the strike. They deserved the party, which after all was really for the people of our fair city and not just the fatcats. The cost of the party would be made up in about ten minutes worth of port revenues, I wrote, and to deny these men the celebration "they so richly deserved" was not only cheap and petty, it was unprofessional and irresponsible journalism as well.

It was a masterpiece of bovine effluent.

The Old Man and his gang loved it. The paper got

phone calls, letters, telegrams. All of the Old Man's cronies, including Murphy, the mayor, and four out of the nine city councilmen the Old Man owned, called. Everybody was happy. I got a small bonus in my paycheck that week, a little something extra they call "lagniappe" down here. Later, when the Old Man shut the paper down, he offered me a job.

That's how I became director of public relations for the First Interstate Bank of Louisiana.

Now let's face it, the director of public relations for a bank simply doesn't have a hell of a lot to do. Press releases on promotions, quarterly reports, annual reports, and making sure the really juicy stuff never gets into the papers is about it. Sally, who came along with me from the newspaper as my secretary, handles most of it herself, leaving me for the more oddball sorts of jobs the Old Man keeps coming up with. And there have been plenty of those over the past ten years. Despite his yelling, I'm not frightened to enter the Old Man's office anymore. In fact, I'm one of the few bank officers who can usually get in to see him without calling first.

The day it all hit the fan began as a typically hot day in August. I drove to work with the top down on the MG I'd picked up cheap from a friend of the Old Man's who owned a car dealership in one of the outlying parishes. I pulled into my reserved spot in the bank's parking lot and ambled across the street, up the sidewalk to the front entrance of the bank, and stopped off at the newsstand to pick up a paper and a pack of smokes.

I was late again, but due to an advanced case of cocktail flu, I just couldn't make myself move any faster.

Inside the building, I said good morning to several people as I walked through the bank lobby toward the row of elevators.

"Good morning, Mr. Lynch." The redheaded teller behind the brass bars of teller cage nine had been flirting with me for weeks, and ordinarily I'd have taken her up on it. But I hadn't been in the mood lately.

"Morning, Mistuh Lynch," Billy Patterson said. He'd been a security guard at the bank for so long he could barely remember having all his teeth. I liked Billy. He was old and wrinkled and seemed to be swallowed up by his blue bank guard's uniform. But he was there every day, all day, standing in the same spot, watching over his empire. He was steadier and more dependable than people half his age.

"Morning, Billy," I answered, stepping into one of the polished brass elevators. The Old Man insisted on polished brass and uniformed operators wearing white shirts and black bow ties, gleaming wing tips, and black pants with a blue stripe running down each leg. Real class.

I took the elevator up to the sixth floor, then walked down the hall and through the frosted glass door that had my name and title hand-painted at eye level.

"Good morning, my dear," I said to Sally. She sat behind her cluttered desk in a bright summery dress looking lovely. She often looked lovely to me. Especially today.

"Well, well. I was wondering if you were coming in before noon."

"You know how I hate to get up early," I said, pulling off my jacket. "Besides, it's only ten-thirty."

"Explain that to Mr. Jennings. He's been screaming down here for you since eight."

"Really? What's he want?"

"What am I, a mind reader? You just better get your ass up there, that's all."

"That's what I like most about you, darling," I said, pulling my jacket back on. "You make it so easy to get through the morning."

"Morning, hell," I heard her mutter as I closed the door behind me. "Morning was over an hour ago."

There was truth in what I'd told her; she did make it easy to get through the mornings—sometimes too easy. A plain, unvarnished prettiness, high cheekbones, light blue eyes, and delicate cat's mouth that held a row of perfect teeth—over the years I found myself looking forward more and more to having her there when I got in every morning. She would pour coffee for the two of us, light her own cigarette as I lit mine, brush her short brown hair behind her ears, and help me ease into the day.

Yet I'd never touched her; don't ask me why.

Sally knew the Old Man as well as I did. If he was as hot under the collar as she indicated, I was in for a long day. This was a prospect that, given my condition, was not a welcome one.

Once on the twentieth floor, I walked down the chilly hall under the bleakness of the fluorescent lights. My footsteps clicked off the tiles and echoed off the walls. Not a soul was in sight. Inside the main suite of offices, though, I found a swirl of activity. Madge was stationed in the middle of things behind her console, her red, close-cropped hair standing crazily up on her head, pencils stuck acutely behind ears, pink telephone messages flying about like confetti.

The Old Man had two kinds of women working for him: either the tough, weather-beaten type or soft, silky young things whose smooth curves and blank eyes spoke of sweetness beyond dreams. The tough ones ran things. The soft ones typed occasionally and always looked pretty. And they served as ego massagers for the Old Man and his battery of lieutenants, of which, I suppose, I am one.

Madge's deep black eyes glared out from under the shaggy hair. I wondered again, as I had for years, if Madge hated everybody or just me.

"What's up, Madge?" I asked.

"He's hot to trot today," she answered. "Better get in there."

"Had his spurs in you, huh?"

"Like a heart attack." She sighed.

I walked quickly down the hall, past all the stuff on the walls I never paid any attention to anymore, and stopped in front of his office. I could hear him yelling.

I stuck my head in; he motioned me to come in and sit down. His tie was pulled down to his second button. His jacket was off and thrown crazily across a chair. His armpits were stained with sweat.

"Screw him!" he yelled into the phone. "Everybody's bellyaching in the oil business! The only difference between a Texas oilman and a pigeon these days is that a pigeon can still make a deposit on a Mercedes!"

There was a long pause as I heard a hapless, muffled voice obviously making excuses for something through the handset.

"You tell him if he can't deliver for the price we agreed on, I'm going to buy him out and fire his ass! You got that?"

Another pause.

"Good!" The Old Man slammed the phone down before the last sound was out of his mouth. He swiveled around in his high-backed leather chair.

"The Houston pipe deal?" I asked.

"Yeah," he said, lowering his voice only a few decibels. "That bastard McClendon is trying to get out of the deal we cut. He told me he'd get that pipe stock to Malaysia cheaper than he really could just to get the business. Then he figured he'd just stick me up the butt with cost overruns. Only it ain't going to work because I got him by the short hairs."

Dumb ass, I thought. Did Buck McClendon really think he could pull that on the Old Man?

"That sonofabitch," he muttered, his eyes flickering over the pile of papers on his desk.

"Is that what all the excitement's about?"

"That?" he asked. "Hell, no. McClendon's a pissant. I'll squash him like a cockroach. I sent Charlie Fergusson over to Houston to handle him."

Fergusson was one of the Old Man's roving operatives. He went wherever there was trouble. One month he'd be at the oil fields in Malaysia, the next in Saudi Arabia, the next at the lumber mill in Canada. Then there was the occasional side trip to Houston to deliver a corrective interview.

"What is it, then?" I asked. "I hear you been yelling for me all morning."

"Yeah," he said, his dark, almost black eyes aimed at me like a sniper's rifle. "And just where the hell have you been? It's almost lunchtime."

"I had a rough one last night," I explained, telling him the stone cold truth. "I took me a little medicinal rest this morning."

He looked straight at me. We had this unspoken understanding between us. As long as I was up front with him, he handled it. The Old Man hated it when people lied to him. If I went and had too many scotch and sodas the night before, which just happened to be the truth in this case, all I had to do was tell him. He didn't like it, but he put up with it.

"Spare me the details," he said.

"Done."

"McClendon's not my worry today, Jack," he said, leaning back in the chair and throwing his hands behind his head. "We got us some real manure on our hands this time." His face tightened.

"What's up?"

There was a moment of silence as he attempted once again to bring the steam down and keep from blowing a valve.

"It's Murphy," he said. "He's decided to buck us on the Iris Project."

As soon as he said that, I understood just what was agitating him. Murphy was a greasy, lecherous, 300-pound hunk of smelly cheese with a taste for expensive brandy,

Cuban cigars, Lincoln Continentals, sweet young ladies—the younger the better—and polyester suits that kept the nervous sweats in so that by the end of the day you just about goddamn couldn't stand being around the sonofabitch.

Besides holding a pretty hefty chunk of stock in the Old Man's bank, he was also the civil sheriff now, a position that was more or less awarded to him after the then-mayor was retired by the mayor we have now, who is not owned by the Old Man and who wanted nothing to do with Murphy.

Smart fella.

Murphy actually had to run for the office, but with the Old Man and the most powerful political machine in the city behind him, that was just a formality. The office is mainly political and ceremonial anyway, a holdover from the days before the city police department became the real law enforcement agency. The civil sheriff's office takes care of foreclosures, evictions, and process serving. Nothing of consequence.

Murphy was also president of one of the strongest political organizations in the city, an eclectic group of old farts who called themselves the Dead Center Deer Hunters Club. Their annual venison feast was a gala evening of politicking, drunkenness, and gluttony.

They'd be a silly bunch of harmless bozos if it weren't for the fact that they had an absolute stranglehold on the 7th, 9th, and 14th wards, as well as the 12th Ward, which was the largest district in the city. Made up mostly of rednecks, yahoos, and future KKKers, the 12th Ward was vocal and powerful and dangerous. And Murphy held it in the palm of his fat, greasy hand.

The Old Man had always held Murphy in the palm of his hand. That is, it seems, until now.

"How's he trying to buck us?" I asked.

"The Iris Project. He wants it. Or at least a bigger chunk of it than he's ever going to get."

I drew a deep breath and settled back in the chair, longing for the cigarette I knew I couldn't have.

The Iris Project was the Old Man's code name for what could wind up being the biggest deal of his entire life; a life, I reminded myself, that had seen some pretty big deals. This was not only big money, it was power politics. Murphy interfering with the deal was the equivalent of a palace revolt.

Iris bordered the 12th Ward over near the river. In spite of its name, it wasn't a pretty place to be. And it was a dead certainty that no flowers as appealing as its name grew there.

Iris was ghetto, the poorest, roughest, cruelest ghetto in the city and one of the top ten or so worst places in the entire country. A grim, dark hellhole of poverty, dope, crime, disease, Iris was practically a war zone. It was the worst scar on a city full of scars, a city that worked hard to hide its dark side from the hustled tourists and conventioneers who kept so much of it alive.

The Iris Project—as the newspapers presented it, anyway—was a classic example of how good men, civic leaders and businessmen, could band together to clean up a city, remove blight, and improve the lives of those less fortunate than themselves.

And if you believe that, I've got some swampland down in Florida I want you to look at.

Sure, the ghetto would be razed, after all the poor people who lived there because they couldn't afford anything else were shipped off to some equally horrible place because they still couldn't afford anything else. Then the buildings would be blown to hell, bombed back to the Stone Age, and the whole area would be crisscrossed with pedestrian plazas, malls, convention halls, and, as the centerpiece of the whole project, another giant domed stadium.

Just what the world needs . . .

The land would soar in value from practically worthless to prime, urban American gentrified real estate. Whoever got in on the bottom floor of the new Iris would become fantastically rich beyond dreams. Wealth measured in baskets of double and triple digits followed by zeros and commas.

And guess who'd spent the last five years buying up the land at bargain basement prices?

"Boss," I said, "I don't understand. What's his problem? Murphy's office, which means Murphy, is going to make a fortune off the foreclosure and eviction fees. What's his gripe?"

"He's not happy with that," the Old Man said, nervously shifting in the chair and tugging at his crotch.

"How do you know he's not happy?"

"Because he's suing me!" he yelled. "The Twelfth Ward Homeowners Association is suing to stop the redevelopment project."

Heading the 12th Ward Homeowners Association was another of Murphy's hats.

"He controls those people," the Old Man fumed. "They do what he tells them to. They're claiming the traffic and the noise will ruin the character of the district. All that historical preservation crap."

"Ruin the character of the district?" I laughed. "You mean the rednecks will have to pull all those rusted-out pickup trucks down off the blocks in their front yards and haul them around back?"

The Old Man had already spent close to $50 million on development costs and land acquisition, and the real construction hadn't even started yet. He'd fought the city planning commission, the Environmental Protection Agency, the city engineers, the Tourist and Convention Commission, and several dozen other bureaucracies, special interest groups, and lunatic fringe organizations. The Old Man had greased an awful lot of palms. The deal was about to go through.

Apparently, he hadn't greased Murphy's enough.

"I don't believe it," I said.

"Believe it."

"He's after something," I offered. "The easiest thing would be to find out what it is and settle. Otherwise, they could drag it out for years. Plus the money and the rotten publicity."

"Publicity, hell! I don't care about the publicity. You know what bothers me, Jack? You know what really chafes me about this?"

"I got a feeling you're going to tell me."

"It's the fact that it's Murphy," he said wearily. "When I met him all those years ago, he was a punk. I gave him a job, then found him a better one. He was nothing. And now he's a big fat-ass. And he thinks he's big enough to take me on. That's gratitude for you."

"You know something, I don't think he's smart enough for this. Somebody's got to be behind him jerking his chain. Who's his lawyer?"

"Hell, I haven't even looked," the Old Man said, sitting up and shuffling through some papers. "My copy of the lawsuit is here somewhere."

He found a stapled pile of legal papers and handed them to me.

"Murphy's not real bright," I said. "But he's not stupid. He had to know as soon as he tried to pull a stunt like this you'd stomp him. He must have."

"You'd think it, wouldn't you? Maybe he figures I'm getting old. Well, he's wrong, Jack, and we're going to show that tub of lard what a crotchety old bastard and a gang of mental cripples can do to him."

He said that without any threat or emotion in his voice. It was a simple statement of fact.

"One of the things I've learned in all these years is to never worry about your enemies. They always want to see a stake through your heart. It's your friends you have to worry about. They're the ones who'll do you in. Even you could be one."

"If money was what I was after," I said absentmindedly, flipping through the pages, "I'd have made my move back when I was young enough to enjoy it."

"Hell, Jack," he said, "you're just a boy and don't know it."

"We've got to find something on him," I said.

"Like what?"

"There's that Kramer girl he keeps on the payroll at thirty thousand a year. I hear she's in his 'Special Services' department."

"He's probably covered his ass on that one," the Old Man said. "He's probably got several sets of books over there, too."

"Yeah, but it's worth a try. The only other thing I can think of is to find out who's behind him and go after that person. Well, I'll be damned."

"What? Who is it?"

"Jimmy—James—Herbert. Of Herbert and Bascomb."

"Yeah, I've heard of him. Good lawyer."

"The best," I said.

"You know him?" the Old Man asked.

"Yeah. He used to be my father-in-law."

Two

It's axiomatic in New Orleans politics that the true test of a man's strength and character is his lawyer. Powerful men got power lawyers; the rest had to settle for leftovers and the LSU graduates.

If Jimmy Herbert had lined up with Murphy on this one, we were in for a hell of a fight. It had been a few years, but I still carried him and his daughter around with me like so many old photos you haul around from one apartment to the other because you just don't have the heart to throw them away.

When I think of Katherine nowadays, I remember that great old W.C. Fields story. A woman accused him of being drunk and he came back with, "Yes, I'm drunk, but you're crazy; the difference is I'll be sober tomorrow and you'll be crazy for the rest of your life." Katherine wasn't crazy, though. She was just eternally pissed.

Still, I learned one thing from the marriage: Never marry a woman whose father is Superman. No matter what you do, she'll always consider you not quite good enough. My next wife, if there ever is one, will be the progeny of underachievers.

Ancient history, redux . . . Oh, well, so it goes. Life's a bitch and then you die.

"These two gentlemen would like to see you," Sally announced as I walked into the office.

They both rose. One wore brown pinstripes that accentuated his inability to put on enough weight to appear prosperous. The other clutched a battered brown briefcase that seemed out of place with his pressed blue seersucker suit. I don't ordinarily see people without an appointment, but just this once I needed something to distract me from my own thoughts.

"Okay, let's go into my office."

Sally gave me a look of exasperation. Like I said, I don't usually see people without an appointment.

They turned out to be drilling equipment salesmen who were trying to get to the Old Man through me. I gave them about five minutes, then discreetly reached under my center desk drawer and pressed a button that lights up a bulb on Sally's console: her signal to rescue me.

My phone rang. I reached for it.

"Hello," I answered.

"There are three tall, beautiful blondes out here who say if they don't have your body in the next five minutes they will simply die."

"Tell them I'll be right with them," I said crisply.

"Gentlemen," I said, lowering the phone into its cradle, "I'm afraid there's an urgent meeting I have to attend. If you'll excuse me."

The two guys bowed out as gracefully as they could, leaving a stack of brochures and advertising crap on my desk. Sally came into my office just as I was scraping all their stuff into the wastebasket.

"Okay, where are the three blondes?" I asked, as she sat down in one of the visitors' chairs and lit a cigarette.

"Got tired of waiting and left. You snooze, you lose."

"That's all right," I said, lighting up. "Two's my limit anyway."

"What did the boss want?"

"It's Murphy," I said, after a deep drag off the cigarette. "He's filed a lawsuit to stop the Iris Project."

Sally's face showed exactly what I expected: nothing.

"He doesn't think he can get away with it, does he? Mr. Jennings'll kill him."

"I don't know what he thinks. Why don't you call him up and ask him?"

"Just what's he suing for?"

I told her the whole story. She was already familiar with what was really going on with the Iris Project. We'd done most of the P.R. work on it.

"Can he win it?" Sally asked, lighting another cigarette with the butt of the old one. Sally smoked too much, even compared to me.

"I don't think the Old Man cares whether he wins it or not. It's the fact that he brought the damn suit in the first place."

"Mutiny?"

"Yeah, kind of."

"What does Carlton think?" she asked.

"I don't know. I've got to call him."

Carlton Smith was the closest thing to a spectacular lawyer the Old Man had. He toadied up to Mr. Jennings something awful, but when you got him in a courtroom, he could be a real wolverine.

"Carlton could tell you for sure," Sally said. "Who's Murphy's lawyer?"

"That's the rub. Murphy's got himself probably the best goddamn lawyer in town. James Herbert. He's getting on in years, but he's as sharp as the shell on a blue-point oyster."

"Sounds bad," she said.

"He used to be D.A. back in the early sixties."

"I was in grade school then. Christ, he must be an old geezer by now."

"Not so old he can't make life hell for us."

I leaned back. Having been mildly depressed most of my adult life, I was no stranger to the wave of uneasiness that drifted over me. I can't quite describe it, exactly, but I felt like a child who'd just done something terribly wrong and hasn't been caught yet. Only he knows it's coming, and sooner or later, there's going to be hell to pay.

She looked at me and gave me a smile that made things better. I flicked into fantasy mode for a second and then turned it off as quickly as I could. Gotta keep that stuff hammered down; after all, I be's a professional . . .

"This has been a shock to everyone." Carlton settled back in the chair behind his immense mahogany desk. His office had the smell of old leather and polished wood and decaying books, all mixed in with the aroma of the Turkish Specials he smoked. We'd worked together for years, protecting the Old Man's flanks as he went forth to do battle with his enemies. Like a couple of old warhorses, we enjoyed the contest and shared the booty. And the politics of it all was beyond our concern. But we'd never really gotten to know each other. I've never been to his house; we've never even had lunch together. He was a lot more than a casual acquaintance, but I couldn't really say he was a friend.

Kind of like most people in my life.

"How bad is it?"

"Lawsuits of this type are getting harder and harder to protect oneself against," Carlton said. "The courts are very sympathetic to the preservationists. There are parts of Iris that can be considered historical landmarks, no matter how fallen into disrepair."

"You think Murphy really wants to stop the project?"

"I doubt it," Carlton replied after a moment. "Knowing Mr. Murphy as I do, I doubt seriously he wants that. This is a bid for power, I'm afraid. A break with the boss. Perhaps Mr. Murphy is setting himself up to run for mayor."

"Murphy? Mayor?" I sputtered.

"Now, just consider. Do you think Mr. Jennings would ever support him? I think not. Mr. Murphy has gone as far as he can with the support of Mr. Jennings. He's breaking away on his own, severing connections. Painting himself as the neighborhood boy taking on the powers that be. And with the Twelfth Ward in his back pocket, Mr. Murphy could pull it off."

"Murphy's not smart enough for this," I said. "There's something here we aren't seeing."

"I couldn't agree more. I think Mr. Herbert, whom we both know has never been a great fan of Mr. Jennings, may have more to do with this than we suspect."

"So you think maybe Herbert's behind this?"

"Possibly." Carlton brought his right hand up to his forehead and gently rubbed his temples. His skin was shiny and translucent, the skin of someone who spent too much time inside and was getting on in years as well.

"What happens if Murphy pushes this?"

He moved his hand to smooth down his thinning hair. His fingers ran across his scalp as if he were trying to erase decades.

"Jack," he said slowly, lighting one of the foul-smelling cigarettes, "I'm afraid we may be in for a fight. We can delay him for a while, but if he pushes, he will sooner or later get his day in court. The delays will be costly and the publicity will kill us, even if we win."

"So we have to get Murphy to drop the suit," I concluded, in one of my customary flashes of brilliance.

"The sooner the better. We can bury him in paper for the time being. If we convince him to drop the suit, the newspapers and TV stations will soon forget about it.

"They have a tendency to do that, you know," he added, raising his eyebrows at the former newspaperman sitting across from him.

"Yes, Carlton," I said, as he leaned back in his chair and made the springs squeak like rusty hinges. "They do."

"Speed is of the essence, my boy, and of equal importance is discretion. No one must learn *why* Mr. Murphy drops the suit. That is where you come in."

He wasn't telling me anything I didn't already know, but I let him go on. He leaned forward and rested his elbows on the desk.

"You must find out what prompted Mr. Murphy to pursue this insane course, and you must convince him that it would be to his advantage to reverse it. Otherwise, my friend, we shall be locked in the stockade, fending off the savages."

"I was wondering if you were coming back," Sally said. "You eating lunch today?"

"Carlton and I had a lot to talk about."

"You must have," she said. "Carlton usually says what he has to, then kicks you out."

"Not this time," I said.

"I'm starved, let's go eat."

"Get somebody to catch the phones for us."

Sally picked up the phone and buzzed Madge.

"I don't feel like eating downtown," I said, as we walked toward the elevator. "Let's drive out to the lake and get some fish."

"I swear," Sally said as the door opened. "If you had to punch a time clock, you'd starve to death."

"One of the joys of being an executive."

"Bullshit," she muttered as we pushed into the lunchtime elevator crowd.

The midday rain was late in coming. This time of year in New Orleans, you can just about count on it raining twice a day: lunchtime and rush hour. But today was different.

Sally and I sweated in the heat as we climbed into the car. My shirt felt like a damp rag stuck to me. The ends of her hair were darkened and matted down on her skin.

I put the top down and we eased out into the traffic. Sally had an unlit cigarette hanging out of the left corner of her mouth.

"You going to smoke that or eat it for lunch?"

She ignored me. I turned on the radio and lit one myself. We limped along until we got to the nearest entrance ramp for the interstate, then I gunned the car and we shot out into the traffic.

Sally's hair flapped in the wind just over her collar. For a second, she looked like she was going to say something, only the whine of the engine and the wind was too loud. She hunched down in the seat and lit the cigarette.

The restaurant stood on the end of a pier overlooking the lake. We ordered fried catfish and a pitcher of beer. The waitress brought the pitcher, wet and steamy and cold, and we sat smoking and sipping on the huge mugs of beer.

Boats on the lake eased by slowly, their sails taut in the wind. Heat shimmered off the pavement outside. Inside, overhead fans struggled to move the air around as the smell of deep-fat fryers permeated the place.

It was a sleepy, hot afternoon in a southern town that fifty years ago would have shut completely down for a few hours in the noonday heat. But this is today and things move faster and nobody can afford to shut down for a second. And I wished I'd lived in the days when men wore real linen and seersucker suits and white Panama hats and the women wore starched cotton and everything didn't move so damned fast. Air-conditioning didn't exist then and people couldn't escape the heat and they were forced to slow down and not run around like banshees, looking for success and hoping the IRS doesn't find out, looking for love and hoping not to catch some awful, incurable disease from it all.

"You know," Sally said, "Murphy's got quite a reputation. I knew about the women, but I didn't know about the vacation home and all that stuff."

"Kind of makes you wonder how somebody can afford a three-story house in town and a condo down in Fort Lauderdale on forty-three grand a year, doesn't it?"

"What I want to know is why the mayor has let it go on for so long. He doesn't care for the boss very much either and it would've been a good way to get back at him."

"It ain't like the old days," I said. "But the mayor and the Old Man respect each other. The mayor's got more sense than to take him on direct."

"Never mud-wrestle with a pig, right?" she said. "You both get filthy and the pig likes it."

"Cute."

"What are you going to do?"

"Try and find out what got into him. What makes a man decide to risk his place on the gravy train? If Murphy'd lay off the booze and lose about a hundred pounds, he'd live to be a rich old man. What we have to do is find out what made him decide to risk that. Then we take away the reason."

"It sounds to me like we're going to be kind of busy the next few weeks."

"Yeah," I answered. "I hope you don't have any hot dates planned for the near future."

"Right," she said. "I'll make sure that my dance card's clear."

I hung around the office until shortly before seven, trying to slog my way through paperwork, proofs, and cover designs for the upcoming annual report. It was hard to concentrate, though, and I mostly just sat, staring and thinking.

Finally, I took the elevator down to the main lobby. Everything was closed, but the clean-up people were there along with a couple of the night security guards. Over in the corner, I spotted Billy and waved to him.

He trotted over, his head bobbing like a cork float in a speedboat's wake.

"Don't see you around here this late very often, Mistuh Jack," he said.

"Believe it or not, Billy, I had work to do. I may be putting in a few late nights over the next few weeks."

"Well, good." His head bobbed faster. "We're always glad to see you, Mistuh Jack."

"Maybe we'll sneak upstairs and have a drink sometime," I kidded.

Billy broke out laughing. "We better not do that. You know how Mistuh Jennings feels about drinking on the job."

"He's told me several times," I said, as Billy unlocked the front door and held it open for me.

Billy was still laughing as I made my way up the sidewalk.

The parking lot attendant had raised the top on my car before the afternoon rains came. There was a slight summer night's chill in the air after the long hot day. I drove through downtown out to the old part of town near my apartment and parked in front of Ray's, an old neighborhood bar where I take most of my evening meals. Thick stone walls held in the dampness as a thirty-year-old yellowed ceiling fan struggled to stir the thick air like a huge cauldron of soup. The waiter brought me a glass of whiskey with lots of ice and a little water. I ordered a hot sandwich, took off my jacket and tie, and settled back to light a cigarette and sip on the cold drink. It cooled my mouth and burned the back of my throat on its way down.

I lost track of time. By the time I finished my sandwich and a couple more drinks, it was almost ten o'clock.

"Leaving early tonight," the waiter said to me as I paid my check.

"Yeah, I got to be somewhere."

The farther I drove, the more tense I got. It was quite a ways from my neighborhood, with its older houses and cracked sidewalks and Spanish moss hanging down from ancient, battered oaks, to the mansions across town. Here was money, both old and new, all intermingled together, safe and happy.

People in Jimmy Herbert's neighborhood didn't buy houses; they either had them built or they inherited them. Their homes were as well-tailored as their suits. Herbert's was a large, two-story house on an acre or so of prime real estate. The backyard sloped gently up toward a row of trees that blocked the view of the neighbor's house. I pulled into the cobblestone driveway that circled around the yard to the front of the house. I parked next to a large silver Lincoln.

The house was dark and I wondered if they'd all gone off to sleep. I remembered Jimmy was an insomniac and often stayed up late. I looked in the front window and saw a light on near the back of the house. I rang the bell.

It took a while, but Jimmy pulled the curtain on the window and looked out.

"Jack," he said, flicking on the porch light and cracking the door. "Is that you?"

"Yeah, Jimmy, it's me."

The door swung open. He stood there in the foyer looking at me.

"Well, I'll be damned, c'mon in, boy," he said, reaching out to shake my hand. His grip was firm, and as direct as I had remembered it. He was smiling at me.

"Well, I'll be damned," he said again.

"How are you, Jimmy?" I asked. "It's been a long time."

"Too long, boy, too long. You look good."

"So do you, Jimmy. So do you."

He did look good. He'd lost a lot of weight and the puffiness in his cheeks from too many brandies and too much work was gone. His straight hair was combed back over his head, and grayer than I remembered. He was older, but a fierce light still shone in his eyes. He was aging well, just like he did everything else.

"Looks to me like Lily's been taking good care of you."

"She has. Let's walk back to the library and have a drink."

I thought how odd it was to once again be in a house that actually had a library. The library in my three-room apartment was a couple of thirty-dollar bookcases from the K-Mart, the kind made out of genuine laminated fiber-board.

"How is Lily?" I asked.

"Fine, just fine. She's asleep right now, though. Says my working late at night bores the hell out of her and she'd just as soon go to bed."

"Oh, I didn't know you were working," I said. "Should I come back another time?"

"No, of course not. I'm just doing paperwork. I don't do much courtroom work these days. We leave that up to the younger boys, but I do seem to have to *sign* a lot of things. I welcome any excuse to put it off."

We walked into the library, a room that had been my favorite place in the house years ago. It hadn't changed much. Shelves of leather-bound law books rose twelve feet high, with rows of classics and hard-bound novels beside them. A chorus line of classical records leaned to the right next to an old KLH stereo. There were two padded leather chairs and a long couch, along with Jimmy's desk. An oriental rug covered the floor. I still felt very much at home there.

"Let me fix you a drink, boy," he said, opening the glass door of a maple liquor cabinet. "If I remember, you take a little scotch with a lot of water."

"I was younger then. It's the other way around these days."

"I understand," he said, laughing softly. "I'll just have a small B&B myself."

He handed me the glass. We sat and I pulled a brass smoking stand over next to me and lit a cigarette.

"I don't enjoy drinking like I used to," he said. "At my age, it just makes me tired."

"You seem to have all the energy you need," I commented. "You've still got more than I ever had."

"Different temperaments," he said. "You were always the more contemplative type."

"Diplomat," I said. "Katherine used to call it depressed."

We sat quietly for a moment. Jimmy lit a small, hand-rolled cigar.

"How is she?"

He looked from the tip of his burning cigar directly into my eyes.

"Still angry," he said.

"Sorry to hear that."

"I've accepted the fact that she always will be. She divorced that rather useless young man she married after you. He did nothing, but his family had money, and I think Katherine simply needed something to hold onto after you were gone.

"I'm glad," he said after a moment, with a slight twinkle in his eye, "that she finally came to her senses. He was a stinker."

"I'm sorry about all that," I said. "I'd heard she got married but didn't know she got divorced again."

"I don't ordinarily criticize my daughter." Jimmy settled back in his chair and held his brandy snifter up to the light. "For one thing, it doesn't do any good. But I think you were both foolish to give up on the marriage so quickly."

"God, Jimmy," I said. "We tried to patch things up for three years. It just wasn't going to work. There was nothing I could do to make her happy."

"Maybe," he said. "Katherine's too smart for her own good. I sometimes think nothing will make her happy. Perhaps if you'd both been a little older. Children these days seem to want to begin life so early."

"C'mon now, Jimmy," I said, smiling at him. "How old were you when you met Lily?"

"Touché," he said, smiling back. "I was seventeen, I think. And I had a blue-steel boner for her."

We sat for a second. Jimmy took small sips of brandy while I smoked quietly and drank my scotch. Finally, he looked up.

"Okay, Jack, why don't you tell me what prompted this little late-night visit? Surely after all these years you didn't decide to just drop in to see how we were."

"You always could get right to the point, couldn't you?"

"That's what the law teaches you, son. When and when not to be direct."

It hurt when he called me "son." Time was when I was as close as Jimmy would ever get to having a son. And my own father's death when I was a baby meant that he was as close as I would get to having a father.

"It's the Iris Project," I said.

"Oh, yes," he said, tapping the ash off his cigar. "The good Mr. Murphy." His voice changed just a bit.

"Yes," I said. "The good Mr. Murphy."

"What have you got to do with this?"

"I still work for William Jennings."

"That surprises me," he said slowly. "I would have thought you'd left there by now."

"He pays me good money. Probably more than I'm worth."

"And that's all you're after, I suppose."

"Everybody's got to make a living." I shrugged.

"That's true," he said. "I just thought that from my past dealings with you some question of ethics might come in somewhere."

"Ethics, hell," I said defensively. "Ethics doesn't pay the rent. I work for Jennings because he pays me well and it suits my habits."

I knew this wasn't true, but I wasn't going to tell him that. I worked for the Old Man because I found proximity to the center of power fascinating. Ethical issues weren't a problem. Truthfully, I'd never had to confront the big ones, and like everybody else, I could slide on the little ones.

"Sounds like you've become a good soldier, Jack. Did he send you here on a reconnaissance mission?"

"He didn't send me here at all. In fact, he'd probably shoot me if he knew. I'm here to find out what's going on between you and Murphy because I hate to see you and Lily get involved in something that could get pretty nasty. For old time's sake—"

"For old time's sake?"

"Didn't they teach you in law school not to get in a pissing contest with a skunk? Murphy's not worth it. He's not worth a damn, in fact."

"Jack—" he interrupted.

"Let me tell you something, Jimmy," I continued, fueled by anger or scotch or maybe a combination of both. "The Old Man has really got his bowels in an uproar over this one. Murphy's dead. Dead in the water. But you can get out and be none the worse for wear. You stay in it, though, and the Old Man will be obliged to burn you both at the stake. It's sort of a matter of honor with him."

Jimmy leaned over in his chair, eyes afire, and pointed his finger at me like a .38.

"Let me tell *you* something, young man. First of all, don't threaten me. I was taking on men like Jennings when you were still trying to figure out what that brown wet stuff in your diapers was. I know Mr. Murphy is not exactly a pillar of the community. But he has a right to pursue this and I think he will win!"

"You mean *you'll* win."

"An attorney is only as good as his client's case."

"But why?" I asked. "You know the Old Man's going to make your life miserable. It can't be the money."

"No, Jack." He laughed. "It's not the money."

He sat back in his chair and puffed a bit on the cigar.

"I'm getting old, young Mr. Jack Lynch, and it seems to me that I don't have too many more fights like this one left. I've always considered your employer little more than a common criminal. I've watched for years as he's skirted the law to build a financial and political empire that's as dishonest and contemptible as he is."

"You need to understand something about the Old Man, Jimmy. He's always pictured mud as something that's there for him to pick up and sling."

"There is no mud, dammit," he flashed. "There is no mud! And I will not sit here in my own house while some child I once knew attempts to intimidate me."

"I'm being straight with you, Jimmy," I said. "I know there's no mud. But the Old Man pays me to look for it. If there's any stink lying under any rocks out there, I'll find it. And when I do, I won't keep quiet about it. You wouldn't expect me to and I won't. That's just the way I am."

"There is no mud," he said quietly.

"Just this once," I said, "I hope the hell there isn't." And I knew full well there wouldn't be.

He led me to the door. As we passed the stairs, Lily called to him. I looked up. Her hair spilled down over her shoulders and she was in a blue silk dressing gown.

"Jimmy," she said, straining to see through the shadows. "Who is it?"

"It's Jack, dear," he answered.

"Jackie," she said, coming down the stairs. "Jackie, is that you? It's been so long."

She hugged me and I hugged her back. In the porch light, she looked older, her face a bit more wrinkled and her hair showing traces of silver.

"How are you, Lily?" I asked.

"Good, Jack. How have you been?"

"Okay," I answered.

"Jack was just leaving, Lily," Jimmy said. "We had some business to discuss."

"You'll come back sometime, won't you?" she asked.

"Well . . ." I said, looking over at Jimmy.

"Of course he will," Jimmy said. "And next time there will be no business discussed."

"Great," I said. "I'll look forward to it."

We said good-bye, and I walked to my car as the front door closed behind me. As I pulled out of the driveway, the porch light went off, and the house was dark.

Three

When I left Murphy's office the next morning, there was a parking ticket tucked under my left windshield wiper. I snatched the ticket, glanced at it, then got in the car and popped the cover on the glovebox. The new ticket was tossed inside to join its brothers. I actually *paid* parking tickets, something that drew hoots from my fellow suits at the bank, but I waited until I had a good stack of them so I only had to write one check.

I don't know what it is with me and parking tickets. Getting a parking ticket fixed in New Orleans is about as serious as spitting on the sidewalk; such a small lapse of integrity in the great corrupt scheme of things. Maybe covering the small lapses in some way made up for the larger ones.

As I pulled away from the curb and into the traffic, I realized I was tying all this into one of those rationalizing inner monologues as a way to decompress.

The civil sheriff's office was in a building next to City

Hall. It was like every other government building I'd ever been in; lots of marble and polished floors, harsh light and cold halls. Portraits of past and present politicians hung on the walls just high enough to be untouchable.

Nothing quite like building a monument to yourself.

Murphy's office was on the top floor, far above the filing cabinets and sweaty clerks in the ill-ventilated offices downstairs. An attractive young blond sat behind a huge desk in the anteroom. Copies of *People* magazine and the *National Enquirer* lay in front of her. She was fanning her hands in the air as I walked in, drying a new coat of fingernail polish.

Busy lady.

"Is Mr. Murphy in?" I asked.

"I'll have to check and see," she drawled. "May I ask who's calling?"

"Jack Lynch."

"Okay, Mr. Lynch, just have a seat." She picked up the phone gingerly to avoid snapping a Lee Press-On nail and punched a button.

Murphy kept me waiting fifteen minutes; about what I expected. I smoked a couple of cigarettes and watched the honey out of the corner of my eye and allowed my mind to speculate on some of the special abilities that got her the job. That's not intended as an exercise in chauvinist rhetoric; I just happen to know what Murphy expects of his female staffers.

God, I laughed to myself, no matter how jaded and cynical I get, I just can't keep up.

Eventually, Murphy buzzed his secretary, who pulled her head up out of an article about how Princess Di was really the offspring of alien visitors to answer the phone.

"Step right through that door," she instructed, turning back to her open newspaper.

I walked into a large office that clearly reflected Murphy's estimation of his own importance. Thick carpet covered the floor, while citations and autographed pictures hung in expensive frames on the walls. On his immense desk sat a crystal paperweight, an expensive gift from the 12th Ward Homeowners Association. The office was cold and the curtains were drawn, giving me the impression that I had just walked into a well-furnished refrigerator.

I didn't much like Murphy; I liked him even less sitting there like he was doing me a favor by granting me an audience.

He stared at me through a cloud of blue cigar smoke. A gaudy diamond tie pin held his shiny tie flat to his belly. His dull gray eyes were embedded in his face, giving him the misleading appearance of being unintelligent.

His bulk never stopped surprising me; it was as if every time I didn't see him for a few weeks, I forgot how huge he was. He looked like the Michelin tire man in a five-hundred-dollar suit.

"I didn't have to let you in here at all, Jack," he said in his low, phlegmatic voice. "I know why you're here."

"Aw, hell, Murph," I answered, walking over and taking a chair without being asked. "All I wanted was a little friendly conversation."

"Get on with it, I'm a busy man."

"Yeah, Murph, so's your secretary outside."

"Stop fucking around, Jack. Say what you have to and get out. I know the Old Man sent you here."

"You kidding? You got the wrong idea. If he knew I was here, he'd have my ass in a sling."

"Then what do you want?"

"I want to talk some sense into you," I said, as coolly as I could muster. His feathers ruffled a bit anyway.

"The way I see it," I continued, crossing my legs, "you have more to lose here than gain. I don't understand it, Murph. You stand to make a fortune off the Iris Project. You even own some of the property down there. And you want to stop it? C'mon, now. Doesn't make sense.

"Now here's the deal. You drop everything. This lawsuit,

the whole nine yards. Fire Herbert. Get the hell out of this case and forget it. The Old Man makes an out-of-court settlement. Some money and a new recreation center for the Twelfth Ward or some such crap like that. You'll be a hero. Then it's up to you to make peace with the Old Man. He might even let you run for civil sheriff again. That is, of course, if you behave yourself and don't cause him any more trouble."

"Tell him I'm not impressed." He sneered at me. "I thought the Old Man had better sense than to send a boy to do a man's job."

Real original, Murph, I thought.

The room was filled with a tension that was as palpable as fog on the riverbank on a steamy summer morning. I was walking the ragged edge here. I knew from years past how dangerous he could be, but I figured the only way to find out what he was really made of was to push him as hard as I could. I gave a big push and stepped off into the abyss.

"Murph, you are without a doubt one of the most disgusting individuals I've ever had the misfortune to run across. If you hadn't had your nose up the Old Man's ass all these years, you would've been lucky to get a job driving a garbage truck."

Murphy's face turned a deep crimson; he struggled for breath and sweat popped out on his forehead. He heaved in the chair.

"Get out!" he screamed. "Get out of my office!"

"Sure, Murph," I said, getting up out of the chair as slowly as possible, but ready to move fast if he blew. "You think about it. When you make up your mind, give me a call."

I reached into my pocket and tossed one of my cards on his desk. In a rage, he spit on the card so hard it skittered over the edge of his desk and onto the floor.

"You know, Murph," I said, calmly. "You ought to slow

down a bit. A man with a weight problem like yours could have a coronary getting that excited."

I shut his office door behind me. There was an explosion behind me against the door, and the shattering of glass. The 12th Ward Homeowners Association would have to spring for a new paperweight.

The cutie behind the desk looked up from the newspaper, where she'd been reading about Michael Landon's past life as a Nazi SS guard.

I leaned over her desk, with a direct line of sight down about an 8.5 on the Richter Scale cleavage. "I think Mr. Murphy's going to need one of your special back rubs, honey. He's in a real snit today."

She folded the paper quickly and started to get up, then settled back down in her chair and glared at me. As I walked out the door, I could see her reflection in the glass, giving me the well-polished finger.

Sally was on the phone when I walked in, obviously preoccupied and irritated. She had on a new dress, a bright, form-fitting dress that was totally out of character for her. The other women in the office seemed to pay a great deal more attention to clothes and makeup than Sally ever did. But lately, I'd noticed her buying new clothes. She didn't look up when I came in.

"What's the matter?" I asked when she came into my office a minute or so later.

She sat down with a look of disgust. "While you go around playing private detective and hobnobbing with your fellow wizards, I have to take care of the ordinary day-to-day stuff like making sure the typesetters don't lose the copy for the annual report—"

"And?" I asked.

"They lost it."

"You want me to call them?" I asked, smiling.

"Wouldn't do any good. I'll just have to stay on their

backs, that's all. How'd it go at Murphy's? You get to see him?"

"Oh, yeah." I laughed. "I got to see him, all right, for about five minutes. And it damn near gave us both a heart attack."

"What happened?"

"One thing's for sure," I said, loosening up my tie a bit. "Murphy's not going to back down easy on this. I made him a good deal. He turned it down; I pushed his buttons. If he could've caught me, I think he would have pinned me on the floor and sat on me."

"Too bad he didn't. Then we could have hung him for murder."

"Very funny."

"You look like you could use some lunch," she said.

"You want to have lunch with me? You kidding? Twice in a row? What's going on here?"

"Just desperate, I guess."

"Call upstairs and have Madge catch the phones for us. Then we'll go."

"By the way, speaking of calls," Sally said over her shoulder, "some lady called right after you left. She didn't leave a name, but she said she'd call back later."

"That's strange," I said. "Recognize her voice?"

"Not exactly." She hesitated. "It may have been your ex-wife. I don't know; it's been a while since I heard her voice."

"Well, was it business or pleasure?" I asked as we left the office.

"What am I, a mind reader?"

We labored through the thick city traffic a gear or two at a time. Sally sat in the seat next to me, her new linen dress matted down with sweat, cigarette drooping in her right hand. She fidgeted with her left hand as if she didn't know what to do with it.

"I'm burning up," she complained, as we snaked through the traffic at five miles an hour.

"I know. Me, too."

Hot air wafted up off the sidewalk, shimmering in the bright sunlight. Finally, we came to the highway entrance ramp.

I jammed the accelerator to the floor; with a whine like a buzz saw, we shot out into the fast lane. The wind blasting past our open windows and the drill of the engine kept us from talking. The feeling of speed, and of things rushing past me, was one of my greatest pleasures.

"Rapid motion through space elates one," Joyce wrote. "So does notoriety; so does the possession of money."

It also relieves one of the terrible responsibility of thought.

It was late afternoon when we returned, just as the sky darkened and the huge dollops of August rain began to fall. We rolled up the windows and watched the wipers struggle without much luck against the assault.

It was one of those late summer thunderstorms with drops big enough to make a splatting sound when they hit the sidewalk. We bolted from the parking lot, across the street, and stood beneath the awning of a store. People crowded up under the awning for protection, but it didn't do much good.

The rain was coming in almost sideways, and as we stood backed up against the plate glass window, Sally pulled her thin arms up around her shoulders and shivered a bit. The dress was plastered down all over her now, like she'd just taken a shower in it, and I saw the outline of her body clearly in the darkening shadows of the thunderstorm.

This one was turning into a real boomer. A bolt of lightning ripped down, just visible over the roofs of the buildings across the street, its jagged streak blazing against the black sky. A tremendous thunderclap followed.

I breathed in quickly through my nose. It was the kind of soaking thunderstorm you could smell.

Sally's hair was a couple of shades darker from the wet. The rain came in on us in sheets, soaking us from the knees down. The canvas awning began flapping terribly in the wind and suddenly, out of nowhere, another lightning bolt hit no more than a block away.

Instantly, a bang like an artillery shell followed. Everybody under the awning jerked like it hit right next to us.

Sally jumped and a sound escaped her that was more like a puppy's yelp than anything else, as if she'd been sitting peacefully next to a closed door and somebody opened it on her tail.

She grabbed me like a trap snapping shut. No problem; I held on to her. Tight.

"Damn," she muttered. "I'm freezing out here."

"Here, take this," I said, pulling off my jacket and wrapping it around her shoulders. "It's wet but it's better than nothing."

I pulled her close to me to warm her. Her arms were still crossed in front of her as she shivered. The rain pelted down even harder; a cab across the street locked up its brakes and hydroplaned right into some idiot in a rusty Chevy who short-stopped in front of him.

There was a terrible smashing of metal, drowned by the blare of horns and the boom of the storm.

Sally turned to me. Our faces were barely an inch apart, each of us dripping water off the ends of our noses. I brought my other arm up across her shoulder and now had her in my own clumsy, soaking-wet version of an embrace.

Ten years, I thought, ten years I'd known this woman, and why was I just now beginning to really see her? I asked myself this question as if I didn't know the answer. Hell, I knew. You walk out of a marriage that at its best was a long stroll on the deck of the *Titanic*, it's going to be a while before you want to set sail again. It took me three years. It'd been six months since I'd even had a casual date, and that was a disaster.

But as Sally and I huddled there in the storm, with the wind howling and the spray drenching us, I finally saw that the parts of me I thought had drowned were suddenly sputtering, clawing for air, for light, for warmth. There was a stirring deep within me. My throat tightened. I realized at that moment I was coming alive again.

The prospect scared the hell out of me.

"I love thunderstorms," she said. "But they frighten me."

"Me, too. Especially the lightning."

"Lightning's not so bad," she whispered, turning to me, looking at me. "Long as it strikes in the right place."

It took me a moment to realize that I couldn't hear the storm anymore.

It was around five and I was fixing to leave for the evening when the phone rang. I'd forgotten about the earlier call. It was only at the sound of her voice that I wondered why the hell my ex-wife would be bothering to call me after all this time.

"Hello, Katherine. How are you?"

"Fine. How are you?"

"Okay, I guess. Pretty busy these days."

"So I've heard."

The voice over the phone was cold and impersonal, but with an undercurrent of tension that you could only read after you'd known her a few years.

"My father told me you came to see him last night."

"Yeah," I said, wary. "We had some business to discuss."

"Oh, he didn't tell me what it was about."

"It was nothing, really. Your father's representing one of the bank's associates in a minor civil matter and I just needed a bit of information, that's all."

"Well, listen," she said, clearing her throat. "I know you're busy and all, and I don't want to take up too much

of your time. I just thought we could have a drink or something . . ."

"Sure," I said, after a moment. "Why not?"

"Good. Where do you want to meet?"

"How about the bar at the Royal Orleans?"

"All right. About an hour?"

"Yes."

She hung up abruptly.

I was on my second scotch and soda when I spotted her.
I'd requested a table in one of the darker corners, away
from the usual happy hour crowd and early diners. She
squinted in the dim light as she looked around for me. I
stood as she walked over, glad that I'd had the chance to
down a couple before she got there.

The three years or so since I'd last seen her barely reg-
istered on her face. She was still pale, slightly freckled, with
a glorious head of deep auburn hair that was thick and fine
and long and brushed straight back over her shoulders. Her
face was long and thin, with high cheekbones and piercing
brown eyes that had once raked me over with every possible
combination of emotions from love to hate to passion to
contempt.

There hadn't been anyone like her since her.

She walked over to where I stood waiting and raised
up on her toes to brush my cheek lightly with her lips, the
same kiss one might give a long-lost uncle or an acquaintance at a cocktail party. I wondered what she wanted
from me.

I pulled the chair out for her and stood as she arranged
the silk peacock-green dress she was wearing and sat down.

"How are you, Jack? Really?" she said, looking directly
at me and giving me the same porcelain smile she used to
give me when she didn't want to let me know what was really
going on inside her. Which was often.

"I'm fine, Katherine. Just fine."

The waiter came over.

"What would you like?" I asked her.

"You don't remember?" she said softly, placing both elbows on the table and cradling her head in her hands.

"Vodka Collins for the lady. Another Chivas and soda for me."

"You come here much?" she asked.

"Not often," I answered, reaching for my cigarettes and offering her one. "Occasionally."

"No, thanks. Was that your car I saw out in the parking lot? The nice convertible two-seater?"

"Yeah, how'd you guess?"

"So, you finally got your sports car."

"Finally. It wasn't the color I wanted, but I didn't want to wait forever."

"Really? What color did you want?"

"I don't know. Maybe something in a deep red."

"I'm sorry you never got it."

"There are lots of cars out there," I said, as the waiter brought the drinks.

"Yes. But how many of them are really special?"

"Damn few," I said, sipping.

"If you didn't want to see me, you didn't have to," she said.

"I don't know what I wanted." It was a condition with which I knew she was familiar. "I think I was more curious as to why you wanted to see me."

"You're still working for William Jennings."

"Yeah. About ten years now."

"That's not at all like you," she said lightly. "To stay committed to a . . . job . . . that long."

"I know. But it's a good job. Pays me well."

"Great," she said. "Is that all you've been doing, though?"

The waiter came and asked if we wanted dinner. I wasn't

really hungry, but the food was a good excuse to avoid more small talk. We ordered two more drinks and decided to go into the restaurant for dinner.

The night air seemed to get more damp and oppressive as the evening wore on. Katherine sat stiffly, eating her food and trying to look comfortable. The dinner plates and the wineglasses, the silverware and the table cloth constituted a demilitarized zone. Katherine shivered a bit in the cool air and I asked the waiter to turn the ceiling fan off.

Afterwards, she ordered coffee and I ordered a brandy. "All right, Katherine," I said, finally. "The restaurant closes in a couple more hours. Don't you think you'd better get to it?"

She had this way about her of looking at me, this shift of her head from one side to another, with just a wisp of hair falling down in her face as she moved. It was a glance, a motion, that was one of a thousand things that first drew me to her. It had taken me many years to learn to fear that look.

"What do you want with my father?" she said suddenly, looking directly at me. That was her style; dance around and dance around and wait for an opening, then land the sucker punch. Only I'd known her too long to be a sucker anymore.

"I can't talk about that, Katherine," I said.

She flared. She tried to keep it under control, but I'd seen it too many times before. The eyes lit up; the mouth curled up revealing the upper incisors. She jammed it all back in, but I knew I'd almost gotten myself bit.

"I want to know what you're doing talking to my father."

"And I told you I can't discuss it."

She softened suddenly, and reached across the table to take my hand. This woman could shift gears faster than anybody I'd ever seen.

"Jack, no matter what happened to us, my father loved you like a son. When we split up, I think he took it harder than we did. All I want to know is *are you trying to hurt him?*"

"No, dammit, I'm not trying to hurt him," I said, angry myself now. "And you might recall, Katherine, that your father is more than able to take care of himself."

"My father treated you like a son. After everything he did for you," she said, digging her nails into my palm. "You're like a hit man for the Mafia. Totally without scruples or morals or anything. I don't know what my father's involved in that's set you animals on him, but I won't let you hurt him, damn you!"

She looked for a second as if she were going to hit me; but I stared her down.

"You never could hold a candle to him."

"Listen carefully," I said, "because I don't want you to have the wrong idea about any of this. I'm not trying to hurt anybody. Your father is involved in a dispute with my employer, and I am trying like hell to put together a settlement that will keep everybody happy and hurt no one. Do you understand me, Katherine? Are you really listening to me?"

She relaxed her grip on me. Her mouth twitched, a smile that held as much cruelty as amusement.

"Of course, I'm listening. I always listened to you, Jack, whether you chose to believe that or not. In fact, it was probably you that putzed out in the listening department."

"Maybe you're right. But that was all a long time ago."

"Let's go somewhere for another drink," she said, almost gaily.

"I don't think so," I said. "I've had a long day and I'm tired."

"Are you sure? We could always go up to my apartment for a nightcap instead."

"No, I think I'll just go home and sack out. Thanks, anyway."

"I swear, you sound like an old man," she said, crossing her arms in front of her.

What the hell was she up to?

"No, I'm just a little tired."

I pulled out one of my gold cards to cover the bill, then we left together. As we walked out of the restaurant, the woman who more than once told me in a fit of temper that she'd like to see me dead took my arm. It was still damp and wet outside and small puffs of fog hung around the streetlights. Katherine's car, a small blue Mercedes, was parked in front of mine.

"Sure you wouldn't like to come over?" she asked, looking up at me as she started the car.

And I was suddenly overcome with the desire to say yes. I remembered how it had once been, in the early days, the days when we were wild and passionate. We stayed up until dawn making love, drinking wine, smoking cigarettes, talking, and making love again, over and over, sweaty and breathless and exhausted and falling asleep in each other's arms for an hour or so until we both had to get up and go to work again.

I'd never had that before and never since and, I thought, probably never would again. But she was there, dammit, right there in front of me. Katherine was my youth, and I'd lost both. And here they were back, tempting me.

Go home with her. Work this shit out.

"Thanks, anyway," I said, slowly and deliberately.

"Some other time then. It was good to see you again, Jack. Call me sometime."

The engine started. The car pulled away. The bitch was gone, having ripped my guts out once again.

I drove back to my apartment, my second-floor flat in an old building down the street from Ray's. I'd lived there for five years now, but it seemed like five decades of clutter met me at the door. I walked through the living room and into the kitchen, fixing myself the scotch and soda that I really didn't need. I walked into the bedroom, a large room that contained my unmade bed, a bureau, a small television on a metal stand, and my stereo. I turned on a late-night jazz station and settled back into a chair and lit a cigarette as Al Jarreau, Chick Corea, Grover Washington, Dave Brubeck, all my old buddies soothed my aching head.

I sipped the whiskey until it was mostly ice water, then got up and made another. I lay back in bed and smoked and drank the scotch slowly and steadily. I felt like an old man, wondering if this was my life now, this being alone with my radio and my whiskey and my memories.

Sometimes sleeping alone is a respite from all the craziness of the world; sometimes it's a bitch. Tonight it was the latter.

I was awake for a long time, staring at the ceiling and thinking. My mind went blank and I dozed off. Katherine came at me first, then Sally, then the Old Man, and finally, James Jimmy Herbert, my friend and mentor, my father and confessor and the only man worthy of my wife. When I woke up, it was four in the morning and I was lying in bed with my clothes on. The cool, damp air flowed in through the open window and it was deathly quiet outside. I got up, turned off the stereo, undressed, and climbed between the sheets.

She'd asked me to go home with her.

Damn, I never could figure that woman out . . .

Four

It only took a few hours and a few dollars to check out Murphy's girl.

"Well," I began, pulling my notebook out of my coat pocket and settling back in the chair in front of the Old Man's desk, "Murphy's playmate is a twenty-four-year-old kitten by the name of Samantha Kramer, Sam for short. Platinum blond, five feet ten, nicely built. Attended Bayou State Community College for two years, but dropped out. Weighs in about one hundred twenty-five.

"It seems she's lived in this very expensive apartment out in the Garden District for about a year. According to the building super, for a while she had a steady stream of, shall we say, gentlemen callers. But that all stopped about seven or eight months ago. About ten days ago, she moved out. At this point, the super's mind went blank until I slipped him a fifty, which jogged his memory considerably . . ."

"Almost like a tonic, ain't it," the Old Man commented.

"It did help," I said. "She packed up all her clothes and

moved out, leaving the furniture. No forwarding address. But the super was helping with her bags and noticed she did have her passport with her. The place wasn't rented out yet, so for another twenty, he let me in. It was clean. I called up Compton over at the personnel office at City Hall. He told me Samantha Kramer's been off the payroll for almost two months now. Murphy started covering his tracks early."

"Yeah."

"Now I could find out where she is," I said, snapping the notebook shut. "But it would take some time. I'm sure Murphy's paid her off. I'm equally sure we could better his offer and get her back here to blow the lid off him. If that's what you want to do."

Mr. Jennings thought for a second.

"No," he said. "Forget her. If every politician who took a mistress wound up in trouble for it, state capitols all across the country would be full of empty offices."

"Well said, boss," I said, smiling dryly at him. "We've also got the limousine and the two houses and Murphy's propensity for long, lazy vacations. But it's all basically small-time stuff. You know what people say around here: anything short of federal indictment is just business. We need something that'll hang him."

"Well, get on it," the Old Man ordered. "And fast. And go to work on Herbert."

"Okay."

"As long as Murphy's ass is well-fed, he doesn't give a damn about what people think of him. Herbert's different, though. We might convince him to change his course with a whole helluva lot less than Murphy might take."

"I'll do what I can," I said. "But you ain't going to find anything on Herbert."

"Oh yeah?" the Old Man asked, lifting an eyebrow. "And why's that?"

"I guess the whole time I was married to his daughter,

he and I were about as close as you can get. He's straight, boss. I know that's hard to accept given the state of the world, but I doubt the guy's ever shoplifted a licorice stick from the corner drugstore."

"Listen, boy. If you ain't up to handling this, I can get somebody else."

We both smiled. Who was he going to get?

"No, let's just take it as an exercise," I said. "Just to prove a point. There's still a few good men out there."

"And the marines are looking for all of them," he said. "Now exercise your ass on out of here."

"On my way," I said, getting up.

"I got to go to a meeting with all my mindless account- ants," he grumbled. "Accountants. Goddamn. I hate every four-eyed one of them."

"So I've heard," I said, and I had. Hundreds of times.

"Stay on top of this. Start digging into Herbert, but stay with Murphy, too."

I expected it would be easy enough to check out Murphy. It's almost as if he anticipated taking the Old Man on one of these days and knew the hounds would be on his trail. He left just enough scent to let you know he was there, but not enough to get you close enough to tree him.

The two houses came first. It would be interesting to see how he could afford two houses on a civil sheriff's salary. As far as I knew, Murphy's never taken outright, obvious graft. Even he was too sophisticated for that; there were other ways to get rich in the public sector.

The Registrar of Deeds was as good a place as any to start. I got copies of the mortgage records and found that, at least on paper, Murphy's properties were heavily mort- gaged. I had the bank run a computer credit check on him; it was as if Murphy were any other honest, solid-working Joe.

I also called down to Data Processing and ordered up

summaries of every account Murphy had ever had a finger in. If he was smart, he'd have his dirty money stashed away in the Caymans where no one could find it. Maybe . . .

But no, he's just another hard-working, honest citizen serving the public. Damn.

I spent the rest of the day checking out one thing after another: all useless, all leading nowhere. This was a new one on me. I'd done this kind of investigative work for the Old Man before, but this was different. I kept running across names of people I'd known and worked with for years. Murphy's tracks were so tangled and commingled with everybody else's that it was hard to keep it all straight.

I finally got back to the office about 4:30 that Friday afternoon, frustrated and tired, and irritated at having to spend thirty minutes in the damn traffic for every five minutes I worked. At this point, I simply wanted it all to go away. I took the elevator up and staggered into my office, wilting and sweaty.

"How'd it go?" Sally asked, following me into my office. "Have any luck?"

"Terrible. Is there anything cold to drink around here?"

"I can run down to the break room and get you a Coke," she offered.

"I'll dance at your daughter's wedding—"

"If she's ever born, I'm sure she'll appreciate it," she said as she left the room.

I loosened my tie and tried to subdue that itchy, restless pants-binding-in-the-crotch feeling.

Sally walked back in and handed me the cold bottle. Beads of water formed on the outside of it. I lit a cigarette and sat for a second, sipping the Coke and trying to relax. Sally sat down across from me.

"It seems Mr. Murphy is as clean as a surgeon's blade," I said. "I've been to City Hall, the Registrar of Deeds, three banks, the central computer terminal office out on Fourteenth, just about everywhere I could think of short of Murphy's bedroom. And that's probably next."

"Well, you'd better find something. Or you know whose head will roll."

"Yeah. The problem is that Murphy knows what the Old Man is after. Consequently, he knows how to hide it."

"The sonofabitch is wise to us," she said, in her best gun moll voice.

"Exactly."

"There has to be a soft spot somewhere."

"The Old Man seems to think it's somewhere in James Herbert's direction," I said. "Maybe. Maybe not. If we can turn Herbert to our side, then the Old Man's right when he says Murphy will drop the lawsuit. That's politics; it's the way things work. But he's wrong when he says we can get something on Herbert."

"C'mon," Sally said. "Everybody's got something to hide."

"I've known him a long time, babe. He loves his wife, pays his taxes, lives clean, and stays home at night."

"Right. That's the ticket. And I buy the queen's underpants." After a moment, she said, "You're wrong. He is like everybody else. He's got something lying around back there that he'd just as soon not have anybody find out."

"Not Herbert," I snapped, suddenly irritated as hell at her. This whole business was starting to tie me up in a knot. Had we all been surrounded by people like Murphy for so long we can't imagine somebody who's incorruptible?

"Why not Herbert?" she popped back at me. "What makes him so damn special?"

"That's just it. He is special! He's got a thing about this ethics stuff. If the IRS overpays him, he sends it back. He finds a ten-dollar bill on the sidewalk, he turns it in or gives it to charity!"

"That's crazy! Nobody's that honest!"

"He is!"

"You're getting all worked up, Jack," she said. "Look, if he's that honest, that straight, then we won't find anything on him. Just do it. Check him out. What's the worst that can happen? We find out that he's human."

"He's not human," I whispered, my eyes suddenly clouding over. "I told Katherine that one time."

"And?"

"It's the only time she ever hit me. Hauled off and slapped the shit out of me."

"God, Jack," she said. "I'm sorry."

I brought my hand up and rubbed my eyes, trying to get the burning to stop.

"Don't worry about it. It's just tough to have to compete against somebody that's infallible."

"Maybe he's not infallible."

"Oh, no." I laughed. "Just ask my ex-wife."

"Actually, I'd like to."

"I was just kidding." I slid forward in my seat and put my elbows on the desk. "Don't you dare call that woman. You're too nice; she'd eat you for lunch."

Sally got up from the chair and sat on the edge of the desk. She put her hands on the blotter and leaned down in my face.

"Don't underestimate me," she breathed. I got a whiff of her perfume; my heart stopped cold.

"And if there's anything out there," she said in a normal voice, after a moment that could easily have stretched on for hours, "it's up to us to find it, that's all. Let's look at this logically. What makes a man do something he's not supposed to?"

"Love," I answered, my heart beating again. "Or at least lust. Greed, money . . ."

"Okay." She sat up straight on the edge of the desk and

crossed her legs. I stared at her for a second and tried to focus on what she was saying rather than how she looked. God, I'm visual. "Love. How much in love with the good Mrs. H. is this guy? Has he ever had a sugar baby stashed away someplace?"

"It's possible," I answered. "But he's sure hidden it well if he did."

"He wouldn't be the first, you know. Age notwithstanding. Just because he's not a Murphy . . ."

"Yeah," I said, shaking my head to try and clear it a bit, "I know that. But when I went to see him the other night, he was home working downstairs with his wife asleep upstairs."

"That doesn't mean he's there every night. Have the boss put a couple guys on him."

"Follow him?"

"Sure. Find out where he goes and who he goes with. If we can get a picture of his car parked at the dime an hour, dollar a dance motel out on Airline Highway, then we got him."

"Seems kind of melodramatic."

"Listen," she said sternly, "either you're going to do this or you're not. And if you're not going to go after it a hundred percent, you may as well pack your bags and hit the streets because that's where he'll send you." Her finger pointed straight up. I wasn't sure which deity she was referring to—the one on the twentieth floor or the one only a bit higher than that.

"Damn, Sally, that's a slimy thing to do to somebody. Besides the fact that I had to respect this guy, I also had a lot of affection for him. He really was like a father to me."

Her index finger was out and pointing at me like a weapon.

"What's it going to be?"

"This is a complete waste of time," I snapped. "Sure, I'd

throw him to the wolves if he'd done something really bad. But believe me, he hasn't. Besides, why should he get nailed over what at its worst is only a casual indiscretion?"

She stared at me, accusing me. "You've done this kind of work before. What's the big deal now?"

"Okay," I conceded. "I'll call Carlton and get a couple guys from security on him. They'd better be damned discreet, though."

My stomach felt like I'd been sucking down the acid out of a truck battery. I reached into my drawer for the old faithful bottle of antacids and popped a few. My mouth was so dry the mints felt like powdered chalk on velvet.

Sally drifted out into her office. I called Carlton, gave him the information, and asked him to put some guys on Herbert as soon as possible. The only thing that kept the whole business from feeling as shitty as it truly was was that I knew they wouldn't find anything. There wasn't anything to be found; I'd been told that for years.

Then Sally was at the door with her umbrella and purse, saying good night. She stood there, with the light behind her shining through the sheer, airy material of her summer dress. She wore a slip beneath the thing, but I could still see her darkened silhouette in the light. I took a deep, imperceptible breath and held my stomach tight to quiet the churning. For a brief moment, I thought of asking her to dinner but it occurred to me that she was probably already booked up and even if she weren't, what woman would go out on a moment's notice, anyway, and let you know she didn't have any other plans?

So I kept quiet and watched her turn and walk away without me. I could've kicked myself.

Saturday night saw me at Ray's, scotch and soda on the table in front of me, a partially eaten dinner pushed off to one side. I noticed that gradually, almost quietly, the days were getting shorter and cooler. The local news came on and led off with what had become a fairly typical story in this city: another gang murder in Iris.

The cops were speculating it was a drug deal gone sour. Very perceptive bunch of guys, those men in blue. One guy from the Bloods sells another guy from the Verdads a half-pound of coke that turns out to have mostly come from an Arm & Hammer box, and the next thing you know you got a half-dozen grieving mothers in front of the cameras again.

But it could be anything. Somebody dates somebody else's sister; she winds up pregnant, somebody else winds up dead. Somebody's raped; somebody's knifed; somebody's mugged. It's a litany of hard work and dreams gone down the toilet. Young blacks and Hispanics who've got a life expectancy roughly half the general population's stand on street corners hawking their own brand of crack. One guy jokes on the street, "How do you spell 'relief'?"

"C-R-A . . ."

Quaaludes, uppers, downers, howlers, screamers, laughers, criers. Stuff that makes you see pretty colors in a gray world; stuff that makes your prick hard and your orgasms better; stuff that makes you feel so good the tingles run up and down your spine like sweet Jesus walking on the water. The weed I used to smoke in my days as a longhair wouldn't pass for pizza seasoning today. I'd be laughed off the street. Or worse.

I'm on my fourth scotch and rambling to myself inside my head. "You're full of shit," this inner voice of mine, the one that only comes out at night after a few scotches, says. "There's no way you can understand Iris or the people that live there. You've never even been through Iris."

So I decide to go. It's late now, around ten, and I'm going to drive right through the roughest part of the roughest town this side of Roxbury and Harlem and the Hough in my sixteen-thousand-dollar sports car with the top down and my little pale white face sticking out from behind the steering wheel and my tender little white ass sitting on a black vinyl seat.

On a Saturday night, no less.

I've got to be freaking crazy, but I want to go. I want to see what's there. I've seen the boss's mansion, and Herbert's house with the leather chairs in the library, the swimming pool out back, the Lincoln in the drive.

High rollers in suits fighting over the fate of Iris.

I want to go see what they're fighting over.

I may be a little drunk, see, but I'm not crazy. The first thing I do is go home and change into a pair of jeans, running shoes, and an old white shirt. Don't want to look too much like an invader from outer space. Then I dig through my closet, to the bottom of a stack of closed boxes, where I keep a .38 Smith & Wesson Secret Service Special in a shoe box.

I'm not exactly sure what good I thought that would do. If I tried to use it, I'd probably get my own head blown off.

Katherine and I bought the gun the last year of our marriage; not to use on each other, surprisingly enough, but because there'd been a bunch of break-ins in the neighborhood. The gun had only been fired at the gun range where the man who sold it to us taught us how to fire it. No intruders ever came, and Katherine and I never got crazy enough to shoot each other. Almost, but not quite.

I load the gun and carry it out to the car. I start to put it under the driver's seat, then think, no, that's too far to have to reach if I need it. I take a chance on not getting stopped by the cops; the gun goes on the seat just under my leg, out of sight.

I sit there for a minute or two, wondering what the hell I'm doing going to Iris. Then I start the car and pull away.

Years ago, when the interstate highway first came

through, the planners ran it right past Iris, which had been there since the war. Thousands of GIs came home to a housing shortage. Iris was the answer to the problem. Only problem with the answer was that everybody moved out as fast as they could afford to, and with each successive generation of tenants, the Iris Projects went further and further downhill.

But the city made sure the buildings that faced the highway were well-scrubbed and painted. Each bit of graffiti was covered before the spray paint had a chance to dry; each broken window was repaired before anyone had a chance to notice. It was only on the inside of the buildings, and the parts that you couldn't see from the highway as you breezed by in your air-conditioned BMW, that the true face of Iris could be seen.

You had to get off the highway, on the exit ramp that curled around back over itself, across the bridge, through the stoplight, and past the no-man's land before you could really get the feel of her.

There she is: Iris.

I go through the stoplight slowly, then east across Blair Avenue. This is the demilitarized zone. It's common knowledge that what goes down on the east side of Blair is treated a lot differently than what happens on the good side. You can sell whatever your clientele wants on the east side, but set up shop across the street and you're popped in a New York minute.

You can feel the change when you cross Blair. It's as if a palpable blanket of oppressive fear and intimidation settles down on you from above. I drive down Ninth, across Mitchell Avenue; the winos stand on the street corners and slug down Night Train like Chateau Lafitte Rothschild at a wedding reception. Sixty-nine cents a pint in a green bottle with the black label pasted on cockeyed.

It pays to buy the best.

Deserted warehouses, shuttered factories, sullen black kids, shot-out streetlights. An occasional blue-and-white cruises by, avoiding trouble and hoping to get through another hot and nasty Saturday night without getting killed. Who wants to see his kids raised on a widow's pension?

I drive slowly, cautiously down Ninth Avenue, through the more-or-less deserted part of Iris down toward the heart and soul of the place: Iris Avenue, a four-lane expanse of asphalt with what had once been a well-manicured median splitting the traffic. Now, of course, the city's given up on greenery and trees; what's still left is overgrown and infested with weeds and who knows what else. Much of it is paved over, leaving a little raised island of asphalt between the two directions of the long parade.

Here's where the pimps and the hookers and the junkies and the crazies call home. Horns blare; soul and salsa boom forth from the restaurants and the bars; the open tenement windows struggle to catch a breeze in the August night. Here is where the hollow-eyed, the hopeless, the hungry, the hustlers, and the hustled hang out. This is what the Iris Project was really about; level it, level it all. Replace it with something that good, God-fearing, middle-class people can come visit without fearing they'll be swallowed up into the dead of night.

The exhaust from thousands of cars, the smell of greasy fried food, the constant chatter and din of the crowded sidewalks, the traffic: it crushes the senses, infiltrates the very air.

NUKE IRIS, the redneck bumper stickers from the 12th Ward read. LET GOD SORT 'EM OUT.

I pull up to a stoplight behind a huge white Cadillac. There's a pickup truck behind me with five or six drunk guys in the back yelling at the babes on the sidewalk. This tall black woman in a tight T-shirt, no bra, day-glo polyester wig, short leather skirt steps off the median and walks over.

She's about four feet above me as I sit in my little wuss of a car. Sweat runs down my armpits, breaks out on my forehead like plague. She walks over and leans down; no, kind of falls onto the hood of my car and drapes herself over the windshield. She looks down at me behind the steering wheel. Her breasts are enormous and spread out over my windshield like great blobs of black ink through the tight shirt. She opens wide; a gold tooth is dead center top. A diamond in the middle catches the marquee of an X-rated theater like a mirrored ball; sparkles cascade around the ballroom of her mouth.

"What you looking for, sugar?" Her voice drips honey and melted butter all over me. The Cadillac up front waits for the light to change. The boys in the truck behind me whoop it up now.

My heart thumps like a bag full of ball bearings tumbling down a staircase. I twitch the right side of my hip to make sure the pistol's still there. Sweet Jesus, I'm a dumb ass sometimes.

"Not looking for anything, babe," I say, mustering as much volume as possible.

"Aw, honey, you wouldn't be down here if you wasn't looking for something now, would you? Here, baby, take a look at these and see if they do anything for you."

And she reaches down and pulls the T-shirt up to her neck; her breasts balloon out on my windshield. The boys in the pickup truck are really getting off on this shit.

"Hey, baby! Back here! He don't want you! Back here!"

She smiles up at the pickup truck.

"Now you don't want to see me go off with them, do you, baby? Le' me get in next to you in yo' pretty little car."

The light changes. The Cadillac pulls away. The driver in the pickup truck hits his horn. The yells and whoops get louder. Two young kids with skateboards and boom boxes stop on the sidewalk to scope us out.

"I got to go, honey," I say. "I can't afford you anyway."

"Oh, it's Saturday night," she coos. "It's my night to give it away. How's about a freebie?"

"No thanks, babe. Gotta go."

I let out the clutch a bit and give it just a bit of gas. The car inches forward with her still hanging over the windshield.

"C'mon baby, I want it bad right now," she whines.

I give it a little more gas. We ease toward the corner now.

"These are for you, sugar."

The light changes back to red. I ease up to it with her still on the hood. All I need is to run over this bitch, I think. Her pimp gets a hold of me and I'll wind up the star attraction in an Alpo commercial.

"Get off the car," I order.

She stands up, pulls the T-shirt back down over her.

"Your little white ass sure got macho all of a sudden," she says, as I hit the gas and shoot through the red light. "Faggot!" I hear her yell behind me.

I get two blocks before I'm stopped at another red light. This wino that's got to be at least sixty or seventy stumbles up, clothes tattered, smell overwhelming, and leans across my windshield and spits on it. He rubs it with his dirty coat sleeve. Christ, I think, what is it with my windshield tonight. Everybody's got the hots for my windshield.

"There you go, Senator," he mumbles. "All clean, now." He holds out his palm. I reach into my pocket and hand him a dollar as the light changes. Iris is a blur of winos, hookers, junkies—the disaffected, disenfranchised, displaced, disoriented—and I realize, in a spike of irrational fear that only the truly scared of life can feel, how close I am to being right at home here.

The world's full of people who are homeless in all sorts of ways. Yeah, I could fit right in here at Iris.

And there's a sadness about it all that won't go away;

for the crazed hooker that won't even remember me to-morrow, the winos that call everybody Senator, the kids that will graduate from skateboards to gang wars, blowing each other away like Dodge City all over again.

The drive home is a lonely one.

God, what a weird fucking place this city is.

Five

Six eggs and some stale bread were the only edibles in the refrigerator Sunday morning. The last thing I wanted to do was get back in my car and go out into the city. I fried the eggs, made some toast, and spent the day drinking coffee, reading, thinking, and watching old Fred Astaire movies on TV.

All this stuff was beginning to get to me. What was going on here? Nobody in their right mind could possibly think there was anything wrong about cleaning up Iris. Maybe some motives and methods were questionable, but the concept itself had to be solid.

Some of the groups that fought the Old Man on the project accused him of being racist, but they missed the point. The Old Man's not a racist; he's a capitalist. And when it comes to this kind of deal-making, there is no prejudice. Everybody gets screwed equally.

And what of Jimmy Herbert? What would a man like Jimmy be doing involved in this mess? If it had been anyone else in the world, it wouldn't have mattered to me. I'd have done my job as best I could and then been done with it. But this was a tighter connection than I wanted. I don't like being this personally involved in my work.

I kept telling myself there was nothing to find on him, while at the same time I was terrified there might be. But that's crazy. Everyone who knew him always told me I should be more like him, and God knows I tried. But as Katherine used to tell anyone who'd listen, I just couldn't cut the mustard.

Sundays are rough for divorced men.

In fact, over the years I found myself looking forward to Mondays. You hear a lot of bitching about Mondays, but I'm always glad to see them.

Thank God it's Monday; the cry of divorced and lonely singles everywhere.

One of the things I've learned over these same years is that success leads to visibility. The more successful you become, the harder it is to hide the things you want to hide. SEC regulations require you to list as public record any stockholdings that exceed 5 percent in a publicly held corporation; if you're appointed a director in a corporation, then you may as well submit to the inevitable strip-search; if you're really successful, somebody from *Forbes* or *Fortune* will be down to do a number on you.

And if word gets out about your IRS troubles, then you'd better accept the fact that an extended trip to the proctologist would be less revealing . . .

With Jimmy Herbert, I had a couple of things going for me that made it easier. First, he'd lived virtually his whole life right here in the city. He'd gone to high school and college here. He'd gone off to Chicago for law school, then straight into an army uniform and the judge advocate general's office—I knew all this from my marriage to the man's daughter—and then back to town. He practiced law for a few years as a struggling young attorney, then ran for district attorney and won. He'd been D.A. for one term, then decided not to run again. Then he opened up his own firm and started getting rich, fat, and happy.

For the past quarter of a century, he'd grown in reputation and wealth and stature. Among local lawyers, politicians, and society types, he'd become an institution, almost an icon. The old money in town had even begun to accept him, despite the fact that he came from a modest background.

Just goes to show; you work hard enough, long enough, and spread enough cash around, just about anything can come your way.

Monday morning, I started at the main branch of the public library with the Martindale-Hubbell, which is a great way to find out where your lawyer went to school. I got his academic credentials and background and the exact dates of his admittance to the bar, his years as a prosecutor, when he'd founded the firm. Then it was on to the Standard & Poor's Directory of Directors, the Dun & Bradstreet, the index to the state bar association magazine. Bits and pieces fell out little by little, chunks of a puzzle that would have to be put together.

I went to the office and tried to make sense out of my notes. I had access to a computer and a modem as well, and logged onto a company in Washington called Disclosure, Inc. Disclosure, as its name implies, can get annual reports, proxies, and 10-Ks about fifty times faster than the SEC, but at a price.

I didn't have to pay for it myself, though, so I ordered everything from every company that Herbert was either counsel to or a director of. That kind of research gets expensive. It's frustrating when it doesn't get you anywhere.

There were a couple of other things to check, but nothing came of it. I fixed a pot of coffee in the office and laid back on the couch that was against the wall across from my desk. I sipped the coffee and tried to relax, to clear my mind, to try and see something that was there and just mixed in with all the other stuff. The tiniest little thing, camouflaged in a jungle of facts, observations, awards, failures, the lifetime of acts and consequences that we all go through, can lead to the treasure.

But not today. Just a blank.

I unplugged the coffee, turned off the lights, walked out into the late afternoon's heat, and the prospect of another night alone.

The newspaper building was only eight blocks from the office, so the next morning I decided to check in with Sally, leave my car in the lot, and walk. Real dumb. The cool Saturday night had been only a cease-fire. It was almost ninety and it wasn't yet ten o'clock in the morning.

You walk into the newspaper building and the blast of cold air hits you like a December wind off of North Dakota somewhere. I took the elevator down to the morgue, the aptly named dark, dusty room where row upon row of filing cabinets, microfilm readers, and old books held the souls of long-dead reporters, editors, people who'd had their brief fling with fame and were now relegated to the cellar. A couple of the younger reporters were digging around, still convinced there was something noble in their efforts.

Maud ran the place. She and I had been friends for years. I was one of the few outsiders she let come and go in her morgue. Maud was short and thin, with scraggly gray hair and a face that must have once been pretty before years of working underground, away from the sunlight and fresh air, got to it.

"Let me see 1958 to 1964, babe," I said, smiling my best lascivious grin at her.

"What, no 'good morning, Maud?'" she said, leaning over the counter at me. "No, 'how ya' been, dawling?'"

"Okay," I answered, "how ya' been, dawling?"

"Terrible," she said, in that curious blend of urban New

Orleanese that sounds more like Brooklyn than anything else. "My lumbago's acting up again. The allergies are killing me this year. And," she whispered, "my period's a week late."

"Whoa," I said. "What's up here? You gone t'have a baby?"

"Nah, I think it's the change setting in. I ain't having no baby at my age. Besides, my old man's been down in Aruba the past month. On the oil rigs."

"Wait'll he gets back and finds out you been messing around."

"Might make him spend more time at home. Listen, babe, six years of reels is more than I feel like carrying right now. Why don't you just take a few months at a time?"

"Whatever, cutie. I don't know if I can stay awake through six years' worth of this newspaper or not."

"You want the subject index, too?"

"Sure. Why not?"

Maud brought a half-dozen or so reels out and a bound volume of cross-referenced listings and dates. She loaded the first reel on for me and flicked the switch, rotated the head, and brought the machine into focus for me.

"Thanks, babe," I said. "Owe you one."

"Knock yourself out. You dumb enough to want to read this rag, I'm dumb enough to let you."

I opened up the subject index and looked up Jimmy's name, then started scanning the filmed newspaper a few pages at a time. Indexes to newspapers—at least for this newspaper—are notorious for being incomplete and inaccurate. I figured the best way to work would be to go from issue to issue, referring to the index, but also putting together my own threads to follow as well. It would be slow, tedious work.

January 1, 1958: local politicos announce Vice President Nixon is going to swing through the city on his next trip.

Whoopee.

World leaders and New Year's wishes, pictures of drunks howling on the front page, celebrating, running over each other, shooting each other in bar fights.

There was nothing of interest until January 20, the day that all the winning politicians from the previous election took office. Jimmy was one of them. There was a short story in the lower left hand of the front page: D.A. PROMISES CRACK-DOWN ON CRIME! It was the same kind of story every D.A. gets right after he takes office and before the complaints start.

I didn't bother to check, but I suspected the newspaper supported Jimmy in the election. He'd defeated an incumbent who was under federal indictment for income tax evasion, which in this state doesn't necessarily mean a hell of a lot. Some of Louisiana's greatest statesmen have been under federal indictment for much of their careers.

I worked as fast and as thoroughly as I could through the next few months. In the middle of February, Jimmy personally prosecuted his first big case, winning a conviction against a murderer who raped the dead bodies of his victims. In the first week of March, the D.A.'s office worked with police to close a prostitution operation that ran six brothels throughout the city. Jimmy had his picture on the front page with the police chief.

As I read more and more of the papers, a portrait emerged of James Herbert that only confirmed what everybody knew. He was everything Katherine always said he was.

The problem was that he was so damn good. He won cases, expanded staff, got more money for his people, attracted good people. He ran a real smooth operation and never gave any appearance of impropriety.

The cleaner he looked, the dirtier I felt. But at least I'd have the satisfaction of showing up the Old Man; something not many had ever done.

I read through the first reel of microfilm, which only

covered the first three months of 1958. The trip back in time had given me a headache. My eyes hurt. I wound the second reel onto the machine and watched as page after page cranked by in front of me.

The stories read like Perry Mason novels, only the defense never wins. A murderer is sentenced to death in April; two days later, another gets life in prison. A rapist gets death; four burglars get ten to forty apiece; a dockworker gets two years for beating his wife; a woman gets life for poisoning her husband. Some poor sucker's popped for selling a shot glass full of marijuana and gets thirty-five years in the state penitentiary at Angola. Jesus, he's probably still there.

It all began to read the same; one conviction after another. Add another scalp to the belt. Not too many that Jimmy went after got off. He was young and thin then, his dark hair oiled straight back.

I worked through lunch, my eyes tired and burning as I sat there reading. Occasionally, some totally irrelevant story would catch my eye and I'd stop and read it out of boredom.

I swung between discouragement and elation. Sometimes it felt like a game, the thrill of the hunt, and at others, the realization that I was screwing around with somebody's life was hard to escape. But in the back of my mind, I still knew there was nothing to find. Yet something drove me on to keep looking.

By 4:30 that afternoon, I'd gone through all of 1958 and 1959. I wondered if it would even be worthwhile to come back and read the rest.

Jimmy told me the other night that he'd been in and out of fights before; I saw now what he was talking about.

I gave up for the day. My notes contained a few names and dates to follow up on, but nothing of any real value. I'm not even sure what I expected.

"What you after, darling?" Maud asked as I piled the stack of tapes on the counter in front of her.

"Just snooping."

"Yeah, I seen that look in your eye before. You on to something."

"I wish I was, babe," I said, half-truthfully.

"Say, when you going to get married again?"

Her question caught me off guard. "Say what?"

"You a good-looking boy with a good job," she offered. "Why don't you settle down?"

"You proposing, babe?"

She blushed. "Sshhee—yit," she said, drawing it out as only a true southerner can. "I'm way too old for you. But I got a niece lives out in Metairie in Fat City. Just divorced, got a cute little boy. She's only twenty-eight, used to be a model. I think you'd like her."

I thought for a second, then suddenly felt tired. "Aw, Maud, sometimes it just don't seem worth the effort."

She reached across the counter and laid her bony hand on my jacket sleeve. I looked down at her liver spots and blue veins and felt her tugging at me through the cloth.

"You too young to be giving up on love, boy," she said. "You too young to be this depressed."

I smiled at her. She was sweet, genuinely concerned, I thought. Not just trying to fix up her niece.

"And you too sweet to be this direct, darling."

"You hopeless."

"I'm just waiting for you to drop that old man of yours," I said, turning to leave.

"Yeah, you just keep right on waiting, sugar. I'm going keep my old man. He got more life in him than you."

"You're probably right."

"I usually am," she said, loading her arms with the boxes and disappearing into the stacks.

* * *

The heat and traffic were worse than before, and I was beginning to feel the onset of a full-scale blood sugar crash. I'd walked barely three blocks before I was covered in sweat and shaky from not eating and the endless, billowing clouds of automobile fumes.

Sally was going over some purchase orders when I walked in, slamming the door behind me.

"You know," she said, "every time you come back in this office you look worse."

"You sure know how to make a guy feel better," I grumbled.

"It's nothing."

"Don't I know it."

"Did you eat lunch?"

"Didn't have time."

"Give me some cash and I'll run down to the snack bar and get you a Coke and a sandwich."

"You're wonderful," I said, meaning it.

"So I'm told," she said back, smiling, reaching for the money I held out toward her.

I called upstairs to see if Carlton was in. His secretary put me on hold for a moment.

"Yes?" he said.

"Carlton, this is Jack. You hear anything from the security men you put on Herbert?"

"Not a thing," he answered. "But I'll call you back the minute we get anything. Did you have any luck?"

"Nothing. This is going to be tougher than we thought."

"Yes, I'm sure it will be," he said, a serious note in his voice. "But remember, my boy, the wolves are at the door."

"I'm doing my best."

"I'd assumed you would."

I'd just lit one after getting off the phone when Sally came in.

"Isn't that how it always works?" she said, setting this

great-looking club sandwich down in front of me. "Just as you light up, the food comes."

I snuffed the cigarette out and began wolfing down the sandwich.

"Jeez, you looked hungry when you came in," she said, settling down in the chair in front of the desk.

"I'm starving," I said with my mouth half-full. "I worked through lunch over at the paper."

"Find anything?"

"Nothing. The guy's Superman. He was single-handedly responsible for getting every bad guy in the state off the streets. I'd have hated to be in the crime business then."

"Not as lucrative as it is now, huh?"

"You got it."

"Well, keep at it. Something's bound to come up."

I finished the sandwich and wiped my hands on the cheap paper napkin. I relit the cigarette and sipped the Coke.

"Oh, that's better." I sighed.

"Good. Listen, I'm out of here. My work's caught up and I'm kind of tired."

"You okay? You're not getting sick or anything, are you?"

She smiled. "No. Just kind of tired. But thanks for asking."

"Sure, take off. I'm going to stick around for a while."

"See you tomorrow, then," she said.

"Hey," I said as she walked out the door.

"Yes?" she answered, turning back.

"Good night."

"Yeah. Good night." She looked at me kind of, well, funny. Then she turned again and walked out.

I loosened my tie as far as it would go without unraveling and laid down on my office couch. I kicked my shoes off, just letting them thump on the floor. My whole body ached from spending the day hunched in front of the microfilm reader.

I closed my eyes and tried to relax, just let images come at me from behind my eyelids like dreams. Jimmy was there, and Lily, and Katherine, and the boss. It must be strange to have that much power over people. Jimmy locked a lot of people away for a long time. Some of them must hate him still. With all the righteousness and vengeful wrath of the system, I wondered if he ever lost any sleep at night. Did he ever worry about locking people away for the rest of their lives? Or strapping them in the electric chair and frying them like a cheap steak?

Another thing that bothered me was the time factor. Here he was, easily the best and most popular D.A. in city history, and he gave it up after one six-year term. He could easily have won a second term, maybe even gone on to become mayor.

Then again, maybe he got sick of it. The politics involved would give anybody a bad case of nausea. The perverse and often contradictory alliances that are made in public life must have offended his innate sense of right and wrong, duty and honor. As long as I'd known him, that had been his thesis, the star of his movie. Right and Wrong. Truth and Lies. There are certain absolutes in this universe, and James Herbert knew what they were.

I'd respected and admired him, loved him and held him in awe. My father died in a car wreck when I was a baby; my mother was never the same after that. Jimmy Herbert became, almost by default, the father I never had. When Katherine and I started dating in college, and she took me home to meet her family, it was as if for the first time in my life I really had a home.

James Herbert treated me like a son, and he gave me the freedom to treat him like a father. No one had ever given me that before. It hurt like hell to lose it.

He also wasn't stupid. He knew what he was getting into

when he went into public life. A man doesn't dive into an open sewer and then come up mad because the stink gets on him.

I'd been thwarted and countered at every move. There was every reason for me to go upstairs and just tell the Old Man to pay up and chalk this one off to experience. Then Jimmy would be safe, Katherine would be happy, and I could get back to whatever structure it was that kept my life moving from one day to the next.

There was something else though, something false maybe, something at least tinny sounding in an ocean of harmony, that kept me going. It was all too perfect. As frustrated and tired of it as I was, something inside me made me decide to keep sniffing around, to search and dig a bit longer for the dead and rotting carcass. After all, with Jimmy's passion for truth and honesty, he'd forgive my staying on the chase. Wouldn't he?

"Jack," Carlton said, motioning me toward a chair, "this is Mr. Burnside of Security."

Mr. Burnside looked like he'd taken a correspondence course in detecting and graduated from the docks, where he'd been employed as a headbuster by the longshoremen's union.

"This guy is handling this?" Burnside asked, incredulously, looking at me as if I'd just broken wind in a crowded elevator.

"Yes, Burnside," Carlton said firmly. "At Mr. Jennings's personal orders."

"Oh, that's different."

So far, I hadn't said a word. It was not the greatest morning I'd ever had; I woke up sick to my stomach from the Mexican food I'd eaten the night before. It took a Lomotil, a Compazine, and a promise to never touch scotch again in the context of burritos to even get me into the office. If this is one of the consequences of age, this business of not being able to eat the things one would have looked forward to just a few short years ago, then I don't think I want to participate.

"Why don't you just tell us what you found out?" Carlton suggested.

"Okay," Burnside said, opening a small notebook he'd taken from the inside of his oversized, somewhat shiny, polyester jacket. "We had a man outside the house from Friday evening on. He spent the weekend either alone at home or in the company of his wife. Saturday evening, he and his wife had dinner with another couple. Nothing unusual. Herbert was followed from about seven forty-five Monday morning until his return home at six forty-five that night. He arrived at his law offices on Park at eight-ten in the morning, and didn't leave again until twelve-fifteen. He proceeded to a restaurant called the Steak Palace at Thompson and twenty-third. He was in the company of two other gentlemen. The three of them ate alone. Herbert ate a small steak, a salad, and had two martinis. He didn't finish the second one. The three men got back to the office at two-thirty. Herbert left his office at six-fifteen and went directly home.

"During this time," he continued, "after Herbert got home, our guy stayed outside until all the lights went out at eleven thirty-five that night. Nobody left the house. Nobody came into the house. The same pattern's been repeated every day. He even eats lunch at the same place. We've got a guy stationed outside Herbert's building now."

Burnside flipped the notebook shut and put it back in his pocket. His deep, gravelly voice seemed to reinforce the general impression that he was a surly and not terribly intelligent man.

"Your men seem to be doing a thorough job," Carlton said.

"Listen, did this guy just watch Herbert's car or did he look for Herbert walking out of the office?"

Burnside looked at me with obvious contempt. Jeez, who pee'd in this guy's Cheerios?

"Both."

"And he found nothing that would indicate Herbert was seeing a woman, perhaps, or maybe some odd clients—"

"If he had," Burnside said, "I'd have told you about it."

"I think we should keep the tail on him for a few more days," I said to Carlton, then turning to the p.o.'d P.I., "that is, if your men can keep from being spotted."

"I don't have to take that from you," Burnside said, menacing.

"Actually, Mr. Burnside, I'm afraid you do," Carlton said.

"This is costing Mr. Jennings a lot of money," Burnside griped. "I ain't so sure he's going to like us wasting his dough like that."

"Mr. Jennings has personally put Mr. Lynch in charge of this investigation. If Mr. Lynch wants something, it's the same as if it came directly from Mr. Jennings. Understand?"

"Yeah," Burnside growled.

My gut took a sickening rumble. I was going to need another Lomotil soon. A ten-milligram Valium wouldn't be a bad idea, either.

"Well, then," Carlton said. "Why don't you contact your operatives and tell them to stay on the job a little longer."

Burnside stood up and towered over the two of us, his hunched, massive shoulders giving him a certain gorillalike appearance.

"What'd I do to that guy?" I asked Carlton, after Burnside was gone.

"He was rather surly."

"Thanks for backing me up."

"I'm just afraid he's not going to find anything," Carlton said.

I didn't know if I was more afraid that he would.

* * *

That afternoon, I was back at the morgue, poring over microfilm copies of newspapers more than a quarter-century old. It's hard to connect with things that far back; I was alive then, but it's not a part of me. I don't remember most of what I was reading.

In 1959, the D.A.'s office prosecuted a fraud ring that had passed $60,000 worth of bad checks in a two-year period. In January 1960, Herbert prosecuted "Axe-handle Mary," a young woman who beat her boyfriend and his new girlfriend to death with an axe handle. He won; Mary got life. In March, Herbert's office prosecuted a gang of burglars responsible for more than $50,000 worth of stolen goods—a lot of money in 1960.

In late March–early April, the office got convictions against an automobile theft ring that averaged almost sixty cars a month. Thirty-six people were involved, nine of them juveniles.

In May 1960, three men were convicted of distributing pornographic literature. Also that month, a prominent insurance broker was prosecuted for embezzlement after being extradited from New York, where he'd been popped while waiting for a plane to Bermuda.

In June 1960, Herbert organized the New Orleans District Attorney's Commission on Organized Crime, beating Bobby Kennedy's time by at least a year. In July, a local gangster was indicted for conspiracy to operate an illegal gambling operation. Later, in August, six members of a motorcycle gang were prosecuted for aggravated rape.

The stories went on like this for reel after reel. All this was in addition to scores of burglaries, muggings, murders, auto theft, and other crimes committed by people who didn't rate a big headline.

It took until Thursday morning to get through everything, the microfilm, the clippings, the files that Maud was able to get for me for a slight under-the-table contribution to her favorite charity. I liked Maud a lot, and wasn't above slipping her a few bucks now and then.

I walked into the office about eleven o'clock. Sally looked up at me and smiled.

"Hey, stranger," she said, snuffing out her cigarette.

"Hi, lady. I finished up at the paper."

"No luck, I guess?"

"No," I answered, walking into my office and settling gratefully into my chair. "It was a waste of time we really ain't got. I'm not sure I expected to find much."

"Still," she said, "it would have been nice."

Sally followed me into the office and set a cup of coffee down on my desk for me. Then she got her own cup and her smokes, came in, and parked herself over on the couch. She crossed her legs; the shorter-than-usual dress hiked up over her knees. I stared at her for a second, feeling the warmth of the coffee cup in my hands, and fought this urge to go over to the couch and sit next to her.

Why was I always fighting it? Maybe Maud was right, I am too young to give up on love, but what do you do with it? Where do you put all the old garbage when it won't go away?

She struck a match and the blaze drew my eyes up to her face.

"I'll be honest with you," I said. "I don't know where the hell to go next. We could start asking around his friends, neighbors, people in the firm, and all that. But we'd be found out in a minute. And if the papers got hold of that, we'd be in worse shape than ever."

"The situation definitely calls for something just a little more subtle," she said. "Let's save the heavy-handed stuff for last. Who knows? Maybe we'll get lucky and something will come out of the tail."

"I doubt it. Besides, those nitwits over at security just might blow the whole thing wide open. I told Carlton I thought it would be best to call them off after a day or two."

"Well, you'd better think of something. Quick."

The air was still for a second as we both sat there looking at each other. The gnawing in my stomach—or was it lower?—started up again.

"To hell with it," I said. "Let's go to lunch."

That's getting to be my answer to everything; the best avoidance of emotional confrontations is to stuff something in your mouth. Food, drinks, cigarettes, it really doesn't matter.

Oh, like I said, to hell with it . . .

There was a nagging, a tugging, that wouldn't go away. That night, I ordered a muffaletta, one of those great New Orleans sandwiches dripping with oil and olive salad, then sat sipping a scotch and soda and smoking. Even that didn't do the trick. Something was kicking up dust that hadn't been kicked in a long time. There was a stink out there that was more than the usual smell of rot drifting in off the river.

The one nerve I had left was getting badly frayed.

As much as I wanted to believe it, the whole story of Jimmy Herbert and his mighty crusades, it just wouldn't all stay together. I desperately wanted to believe him, to have someone in this whole shitty escapade to depend on for some kind of purity and nobility of purpose. But I've been wallowing around in the muck for too many years. Was I missing something? A piece that wasn't there yet? I wanted a fact that would confirm it for good; I was afraid of one that would blow it wide open like an infected wound that finally erupts in pus and blood.

No matter how hard I tried to dig it up out of that muck, it seemed to sink deeper as I got closer to it.

It was no good, though. I was getting real pissed at myself. It seemed as though the urgency of the situation and my closeness to Jimmy had put up some kind of mental block; some bizarre and terminal form of psychic impotence. Goddammit, I used to be smart and quick. What happened? Too many years, too much booze? Are the circuits burned out, the fuses hopelessly blown?

Disgusted, I had one more drink, paid my check, and went home, prepared to give the whole thing up. Just bag it. I was surprised to find that it was well past midnight.

It came drifting up toward me out of an uneasy, troubled, half-sleep.

Zimmerman.

The clock read 3:30, the orange glow of the digital numbers pulsating in the darkness.

I'm on an airplane. No, I am the airplane. I'm landing in a church parking lot, picking up passengers.

I got all these people running around inside of me.

Zimmerman.

Katherine's there, and she's inside me. Running around, tearing things loose, ripping me up inside.

Sally's there, too. She's wearing a bright paisley silk dress that's flapping in the breeze, around her legs, the dress rising higher with the wind. I get glimpses of the inside of her thighs; I want to see more. C'mon, dress, I think, go higher.

And then I realize I'm standing on a stage, before all these people. Nude. Exposed.

I try to hide.

The Old Man is there, coming at me with an axe. I try to run, grab a stage curtain, pull it around me. Katherine's laughing.

My mother, the crazy, is in the back of the auditorium—

Zimmerman.

—directing all this mess. Her hands are held out before her like a witch's. Her hair blazes with electricity; there's madness in her eyes.

But she's been dead for years.

Zimmerman.

What is it? What's going on here? Is this insanity, dementia? I shoot up out of bed in a cold sweat. And there, stuck in the back of my throat like a piece of eggshell, is that name again: Zimmerman.

I grab a pen off the nightstand and fumble for a piece of paper.

I wrote the name on a scrap of paper and laid it on the nightstand. Three hours later, the alarm clock goes off like the call for Armageddon. I roll over and sit up, the skin over my face stretching like old elastic. My eyes burn; my mouth is full of fur. What an ugly way to wake up.

I've all but forgotten the details of the dream, but the way I felt in the dream—exposed, terrified, threatened—hangs on to me like fog that won't dissipate, snow that won't melt. I reach over and snap on the light, squinting to protect my tender, bloodshot eyes.

And there on the table, the scrap of paper sits.

Zimmerman.

Six

"Good morning, Public Relations." Sally's telephone voice was as effectively cold and impersonal as any I'd ever heard.

"Good morning, darling."

"My, someone's awfully chipper this morning, darling." The voice changed back to the real Sally. "By the way, who is this?"

"Oh, I see. You'll just return a darling to anyone."

"You got the money, honey, I got the time."

"Right," I said. "Listen, I'm going to be in late this morning. I got to go back to the newspaper."

"How come? Come up with something?"

"Probably not. I just thought of something, that's all. If anyone should call, don't let them know where I am. I'll be in later."

"Yeah. I'll keep the door barred."

"You're wonderful."

"So I'm told," she said, hanging up.

Alton Valentine Zimmerman. What in hell ever happened to him?

Big Al Zimmerman. At one time, in the late thirties and forties, Big Al had been it: the King of the New Orleans Jewish Mafia. And this group of guys wasn't no carnival krewe. Dey wuz serious.

"Maud, darling, let me have your file on Al Zimmerman."

"Big Al?" she asked. "You got a wheelbarrow?"

"C'mon, there wasn't that much on the microfilms."

"Well, hell, by the late fifties, Big Al Zimmerman was getting along in years. He must have been in his sixties or something."

"Let me see what you got on him, okay?"

"It's going to take a while," she said with an edge of complaint in her voice. "A lot of these files are really buried deep. Big Al's been dead a long time, you know."

"This is important to me, babe. I'm grasping for straws here."

"I love the way you talk to me. You know that?" she said, wrinkling her nose at me, adding more lines to the ones already around her eyes. "Why don't you and I get together? My old man's never around anyway. I'd just as soon dump the old fart."

"Maybe we'll do that sometime," I said, smiling back at her. "In the meantime, take yourself out to dinner and think of me."

I palmed a couple of twenties and handed them across the counter to her. Maud looked around the room to make sure nobody saw her take what could possibly be misconstrued as a bribe.

"I really *do* like the way you talk to me," she said, taking the bills.

"Girl's got to make a living, right?"

"Damn straight," she said, turning and disappearing into the stacks.

Ten minutes and two large file cartons later, I had the sum total of a bad man's life on the table in front of me. Yellowed clippings dating back over a half-century; black and white file photos showing a greasy young punk with slicked-back hair and sharp features and curious black circles under his eyes; photocopies of arrest records, indictments, lawsuits, reports, accusations, suppositions. It was all there. Except for a few missing pieces I still had yet to find.

Big Al, so-called because he was barely five-feet-five, had it all at one time. He grew up in the Quarter in the early days of the century. Storyville was big then; legalized, safe, regulated, and above all, lucrative prostitution. Everybody was getting rich—the girls, the brothel owners, the city officials and cops who were paid off to keep Storyville alive.

Alton Valentine Zimmerman delivered beer, buckets of beer, from the saloons to the barber shops, the stores, the smaller brothels that weren't equipped with their own facilities. It was nice work that paid well for a young boy. When World War I broke out, two things happened: Storyville was shut down because of the cries of mothers across the country who feared for the morals of their brave boys encamped at the naval station in New Orleans; and Al Zimmerman was drafted into the army.

Somehow, he got out of serving. There's no record of him ever having been in the military. How he got out is anybody's guess; I only know that there's a picture of him back then, a faded glossy of a kid in his late teens/early twenties wearing a hundred-dollar suit. Anybody who could afford those kind of duds at that early age could probably bribe some geek in the local draft office, or maybe a doctor to help him flunk his physical.

Anyway, he got out of it, a pattern that was to continue all his life.

They never nailed him. As far as I could tell, he never did a day's worth of serious time. He got arrested a couple of dozen times, occasionally having to even spend a night in jail. But they never got him. And he was into everything: numbers downtown, prostitution everywhere, drugs—real serious, hard, nasty shit—down in the bad parts of town, loan-sharking at the docks. There was no part of graft, vice, or corruption that escaped Big Al Zimmerman's involvement. The man was a genius, an entrepreneur in the truest sense of the word. You had to give him that.

Apparently, he carried himself with a certain style, finesse, grace. He was a small man, with a face that couldn't be described as handsome by the kindest of grandmothers. And yet, his newspaper pictures remind me of a young Cary Grant. Did he cultivate this intentionally? The young boy came out of the roughest parts of the city. Could he have known real style? Can that come to some people instinctively? Or did he just watch a lot of movies?

I dug back through the files while rolling back the reels of microfilm, trying to correlate notes, pictures, reports, typed articles, with the actual published stories. I had no idea if any of this was going to work. Reporters aren't now, and certainly weren't then, required to turn over all their notes to morgue librarians. A reporter could have spent his entire professional life following Alton Valentine Zimmerman, and not one speck of material would have to wind up in a dusty file in the basement. That's just the way it worked.

But there was one attempt to nail him, and somehow it was that one attempt that hung around in a corner of my mind unresolved, like a hiccup on a disk drive that causes the screen to blink suddenly and inexplicably out of nowhere. My disk drives had hiccuped on me in the middle of the night: an unexplained system error that needed to be resolved. And the way you resolved these things, in human minds and computer brains alike, is to go back over the data, lift it up off the tracks, examine it for bugs and little things that go bump in the night, then lay the cleared data back down on a clean track. It was time to reexamine the data.

July 20, 1960. A Wednesday; probably a hot-as-hell-in-the-south Wednesday, with people fanning themselves and moving slowly and reading the papers with one hand while sipping a co-cola with the other. And there it was:

RACKETEER INDICTED IN GAMBLING CONSPIRACY

Prominent racketeer and underworld figure Alton V. "Big Al" Zimmerman has been charged under an indictment filed by the District Attorney's Commission on Organized Crime.

The indictment, which charges Zimmerman with conspiracy to operate an illegal gambling operation, was announced by District Attorney James Herbert today.

If convicted, Zimmerman faces up to 25 years in the state penitentiary.

The Orleans Parish Grand Jury refused to indict Zimmerman on similar charges last year. D.A. Herbert said today that new evidence recently found makes an indictment possible.

He also told reporters that his office indicted Zimmerman because the recent Grand Jury term has expired and the next will not convene until next summer.

Blip. That's it: five quick paragraphs in the evening paper. Two more hours of digging through the files and going through the blasted microfilm reels one more time to make sure that what was bubbling around underneath was true and real and not some screw-up on my part. But there it was.

There was no trial.

Why?

Could there have been a trial with no coverage? Not likely, even given the crappy newspapers in this town. Big Al was too big a name in the city; he sold too many papers. If anything, every step and moment of the trial would have been splattered over the front page like goo at the slaughterhouse.

So what the hell was going on here?

"Maud," I said, laying an armful of files on the counter. "You're wonderful and I love you." Then I leaned across the counter and kissed her on the cheek. She blushed and giggled.

"Later, babe," I said, walking out the door.

"You wish . . ."

Fred Williams, over at the D.A.'s office, was a different kind of man from the type you usually saw at the courthouse. Politics is changing everywhere, even down here in Never-Never Land, and Fred was the new kind of up-and-coming political animal. A lawyer by trade, but with that special kind of fire-in-the-belly passion that marks the new young breed, Fred Williams didn't even look like a southern politician. He didn't smoke smelly cigars; he didn't wear cheap, shiny suits; he didn't shear his hair off short enough to show the red around his collar. Daily racquetball games and jogging kept off the excess poundage that one invariably picked up from the rubber chicken and bourbon whiskey circuit. In fact, blasphemy of blasphemies, except for an occasional beer, Fred Williams didn't drink. Even ten years ago down South, this would have marked him as at least a wimp, or worse yet, a faggot. Jesus, in this part of the country even the Baptists drink on Saturday night, then pray for forgiveness the next morning.

Fred was a good guy and I liked him. He was probably dangerous; all competent politicians are. But Fred scared me less than the rest of them, and until he gave me reason to think otherwise, I'd keep on trusting him as far as I trusted anybody in his line of work.

Over the years, we'd swapped a few favors back and forth. Fred was a new age politician, but he still had sense enough to cultivate the people behind the people with the real power in this town. And I happened to be behind one of the biggest.

"God, Jack, Big Al Zimmerman," Fred said, leaning back in his leather assistant D.A.'s chair and folding his hands behind his head. "That's ancient history for sure."

"Yeah, but you can learn a lot from history."

"You don't have to tell me that, Jack. I double-majored in it as an undergrad."

"What?" I said, kidding. "You got two history degrees?"

"No, dumb ass, history and political science. Did I ever tell you my granddaddy loved football? He helped finance the last big renovation of the Sugar Bowl. Back when there was a Sugar Bowl, you know."

"And since then has been promoted to God."

"Or at least to Glory." Fred sighed. "C'mon, Jack, I don't have time for this happy horseshit. What do you really want?"

"Al Zimmerman was indicted by the D.A.'s office in July 1960. There was never a trial, at least not one that showed up in the papers. I want to know why."

"Not asking for too much, are you?"

"It's important, Fred," I said. "To me. To my boss."

"Well, I never pass up the chance to help a citizen if it's not illegal and doesn't cost the taxpayers too much. But records that old aren't even in the courthouse anymore. All that stuff's been moved into the new storage warehouse out by the landfill."

"Great, that means it's probably covered in mold by now."

"That's what happens when the city lets a contract go to one of your boss's cronies—"

"Find out for me, Fred, will you? You're the only one in the D.A.'s office that has the authority and that I trust."

"Lucky me," he said. "I tell you what. I'll get you a copy of the indictment and the file, if—and that's a big if—my girl can even locate the records out at the warehouse. But Lucy's not going to be too happy about having to dig around in a building full of musty papers."

"Let her wear jeans out there," I said. "I'll send her some roses or something."

"It may take more than that, guy. It may take a couple racquetball games with me next week."

"What? You need an ego boost or something?" I said. "The last time we played, you skunked me three games and I couldn't bend over for a week."

"Yeah." He grinned. "Great, wasn't it?"

Back at the office, I wondered which way to go. The maze was getting more convoluted than ever, and only one thing was certain: either I was getting closer to the truth or farther away from it.

"Sally," I called. She came in and sat down in front of me. "I'm going upstairs. I haven't seen the boss in a few days."

She laughed.

I went straight up to the executive suite. "Is he busy?" I asked Madge. "You think he'll want to see me?"

"He's been asking about you lately," she said soberly. "Wondering if you still worked here."

"Oh, shit," I said quietly.

"You don't have time," she said. "I'll announce you."

The Old Man was standing up in front of his desk, pacing back and forth. His tie was pulled loose at the neck. One of the flaps of his collar was turned up and his hair splayed in all directions, like he'd been running his fingers across his scalp all morning long.

"Where in the hell have you been the last week or so?" he boomed.

"Playing bloodhound," I answered. "Doing what you pay me for."

"Have you found anything?" he demanded, sitting down behind the desk.

"I don't know."

"You don't know!" he yelled.

"I may have," I said quickly. "But then again, I may not have. I don't know yet."

"What is it?" he demanded again.

"I'd just as soon not say yet, if you don't mind."

"Goddammit! I mind!"

"Now you told me when I started this," I said, desperately wanting to light a cigarette, "to do anything I had to to get this thing taken care of. Now I assumed that meant to do it any way I saw fit. And I see fit to not talk too much or get too excited until I've gotten something solid. Now if I was wrong about that—"

"All right," he interrupted. "You've made your point. Just tell me one thing. Is it solid? If it's solid, will it nail that S.O.B.?"

"It's too early to tell."

"When will you know?"

"I'm not sure."

"You are the be-jesus most damn difficult person I've ever met in my life. Will you just do me one favor? Take a bath every morning."

"What?" I asked.

"Since I have to kiss your ass to get anything out of you, I'd like it to be clean. Now get out of here."

Downstairs, Sally was behind her desk, having hung up the phone just as I walked in.

"Hey, how are you?" she asked.

"I think I'm getting an ulcer."

"Boss pretty hard on you?"

"Yeah. Had he been calling down for me while I've been gone?"

"Madge called a couple times looking for you."

"Jeez, give me a little warning next time. I really have to walk a line with him sometimes."

"One of these days you're going to push him too hard."

"Or he's going to push me. One or the other."

"You look tired," Sally said.

Come to think of it, it had been a long week. I was beat; I just never thought she noticed things like that. "I'll be all right."

"Right, sure."

"I'm not physically tired. Just mentally."

"I'd hate to see what would happen to you if you really had to work for a living," she said, grinning.

"Maybe we can both get a vacation soon."

She looked up at me. "Together?"

"Depends," I said. "Where would you like to go?"

"I'd like to go back to San Francisco someday."

"I didn't know you'd ever been there."

"Yeah," she said. "I was there once on my honeymoon. But I liked it anyway."

She looked at me and there was a moment of silence between us. The flowered print dress she wore was very sheer and light, almost airy. She'd pulled her hair behind her and tied it with a hairband.

"Got a date tonight?" I asked out of nowhere.

"No, just going home."

"Want to have dinner?"

She looked at me for what seemed like a long time, as if she were really mulling it over hard.

"Sure. Why not?"

I smiled at her. "Don't get too enthusiastic here. I wouldn't want you to get overheated."

"Well, I am hungry. And I don't know about you, but I could use a drink."

"Sounds good to me. Let's go suck down a chili dog or something," I said, getting up and pulling my jacket off the chair behind me. Sally made a face at me.

"You're gross, you know that."

"I promise to behave myself tonight."

"Oh, great," she said, turning and walking out of my office. "Now I know it'll be a boring evening."

We drove to a place in the Quarter, deep down in the residential, old part, away from the loud tourist dives and jazz joints. This was an out of the way place with thick stone walls and lots of plants. It was lush and damp, thick and sleepy, with a wonderful piano-playing singer who reminded me a lot of the time I saw Bobby Short at the Carlyle in New York with Katherine. It was one of our last good times together, years before we split up. We flew to New York to play tourist for a week. It was the last time it was ever her idea to make love; we'd come in half-loaded and stuffed from a wonderful evening out. She reached into her suitcase and pulled out the little blue plastic case that held her diaphragm. "Don't go away," she said. "I'll be right back."

But eventually I did go away. And nothing had ever been the same since. Sometimes I felt like a damn fool; near middle-aged men are supposed to be self-sufficient and strong, and able to cope with broken relationships. I could never seem to shake the sadness of it, though, except in work. The mindless pursuit of something that in the long run makes no difference to anything; the endless burning of energy.

Only this was different now. Searching for the truth about Jimmy Herbert was like throwing dice in a dice cup and shaking them until the edges were worn off. My edges were worn off. The stable little predictable world I'd created for myself was getting the foundations kicked out from under it. I was itchy and restless and I wanted to see what came out of the dice cup, what numbers would be on top when the dice stopped rattling.

And I didn't want to be alone tonight. Something in the way Sally looked at me, or maybe it was just the way she looked period, made me finally speak up and ask her out.

Suddenly, our relationship had changed. I could feel it even as we walked toward my car. This was a social occasion now. It was after hours and we were still choosing to spend time with each other.

Some dangerous shit here.

My stomach was in a knot. But I fought it and made

myself calm down. This was just a night out, that's all, a night out with an attractive woman I spent a lot of time with in my work.

Over drinks, we talked. Mostly work, the constant changing ebb and flow of power in the corporation. Who was in favor, who was out of favor, who was an up-and-comer, who to watch out for. The same kinds of games millions of people play in thousands of companies every day.

She ordered white wine; I my usual scotch and soda. I reached across the table to light her cigarette. She held out her free hand to steady mine as it held the lighter. Her fingertips brushed the back of my hand and I was left speechless.

I had been out lots of times with lots of women since Katherine. But it was always just for a night out, or casual sex, or just somebody to be with. It's not that hard to find that sort of thing, if that's all you're looking for.

This time was different. This was someone who knew me, or at least knew me as well as anyone did these days.

"Have you heard any more from your ex?" Sally asked.

"No, I think she just wanted to pry," I answered. "Just wanted to know why I'd be talking to her father after all this time."

"I don't hear from my ex very often. It's something that will bring me great comfort in my old age."

"What happened to you guys?" I asked.

"Well, let's see," she said, looking around for our food. "I met him back in the little town I came from. This was way before I came to the city. I'd graduated from high school and had a job as a secretary at the local weekly newspaper. He worked on the oil rigs, which meant he was gone for two weeks, then back for two. In the beginning I missed him so much during the two weeks he was gone. In the end, though, I dreaded the two weeks he'd be back."

"That bad, huh?"

"Life on the oil rigs is pretty weird. The three cardinal

rules: no booze, no women, no guns. And he loved all three. By the time he got home, he had a ton of bundled-up nervous energy just waiting to bust loose."

"Must have been fun when you were newlyweds. There's nothing for preserving passion like being away from somebody you want."

"In the beginning, yeah." She laughed softly. "After a while, though, I got the feeling it could be anybody. He was just looking for release. After a time, it was anybody. Anybody he could get his hands on. He'd be home an hour or two, then he'd be down at the bars drinking beer and slutting around with some greasy waitress."

"Must have been tough."

"It was. I fell out of love with him real quick. He was just a bayou redneck that worked on the oil rigs. And to tell you the truth, I wanted more."

"I can understand that."

"Eventually, things got real bad between us. He beat me around a little bit, but I didn't put up with that too long. He knocked out three of my front teeth one night and I laid him open with a pipe wrench. We decided to call it a draw and get divorced."

"Jeez, I didn't know that. How long have we worked together now, almost ten years? I never knew he hit you."

"Yeah, well, you never asked. These three upper fronts are a partial," she said, pointing at her mouth.

"You can't tell," I said.

"It pays to buy the best when it comes to dentists."

We continued making small talk as the food came. We were both hungry, strung out from the week, glad to have some time alone. After dinner, we smoked and had coffee and a brandy.

It was nearly eleven when we finally left. In the distance, we could hear the yelling and loud music that defined that part of the Quarter the tourists saw. But we were in the old part, the residential part, the places where the Stanley Kowalskis lived. It was quieter here, although an occasional yell or a radio turned up loud pierced the night's silence.

I paid the waiter and we walked out into the cool night air. They say that in New Orleans the only way you can tell the change of seasons is when the temperature of the rain changes. We were coming up on that part of the year I loved the most. Autumn in New Orleans almost makes me happy.

The sidewalks were mostly deserted as we walked back to my car, which was parked, as usual, four or five blocks away. In the Quarter, you're lucky to find a space at all.

The yellow of a streetlight cut through the mist as we walked under it. We walked side-by-side, close, our arms brushing as we stepped. Our hands touched and I took hers in mine. We walked down the street holding hands like two teenagers on a first date, which except for a couple of quick decades, we were.

"Thanks for dinner," Sally said.

"Thanks for being there with me. Old bachelors get tired of eating alone."

She laughed. "It's not much fun for old divorcées, either."

"Listen to us, we talk like we've got one foot in the grave and the other on roller skates," I said. She stopped on the sidewalk and turned to me. We were in the shadow of a building, halfway between streetlights. I turned and looked at her, into the light that seemed to come straight out of her eyes, from someplace deep down inside her. I put my hands on her shoulders and felt for the first time how slight and thin she was. She brought her arms up and wrapped them loosely around my waist and lifted her head up to me.

"We're being silly," she said.

I smiled, almost a grin, unable to help myself.

"I know. Life's too short."

"Yeah, too . . ."

And I leaned over as she started talking and very softly

kissed her. Something shot through me like a jolt, and I flashed on this stupid, fleeting thought that here I am in some incredibly romantic moment with this woman and I'm going to have a freaking heart attack.

She kissed me back. Her mouth, like the rest of her, seemed so tiny and delicate, her lips thin like a cat's mouth. But she kissed me back with a passion that surprised me, that brought out my own desire, a desire that had been very quiet for a long time.

Suddenly my arms were around her and we were locked together. She held me tightly, as tightly as anyone had ever held me, and I felt my knees going wobbly as her mouth opened and pulled mine along with it.

Her eyes were closed. Her head was back and I could feel that her legs were going limp as well. I held her up, looking at her through my own half-closed eyes.

"You're incredible," I said. "I've wanted to do that for a long time."

"So what took you so long?" she said, smiling.

We turned and started walking, my arm around her shoulder, her head turned slightly in toward me. We walked in time now, our bodies moving in an effortless, graceful way. It was a way I hadn't walked with anyone in a long time.

Finally, we got to my car. I opened the door on her side and she got in. I carefully closed it, then walked around and got in on my side. The top was up.

Sally took my hand after I closed the door. I turned to her, barely able to see her outline in the pitch black inside my car.

"It's getting late," I said. "I guess I need to take you home."

"My car's still in the bank parking lot," she said.

I leaned over and kissed her again, a long, slow, soft, and wet kiss that she returned with no hesitation, no complication. Part of me wanted to go very, very slowly, while the other part wanted to let loose all the pent-up feeling I'd had for years. Her hair was on my cheek now, touching my skin like a thousand tiny fingers.

"Would you like to come over for a drink?" she asked.

"Of course," I said. "You know that."

"My car . . ." she said, as she felt me moving toward her again.

"We could get it in the morning."

I wrapped her in my arms and held her, feeling at that moment as if I could hold her there safe and warm for a thousand years. This was a new one on me. It had been one hell of a long time.

"Okay," she said. "We'll go get the car tomorrow."

And I realized, as we drove away, that I hadn't thought about the Old Man or Iris or Jimmy Herbert or any of those other damn people all night long. Just completely forgotten about them.

Seven

I have to ask you something," she said as we lay there in
bed the next morning.

I'd come up out of the deepest sleep I'd had in years
just a few minutes earlier. There she was, back turned to
me, brown hair splayed in a million directions over the pillow.

I had to stop for a second and remind myself where I
was.

The sheets were tangled all around us like storm clouds
broken loose. She was still asleep when I woke up, with the
top sheet pulled around her shoulders and down her back,
and her bottom and legs uncovered. Sleep was in my eyes,
like looking out at the world through a dirty fishnet. My
mouth felt as if the Third Armored rolled through it last
night on its way to maneuvers.

I'd never felt better in my whole life.

Sally lay there asleep, with me not moving, not wanting
to wake her up. It was early. Sunlight was barely making it

through the sheers; there was no traffic outside yet. Cool and damp and lush, it was a New Orleans morning at its best.

She lived on a side street near the park. Located in a converted, turn-of-the-century house, the apartment had a huge fireplace, wooden floors, and ceilings so high you couldn't jump up to touch them. She lived there alone. It was warm and comfortable, plain and simple. Wall-to-wall bookcases lined the living room and one wall of the bedroom. They were full of everything from the classics to dime-store paperbacks.

She'd been full of surprises that night. And I found, much to my astonishment, there were still a few left in me.

I watched her sleep for a few minutes, then raised my head up on my arm, with my elbow digging into the soft mattress. She stirred at that and woke up slowly, then rolled over to face me, being careful to hold the sheet up over her. I leaned down and stared into her sleepy eyes for a second, then kissed her ever so softly.

"Nice kiss." She sighed. "Terrible morning mouth."

"I'm sorry."

"Not you, dummy." She smiled. "Me. I feel like somebody did an oil change in my mouth. Mmmm," she hummed, snuggling in close to me. "Which I suppose is not too far from the truth . . ."

"Okay," I said, after she brought up her question. "What was it you wanted to ask me?"

"How did you . . ." Then as if suddenly becoming terribly shy, she nuzzled down in my arm and hid from me. "Go so long? I mean, I'm not complaining. Believe me. It's just a new one on me."

I settled down in the pillow next to her and stared up at the ceiling.

"It just takes me a long time to let go, I guess. Sometimes it's been a problem."

"Heavens." She laughed. "All men should have that problem."

"I suppose I should feel flattered," I said. "Usually it works the other way around. I have trouble letting loose and really losing control. Which, I think, is one of the things you do when you make love."

"Yeah, well, you lost control just fine last night. You just took a deliciously long time doing it."

She came up on an elbow herself now and looked down at me. I slid my arm up under her and pulled her toward me, and she kissed me slowly, sleepily. I brought my other arm up and around her, pulling her even closer. We settled into making slow, sweet, early morning love.

We drank coffee and talked and made love again. We went over to my place for a change of clothes for me and then out to dinner Saturday night, a long, lazy dinner, and then back to Sally's apartment. We drank brandy and smoked, watched an old film on TV, stayed up half the night, and slept until almost noon Sunday.

It was late Sunday night before we got Sally's car back from the bank parking lot, and even then only because it would look just a tad too suspicious for her car to be in the same spot all weekend, with her driving in to work with me Monday morning.

Romance is even sweeter when corporate reality is headed off at the pass.

It was a weekend that made me alive again.

I swear I really thought I'd lost interest there for a while. But Sally woke me up, breathed life into me. I'd known her for ten years, but never really known her. Not until this weekend.

It had been coming for months, I think; this gradual realization that in all my years of looking for something, someone, to anchor my life to, all the time the moorings were right next to me. I felt silly and giddy, embarrassed at my show of emotion but unwilling to hide it a second longer.

I was in love.

Then reality hit.

Monday morning, back to the office, I walked in twenty minutes late.

"Well," she said, "where have you been?"

"I had to drive home and change," I said, walking over behind the desk and putting my hands on her shoulders, rubbing them in a distinctly nonprofessional manner.

"You had a shower at my place," she said.

"I know."

"You dawdled," she chided. "I know you, you dawdled."

"Only a little," I answered, leaning down and nuzzling her neck.

"You've got to quit that," she said, pulling away from me, serious now. "We're liable to get in trouble, anyway. But we will for sure if someone walks in and catches you doing that."

"You're right," I said, appropriately chastised. "I'll be good."

"You can do that later. Right now, call Fred Williams."

Less than a minute later, I had Fred on the phone.

"That was quick."

"I got curious," he said. "Kind of wanted to find out myself. So I put on my grubbies and went over to the warehouse Saturday."

"And?"

"You want to tell me what this is all about, fella?" Fred asked.

"Sorry, pal. If I could, I would. But I can't."

"Jack, those files are gone."

There was a long moment of silence on the phone; it took a bit for what he was saying to soak in.

"Gone?"

"Yeah, gone. Stolen. Missing. Absent without leave—"

"Are you sure you just couldn't find them?"

"I was on staff when we opened the new warehouse. I helped pack the files up. We had a system; two people signed off for packing and each box was sealed with tape. The case files on Zimmerman took up a half-dozen boxes. A chunk that big doesn't get misplaced."

"What does it mean?"

"Well, offhand, bucko, I'd say somebody didn't want those files ever found. And it was somebody with the clout to get to our security people."

"Jesus," I muttered. What was going on here?

"Jesus hasn't got nothing to do with it, babe. What are you up to?"

"I told you I can't tell you that."

"I like you, Jack. Whatever you're up to, you're in the game with some major league players."

"Apparently so."

"Keep your jockstrap tight, buddy," he warned.

"I will, Fred. Thanks."

"Oh, there is one thing. Whoever took the boxes got all the files. But the staff assignment sheets for that year were in a different place. The assistant district attorney in charge of prosecuting Zimmerman was a guy named Lubbock Powell."

"You know him?"

"Hell, Jack, I was just a kid. Never heard of him."

"Lubbock Powell," I said. "Okay, Fred. I owe you one."

"You watch your ass, you hear?"

"Yeah. Thanks, buddy."

The hair on the back of my neck bristled. How long had the files been missing, I wondered. For years, or did my poking around cause someone to get the files last week?

"Sally, I'm looking for an attorney."

I heard a laugh from the outer office.

"You can't shake a stick without hitting a lawyer around here. Come to think of it, that's not a bad idea."

"No, a particular attorney. His name's Lubbock Powell."

She scribbled the name down in her notebook.

"Lubbock, like in Texas?"

"I guess."

"Right on it."

I started digging through the paperwork on my desk while Sally played bloodhound for a while. An hour or so later, she walked into my office and slapped her notepad down on my desk.

"He doesn't exist."

"What?"

"You heard me, baby," she said, lighting a cigarette. "There ain't no Lubbock Powell."

"How could that be? He was an assistant D.A."

"I checked the Martindale-Hubbell, the Yellow Pages, the state bar association. I even called information for every big city in the state. There is no lawyer named Lubbock Powell in the state of Louisiana."

What did it mean? Had he died, moved away, retired?

"There is one thing," she added.

"Yeah?"

"Stop looking for a lawyer named Lubbock Powell. Just look for the man. With a name like that, there can't be too many of them."

"Driver's license bureau?"

"Yeah, only you got to go down to the State Office Building for that. They won't give you that information over the phone."

"I'll go check it out," I said, getting up and reaching for my coat.

She walked around back of the desk and straightened my lapels. I sensed she was just looking for an excuse.

"What's this guy got to do with the price of tea in China?" she asked, coming into my arms.

"He used to be an assistant D.A."

"Yeah, I got that much. How come you're looking for him?"

I hesitated for a moment. It wasn't a matter of trust with Sally; I'd trust her with the rent money. It was more a matter of how much I wanted to tell anybody. This whole business with Zimmerman made me nervous.

For the first time, I saw something that didn't make sense.

Hell, there's no point in kidding myself anymore. I knew there wasn't anything out there on Jimmy, but I was compelled to look anyway because part of me hoped there would be—and part of me hoped there wouldn't. This had raked up so much garbage and muck inside of me that the only way to resolve it was to follow it through to the outer limits of the envelope. We're talking extremes here; if there was anything out there, I was going to do whatever the hell I had to to find it. I wasn't even sure I'd tell anybody if I did, but *I* had to know. Jimmy was a great man in my life. Funny thing about great men; you want them to be great and human at the same time. We all loved Jack Kennedy, but at the same time everybody wants to know who he was boffing between appointments in the Oval Office.

My gut swirled like an incoming tide as I stood there, suddenly realizing that I was squeezing Sally so tight she could barely breathe.

"Hey," she said, her voice muffled by the fabric of my coat. "Passion's great, but I need to come up for air every few minutes."

I eased up on her and relaxed. "I'm sorry. I was just thinking and got carried away."

"Next time, carry me with you," she said, backing

off and straightening her dress. "What's the matter with you?"

"Just tense."

"I gathered that. Want to talk about it?"

I thought for a second. "No."

Her face tightened. "Okay, fine." And she walked out of the office.

Her cigarette still burned in the ashtray behind her.

"I've got an uncle who died a few years ago and I'm preparing a genealogy. Is there any way I can get a copy of the death certificate without knowing the exact date of death?"

The woman behind the counter at the Bureau of Vital Statistics eyed me suspiciously.

"You don't have a date of death?"

"No ma'am. In fact, it could be any time in the past twenty-five years."

"Twenty-five years!" she snapped.

"He was kind of the black sheep of the family. He disappeared about 1962. We're pretty sure he's dead, but we can't say for sure."

"So this is really missing person stuff."

"Yes, ma'am, kind of," I said, in my sweetest southern voice. It was the same voice I'd used lots of times to get bureaucrats to help me when they didn't want to. I didn't know if it was going to work this time.

Finding Lubbock Powell was turning out to be a big pain in the butt, just like everything else I'd been doing for the past few weeks. No record of him in any of the places where you'd find lawyers. No record of him having a driver's license. It was as if the earth had swallowed him up, along with all his traces.

Finding a death certificate with his name on it would mean the swallowing had been literal.

The woman looked over the top of her glasses. She was

short, with close-cropped black hair and tear-drop eye-glasses that were popular back when Powell was still working for the D.A.'s office.

"That'll take some looking," she said. "I'll have to check under P for each year."

"I'll be glad to wait," I said sweetly, as my shoulders tightened up and I thought to myself, 'Excuse the hell out of me, bitch, for making you work.'

She muttered something to herself that I didn't bother to interpret and walked over to the microfiche machine. She pulled out boxes of little plastic cards, each card holding the death records for a year. She searched through twenty-five cards in about an hour, counting interruptions, then turned around to see me still waiting.

"I can't find him," she whined, frustrated. "Are you sure he died in Louisiana?"

"No, not at all."

"Jesus, you think I got records here for the whole country?"

"Thanks, lady," I said, walking out. "Check you later."

So he ain't dead and he ain't practicing law, not that the two are mutually exclusive, anyway. And he doesn't drive, which given the way people drive in this state may explain why he's still alive.

So where the hell is he?

Fred Williams leaned back in his big leather chair and looked at me hard.

"So you can't find him?"

"Yeah. That last address you had on him was good until about 1965. I lost him after that."

"Why don't you tell me why this is so important to you?"

I had a cramp in the back of my neck; living with tension had always been easy for me, but not this much and for this long. I thought how irrational and counterproductive it would be to start screaming at Fred.

"Fred, listen. Maybe one of these days over beers, okay? It's not that big a deal. I'm just digging up a little ancient history, that's all."

"You're going to owe me one, buddy. You know that?"

"I already do, Fred. Just help me out here if you can."

"There's one other person," he said, reaching for the phone. "He's the last guy on staff who worked here back then. Old guy named Shelton. One of the clerks. He's going to retire in six months."

"Has Mr. Shelton gone to lunch?" Fred said into the phone. "Good. Ask him to come in here."

Julius Shelton knocked timidly on the door, then opened it a crack. From the moment I saw him, I realized how he'd managed to survive more than twenty-five years in the politically electric climate of the D.A.'s office. He'd fade into the background anywhere.

The gray-haired, stooped man stepped in.

"Mr. Williams? You wanted to see me?" The look on his face was one of nervousness, as if getting called into Fred's office meant nothing but trouble.

"Yes, Julius. Have a seat."

Julius took little old man steps over to the chair and shakily eased into it.

"Julius, this is Jack Lynch of the First Interstate Bank of Louisiana. He's making some inquiries we thought you could help us with."

I took his outstretched hand. "I'm one of your customers, Mr. Lynch."

"Good, Mr. Shelton," I replied lightly. "I'm pleased to hear it."

Fred explained what I was doing here. "And we hoped you might give us some idea of how to locate Mr. Powell, since you did work with him back then."

The tired old man hesitated. "I don't know. It's been such a long time and I don't have too much time until retirement."

"Don't worry, Julius," Fred reassured him. "There's no trouble here. We're just trying to find out what happened to the Zimmerman case."

"Well, best I remember the charges were dropped."

"Yes, we know that."

"What we were told was that Mr. Powell messed the case up. He drank."

"Drank?" I asked.

"He got fired after that," the old guy offered. "They had to drop the charges because of the way he mishandled the case. I don't know the details."

"But he did get fired?"

"Oh, yes, Mr. Herbert threw him out. He left the city a while later, I heard."

"Do you know where he went?"

"No." The slightest hitch in his voice said he knew something more.

"And?" I said quietly.

"He was from a small town up in the northern part of the state. I heard he went back there, but I never knew for sure."

"Which town?" Fred asked.

"Brecksborough," Julius said. "Brecksborough, up north near the Arkansas border."

Back at the office, Sally was still fuming at me. Nothing serious, I hoped, just a low-grade irritation.

"You ever heard of a town up north called Brecksborough?" I asked, walking past her into my office.

"Yes," she called. "It's near the town where I grew up. Before I moved to the bayous."

"What's the area code up there?"

"Three-one-eight," she answered. I heard her footsteps behind me as she came into the office.

"I've got a line on Mr. Powell. Maybe."

I dialed long-distance information.

"What city please?"

"Brecksborough."

"Yessir?"

"I'm looking for a Mr. Lubbock Powell. Not sure of the address. You got a listing?"

A moment's pause. "I'm sorry, sir. That number is unlisted."

So Lubbock Powell, of Brecksborough, Louisiana, didn't want his phone number released.

Bingo.

Driving from the southern part of the state, with its large cities and freeways and tourist attractions and millions of people, to the northern part was like entering another world. It was scrub brush and farmland up there, mixed in with the unforgiving bayous and the packed red clay that brought ruin to more than one hardworking, poor dumb sonofabitch who didn't have sense enough to get out. Even the character of the sun changed; the same sun that brought young girls in tight bikinis to the beaches down south turned young beauties into wrinkled old women up north. One could feel the hardness of life up there, as if it were in the air.

The roads turned bad as well. You take I-10 up to Baton Rouge, then on to Lafayette, then turn north on 167. You drive forever, through Alexandria and Winnfield and Ruston, then through a bunch of little towns that have one or two stoplights, a cafe, a lone cop patrolling a few hours a day trying to catch the high school kids drinking beer or balling in the backs of their jacked-up cars. The turnoff to State Route 48 was a fight not to tear the car up on a two-lane concrete highway deeply pitted with cracks and chuckholes, and patched with little strings of black asphalt that slithered across the dirty white surface like snakes.

The sky was overcast and dreary. Crosswinds pushed and shoved the car around; the beginnings of the northers that would soon rake this part of the country like nails on a blackboard. I'd spent enough time up here to know what it was like. It was a hot, dusty, mind-bending wind in the summer that could pop up into a tornado or a fierce thunderstorm with about a minute's notice. Later, in the terrible winter, the wind would cut through you like the jagged edge of a block of ice, pushing snow into twenty-foot drifts and literally killing the ones who couldn't afford to pay their heat bills.

It was a tired, beaten, desolate place, the kind of place that would gladly welcome a leaking toxic waste dump just for the jobs it would bring in. For two hundred years, people had been trying to make a go of it. And it still held the biggest pockets of desperately poor, the highest illiteracy rates, the least hope. It was a rural version of Iris.

And ahead of me, on a faded wooden sign stuck in the dirt shoulder of the road, were painted the words BRECKSBOROUGH—18 MILES.

That eighteen miles took almost an hour to drive. The road was bad enough, but the traffic on State Route 48 was mostly battered pickups and tractors pulling hay balers and farm machinery I didn't recognize. There was a stretch of the road that was down to one lane because of repaving. The guys on the work crew were standing around leaning on their shovels. I couldn't blame them; it's hot as hell out here and if you work fast and hard, then the project finishes early and you're back on the unemployment line.

Finally, I came to the wide place in the road that was Brecksborough. The main street was the state route, with a couple of side streets. There was one stoplight, a gas station, a diner, two variety stores, and a church. Farther up the road a bit was a bank, another store, two more churches, and several houses. As far as I could tell, that was it.

I pulled into the gravel lot of the gas station. A tan, stout man in greasy blue jeans, a T-shirt, and a cap advertising some kind of smokeless tobacco walked up to the car. The man's teeth needed a lot of work, but other than that, he looked healthy.

"What can I do for you?"

"Fill it up, please, and maybe some directions."

"Yeah?" he said, sauntering around to the gas pump.

"I'm looking for somebody. Guy named Lubbock Powell? You know him?"

"Sure." He laughed. "Our notary public and resident town drunk."

Town drunk, I thought to myself. What the hell am I doing up here?

"I'm an old friend of his from New Orleans. Thought I'd drop in, surprise him, you know."

"Sure," the guy said, screwing my gas cap back on. "Go to the light, turn right, go down a half-a-mile or so, make a left. Poplar Street, about number thirty-six, should be about the fourth house on the left."

"Thanks. Is there a place I can get a room for the night?"

"There's a motel about three miles down 48."

I paid the man and left. Rows of what were once beautiful turn-of-the-century houses now sat baking in the sun, paint peeling, in various states of disrepair. Lots of dogs barked, and there were chickens scratching around the front yard of one house.

Lubbock Powell's house was down the road on the right, not left, side of the street. I wondered if I had the right Lubbock Powell. Piles of dog droppings, loose car parts, beer bottles were scattered about amidst the barren dirt and crabgrass front yard. There was a screened-in front porch, but the screen was loose at the edges and curled up in places. The sound of some mutt yapping could be heard from inside.

I parked the car across from his house. The heat and the dust made me feel, and probably look, like I'd spent my life in Brecksborough. How did a high-powered attorney in a big city wind up in a place like this? And disbarred, no less. Judging by the shape of the house, that was probably what had happened to him.

I'd find out tomorrow. For now, I needed a shower and a drink. Then I'd come back, to dig up again what had laid buried for all these years.

And there it was again, the question that kept coming up like the verse at a stuck place on a record . . .

What the hell happened?

The glazed, bloodshot eyes behind the screen door stared back at me suspiciously.

It was 9:30 in the morning and already the hot sun was beginning to make waves dance up off the pavement. Dust clouds blew across the yard.

I'd had a bad night's sleep and a terrible cup of coffee at the diner in town. I wasn't looking forward to this the least damn little bit. But Lubbock Powell was standing there before me now, and I had to either say something to him or continue standing there looking stupid.

"Mr. Powell, my name's Jack Lynch and I'd like to talk with you if I may."

The mutt standing next to him barked at me.

"Shut up, damn you!" Powell barked back, swiping at the dog with his hand.

"I'm not taking any clients today," he said.

"Good," I answered. "I'm not giving any away."

"What do you want?" he demanded.

"It's kind of complicated. But it won't take up too much of your time. Can I come in? It's kind of hot out here."

He looked at me through the door. It was dark inside the house. He was getting a better look at me than I was at him. Lubbock Powell leaned down and grabbed the dog by his collar and pulled him back. With his other hand he pushed the screen door open.

The man who stood before me was a mess; my height, with a massive beer belly and a three-day growth of stubble. He wore no shoes, a dirty T-shirt, and a pair of stained green pants that were a size too big for him. The waist of the trousers curled up and over his belt, with his stomach hanging over like a sack of grain. He smelled of cheap whiskey and sweat. His eyes were glazed over, his hair uncombed.

Yeah, he drank.

"C'mon back," he ordered, leading the way into the house. We entered a room that was dark and musty, lit only by an old, flickering black-and-white television. Rows of dusty, worn books lined the walls. Some of them were law books; huge, threatening, and unused for some time. Equally worn furniture dotted the room, along with a worn carpet that was stained with what appeared to be and smelled like dog urine.

Powell walked over and turned the television down, then eased into a beaten leather chair that must have once cost a lot of money. On the table next to him, an over-running ashtray sat next to a dirty glass full of pale liquor. I sat across from him on a torn couch that smelled of wet dogs.

"Want a drink?" he asked.

"No, thanks," I answered.

"What'd you say your name was?"

"Lynch. Jack Lynch."

"Okay, Mr. Lynch. What do you want?" he asked, easing back into the chair with a grunt and picking up the dirty glass. He sipped on the liquor as if it were an after-dinner Courvoisier at Lutece.

"I'm doing some research for a book," I said. "A book on a gangster by the name of Alton V. Zimmerman."

He looked at me suspiciously. "Big Al Z." Powell grunted, "Yeah. I remember him."

"And I've come across something I can't figure out. I dug through newspapers and articles and court documents and there's just nothing to explain this. Your name appeared in some of the documents and I just decided to track down the original source. Mind if I ask you a few questions?"

"I don't know. All that was a long time ago."

I noticed as he reached for a cigarette that he was having a little trouble looking me in the eye. I took this to mean that he knew a great deal more than he was willing to let on. At least for free.

"Maybe if I compensated you for your time. I figure an attorney with your background must charge something in the neighborhood of two hundred an hour for consultations. Can I buy an hour of your time?"

His face brightened considerably as he lit the unfiltered cigarette and inhaled deeply. A cough rumbled around inside his massive, flabby chest and finally came out. It was a wet, hacking, throaty sound, the kind of cough that made me wish I'd never lit one in my entire life. He raised the glass to his lips and washed the phlegm back down with a swallow of whiskey.

"Cash?" he asked.

I reached into my jacket pocket and took out my wallet, then laid two one-hundred-dollar bills down on the coffee table in front of me. The corner of one of the bills touched something wet, and the dark stain spread slowly across the bill as he sat there looking at the money. But he didn't touch it.

"Okay, talk," he said, finally, leaving the money sitting there.

So I told him the story, everything I knew. It took a few minutes, with him sitting there like a drunken Jabba the

Hut, never looking at me directly, staring first at the ceiling, then at the floor, and then back to the money.

"I'm trying to find out the real reason those charges were dropped," I said, finishing.

He looked at me a second, the smouldering butt of the cigarette held in his yellowed, stubby fingers.

"You ain't writin' no fuckin' book," he said. "Just who the hell are you, and what the hell are you up to?"

He caught me by surprise and my face must have showed it.

"All right," I said after a moment. "I'm not writing a book. I work for a man who has his own reasons for wanting to know why those charges were dropped. He's paying me to find out why and I'm not at liberty to discuss why with anyone. He's more than willing to pay, and pay well, for information. But if you expect to get any money out of this, you've got to tell me what you know. Or that two hundred sitting on the table will be all you see."

I looked around the room, at Powell's obvious penury, and hoped that by going directly to the question of money, I'd done something to convince him to cooperate with me. If he wouldn't, I had nothing to fall back on.

"So how much more we talking about?"

"Depends on how valuable the information is. And whether it checks out or not."

"Well," he said slowly, after a moment, "I do happen to be a little short of funds right now. Business has been kind of slow lately."

"Two hundred right now, and a check for whatever else I get, depending on how much I think it's worth."

"I don't know about taking no check—"

"It'll have to do."

He took another long slug of the drink, draining the glass, then sat a little upright.

"When was that?"

"July 1960," I answered.

"You sure it wasn't 1961?"

"I'm sure."

He belched, then lit another cigarette.

"Yeah, I remember," he said. "Big Al was a punk even then, even if he was an old man with a lot of money. Once a punk, always a punk."

"Yeah."

"I hated the little sonofabitch. You know, he always tried to tell people he was born right there in the city. But he wasn't."

"Really? I didn't know that."

"Aw, hell no. He was from somewhere overseas, somewhere in Eastern Europe. He wasn't no American. And he came over here and did pretty good for himself. Always managed to stay just a short hair away from the law. He was indicted something like eight times, but he managed to get out of it every time. He'd bribe jurors, judges, ice witnesses. Whatever it took—

"I was thirty, you know," he continued. "Had just turned thirty. Only been out of law school three years. I was a late bloomer, you know. I had two years in with the D.A.'s office. I had real good prospects for after I got out. Then this shit came along . . ."

"What came along?"

"We had Big Al Valentine Zimmerman nailed. This punk was dead in the water. One of his people turned on him. A clerk, a lousy bloody clerk, but he turned on him. Big Al iced his brother-in-law or something like that over a bad debt or a dame or something. Hell, I can't remember. But I remember the clerk."

"Yeah?"

"Yeah. He came to the commission and said if we'd put him in a witness protection program, he'd get us copies of Big Al's books. Can you believe it? The *real* books. Everything. Where every nickel came from. The broads, the dope, the sharking, the dice games. We had enough to put him away for a hundred years, then we were going to turn his ass over to the IRS for whatever was left."

I checked the tape recorder I'd set up on the coffee table when Powell started talking. He hadn't even noticed it as it sat there turning, taking down every word.

"That must have been the new evidence I saw mentioned in the newspaper article."

"Yeah," he said. "That's it. Jim Herbert assigned me to the case to arrange all the paperwork for the trial. But he was actually going to prosecute it himself. Which was okay with me. Hell, I was too green. I was going to be his assistant, though, and let me tell you, buddy, we were all going to come out of it smelling pretty goddamn rosy."

"So what happened?"

Powell looked away almost dreamily, in a liquor fog. His eyes wandered, but his voice wavered only slightly.

"I guess it must have been a couple weeks or so before the trial was scheduled, I got this memo on my desk telling me the indictment had been withdrawn. For lack of evidence! I about blew a gasket. I went into Herbert's office and raised hell. I told him I'd go to the presiding judge of the state supreme court if I had to. I was gonna raise hell, cause an investigation, take it to the grand jury!"

"And?"

"Well," Powell said, easing back, "he stood up and fired my ass on the spot. Told me to clean out my desk and get out. The evidence had been determined to have been taken illegally, or it wouldn't stand up on the rules of evidence, or some such bullshit like that.

"I didn't believe him for a minute. But he said if I ever mentioned word one of this to anybody, he'd personally see that I was cited for misconduct and that I'd never work again in the city. So I went down to the basement of the D.A.'s office, before word got out that I was fired and my keys confiscated, and went into the evidence room. I was going to take the ledgers and the papers we had and scoot with them."

"So what happened? Did you?"

"They were gone."

"Gone?" I said, sitting up.

"Gone. No sign of them having ever been logged in. The books had been tampered with, I'm sure. But they were gone, all of them, from the face of the earth. As if some mighty hand had come down from above and erased them."

"What happened after that?"

"I got fired. There was no way I was ever getting a job with another firm in the city, not after getting canned from the district attorney's office. You got to remember, this was 1960. You couldn't go to the newspapers and talk to a reporter and get your story in like you could now. The newspapers cooperated with the government back then. I've thought of trying to get it in the papers now, but Herbert's such a damn big shot he'd probably sue me for libel. I got no proof. You understand that, don't you? I got no proof. I just know it happened."

"Lubbock," I said. "That ain't exactly the way I heard it now."

"Yeah?"

"I heard you botched the case. Something about drinking. To tell the truth now, I'm inclined to believe it."

He shook in the chair. "Get out! I don't need this shit from you!"

I got up slowly and pocketed the small recorder, but left it running. "I'll be glad to go, Lubbock. But if you can't tell me any different, I got to assume what I've heard from other people about you was the truth."

The Truth. It seemed, I thought as I walked toward the front door, that the only little bit of stink I'd been able to find in Jim Herbert's life had been put there by someone else. Game, set, match . . . I was relieved to be able to go back to New Orleans and tell the boss he was just going to have to eat it on this one.

The squeal of the rusty screen door was at its peak when I heard the rumbling voice behind me, then heavy footsteps. I tensed, wondering what he was up to.

"Wait a minute," he said. I stopped with my hand on the door and stood there motionless.

"You want to know what really happened or not?"

I turned. He was standing there, eyes blazing with the liquor like a madman.

"Well?" he demanded.

"So enlighten me, pal," I said.

"What's it worth to you?"

"You tell me."

"Would it be worth five thousand to know what *really* happened?"

I sputtered. "Pardon me, you mean American dollars?"

His eyebrows came together into one long furry line. "That bastard ruined me!"

"And now you're going to give me some line of bullshit to get back at him. Listen, Lubbock, it looks to me like Jack Daniels did more damage to you than Jim Herbert."

His arms snapped like a Cy Young candidate's and the half-full glass of booze streaked by off to my right. It shattered against a closet into a puddle of 90 proof jagged edges.

"You want the truth or not?" he yelled.

I stared at him for a second, my senses going numb at his outburst. What can make a man that kind of crazy, I thought. Powell's was the kind of crazy that drove a man to climb on top of a building and pick people off with a deer rifle.

"I don't have that much cash on me," I said.

"Are you good for it?" His voice was a stone floating in the air.

I let the door swing shut behind me.

"Yes, I'm good for it. If what you have checks out."

"It'll check out. But it'll be your job to do it."

"That's what I get paid for, anyway."

He leaned back against a corner where two walls met. His flabby body folded over the point and seemed to hang there suspended. He was a man drained, exhausted, beaten.

"Herbert was broke," Lubbock Powell said.

My heart jumped like I'd been jammed with a live cattle prod. My hand rolled into a tight ball.

"What do you mean broke?" I asked.

"I mean broke, boy. You deaf or what?"

"Broke," I said. "You expect me to believe that?"

"Stone cold damn broke, that's what I mean. Busted flat."

"How could that be? He was the district attorney."

"That's why he became D.A. in the first place," Powell said, leaning toward me. "Don't you understand? He needed the money. His law practice wasn't doing any better than any other young lawyer's at that time. And he had a family, and a wife with real expensive tastes and a sick mother. He had this 'image' he had to maintain. So he decided to run for D.A. and that wound up costing him a bundle. He was in hock up to his eyeballs."

"That doesn't make any sense."

"He figured a term as D.A. would either get him into a good firm or attract some high-rollers if he formed his own firm. And he was right. It worked. That's why he didn't take a second term. Hell, the job only paid twelve grand back then. Even in 1960, that wasn't the kind of money Herbert needed."

"I'm having some trouble with this, Lubbock."

"Track the records down."

"Records? What records?"

"He filed for bankruptcy."

I felt my lip curling on its own. "Get real, Lubbock. Try."

"Why are you having so much trouble believing it? Is

he that highfalutin these days? Christ almighty, boy, he ain't God."

Lying sonofabitch, I thought. No way was this guy getting a nickel out of me.

"You want five grand for telling me that?"

"It's worth it if you're trying to nail that bastard."

"What makes you think I'm trying to nail Herbert on anything?"

He looked right through me. "Why else would you be here? Why else would you keep listening to me?"

Something cold and hard ran up my back and into my skull. Both fists were knotted up now and I was beginning to see little red waves in front of my eyes.

"You're lying to me, you won't see a fucking cent," I growled.

"It's solid," he muttered, then louder, drunker. "And don't send me no check, either. Unless it's certified. They got a law in this state against passing bad checks."

"They got a law against practicing law without a license, too."

"What the hell you talking about?" he demanded.

"Not taking any clients today, eh?"

He moved toward me.

"Try it, Powell," I warned. "I'm half your age and twice as sober."

He stumbled over and sat down on one of the steps leading upstairs. The dog trotted in and tentatively nuzzled up to his master. Powell held his head in both hands, then reached down with one hand without raising his head and gently scratched the mutt's ears. A mongrel tail started bouncing around like a loose high-tension wire.

He looked up. There were tears in his bloodshot eyes, an ache that I could fathom only in my mind, not my heart.

"That bastard ruined me," Powell said, as if explaining himself. "He ruined me."

"Good-bye, Lubbock," I said. "Take care."

My anger rose again as I saw the grown man sitting there now blubbering out loud. Five thousand dollars; he could drink himself to death three or four times over on that kind of money.

I slammed his door as I left, then threw dust behind me for twenty yards after peeling away in the car.

Eight

Sally was in the office late that afternoon when I got back. She looked up from her desk and smiled when I opened the door. In a moment, I was behind the desk with her, holding her in my arms. It felt like a year had passed.

We kissed longingly, tenderly. I backed away from her a step and just kind of took her all in.

"Is that new?" I asked, noticing the new, shorter, lighter dress she had on.

"Yeah," she answered. "I went shopping last night. Bought five new dresses."

"Sally, I'm shocked. That's not at all like you."

"You're a bad influence on me. Like it?"

"It's very pretty. Makes you look so much less serious."

"Trying to recapture my lost youth."

"I missed you," I said, impulsively.

She blushed slightly. "You were only gone overnight."

"Well . . ."

She walked over to the table where the coffee pot sat. "I'll make a fresh pot of coffee. Have you eaten?"

"Yeah, I ate on the road."

"I never know about you. I have to check, you know."

I went into my office and sat down. There was a stack of pink telephone messages on my desk, none of which looked particularly urgent or troublesome, and some opened mail.

"So what happened upstate?" Sally asked, bringing me a cup of coffee. "Did you see Mr. Powell?"

"Oh, yeah, I saw him. He's a pretty broken down old guy. I feel kind of sorry for him."

"Did he give you any help? Any information?"

Here was my chance; all I had to do was say no, he was too drunk, senile, demented, whatever to remember anything and that would have been the end of it. Let it go. Don't dig any further. Just take the Old Man's yelling and screaming over it as much as I could, then either quit or stay, one or the other. But I had come this far in my search for this one particular truth, and I wasn't willing to go back.

"If what he told me is true," I said, picking up the phone, "then we may be on to something. I don't know, though."

I flipped through my Rolodex until I found the number for the records office over in City Hall.

"Recordations, Wallace speaking," an anonymous voice said.

"Mr. Petersen, please."

"Sure, hold on."

Petersen was an acquaintance of mine who owed us a favor. It was time to call a marker in.

"Petersen here," a voice clicked in.

"Mr. Petersen, this is Jack Lynch over at the bank. How are you?"

"Hello, Mr. Lynch. How are you?"

"Just fine."

"And Mr. Jennings?"

"Cantankerous as ever," I answered.

Petersen laughed. "I'd imagine so. What can I do for you?"

"I need a deed checked. In a hurry, sort of."

"Shouldn't be a problem. Why don't you drop over to-morrow?"

"There's a time problem here. I need it before the end of the day." It was nearly five already. I heard Petersen hesitate on the other side of the line.

"What do you need to know?"

"Sometime between 1957 and 1960, a man in town named James Herbert bought a house located at 5613 Commission Avenue. I need to know the original purchase price of the house, the recorded lien at the time of purchase, and the status of the mortgage."

"That's a tall order on such short notice, Mr. Lynch."

"I know. But Mr. Jennings would sure appreciate it."

Petersen sighed.

"I can't give you the outstanding balance on the mortgage, of course, that requires an actual credit check. I can only tell you if there are any outstanding liens on the property now. The rest will take forty-eight hours."

"If you could just give me what you can, I'd appreciate it."

"It's going to take an hour or two. Can I call you back?"

I gave him my office number, thanked him, and hung up.

"Nothing like making a civil servant work past five," I said.

"So what happened up in Brecksborough?" she asked.

"For one thing, it cost a couple hundred up front just to talk."

Sally whistled. "Boy, that's not going to go over too well."

"It will if it turns out to be worth it."

"I'll get an expense voucher made out and upstairs be-fore I leave. How come you're checking out Herbert's mort-gage records?"

"I want to know how much the house cost and how deep he was into the bankers. How much cash he had to raise to get the house in the first place."

"That's what. Not why . . ."

I stared at her a second; that same tension I felt earlier at Lubbock Powell's was back.

"Not talking, huh," she said, turning away. She was gone a few steps when I spoke as if in a trance, very softly and detached, like hearing myself as another person.

"Powell said he was broke."

She stopped and turned. "Broke? Powell or Herbert?"

"Herbert. He said Jimmy was broke." I raised my head up and looked at her.

"You believe him?"

"No. Not for a second. But I have to check."

"How you going to do that, ask him?"

"Powell said he declared bankruptcy."

"Oh, hell." She sighed. "Can you check it out?"

"The records only go back seven years, as far as I know. Beyond that, I'm not even sure if there's a way to check."

"If they do keep all that stuff, it should be a matter of public record."

"Yeah, but who knows how much trouble it'll be. We have to keep this quiet," I said. "If we start raising hell, everybody in the world will find out about it."

"Just grease some palms. It's one of your best talents, anyway."

"So I'm told."

"Even if this is all true, it doesn't mean anything."

"I know that," I said, sipping the coffee. "But it's all I've got to go on now."

Sally went into the outer office and began typing up my expense reports. I read mail and smoked and drank my coffee and waited for Petersen's call. Finally, about 6:15, it came.

"It's Mr. Petersen," Sally called.

"Put him through."

"Petersen here," he said curtly. "I've got the information you need."

"Okay," I said, reaching for a pad. "Shoot."

"The house on Commission Avenue was purchased in February 1958, at a purchase price of seventy-five thousand dollars, with a down payment of ten thousand. In January 1960, a second mortgage of twenty-five thousand was taken out on the house. At that time, only seven thousand of the original mortgage had been paid off. At that time, then, Mr. Herbert had an outstanding lien of approximately eighty-three thousand."

"Pretty good chunk of change in those days."

"The second mortgage was retired in August 1960. Only eight months after it was taken out."

"Retired?" I asked.

"Paid off. In full. And according to our records, the original mortgage was paid off almost ten years ago. There are no liens or mortgages on the property of any kind now."

"Mr. Petersen," I said, ringing off. "I owe you one."

"Anytime, Mr. Lynch. Glad to be of help."

Sally walked into the office and sat down with expense forms for me to sign.

"What's the word?"

"In January of 1960," I said, "Herbert was in hock up to his eyeballs."

"Wow," she said. "What next?"

"Tracking down the alleged bankruptcy."

"That'll have to wait until tomorrow. Right?"

"Yeah, it's too late to do anything about it now."

Sally looked down at her watch and shifted uncomfortably in the chair.

"By the way," she said, "there's a couple messages in there from the same person. Guy's called a couple of times. Won't say what it's about, just that it's important and he wants you to call him."

I shuffled through the stack of pink messages.

"There," she said, pointing, "that one. His name's Bob. Wouldn't even leave a last name. He also said you couldn't get him at his office. He wants you to call him at home."

"Weird," I said, staring down at the slip. "Wonder what he wants."

"I don't know. Normally, I wouldn't bother you with something like this. But he sounded desperate."

"No, it's okay. I just wonder what it's about."

Sally got up from the chair and walked around to the back of my desk. I eased away from the desk and reached out to her from my chair. She slipped into my lap as if she'd been doing it for years and put her arms on my shoulders.

"I missed you, too," she said.

I looked up at her. She grew more lovely to me every moment.

"Dinner?"

"Yeah." She smiled, nodding. "What would you like to do?"

"Anything. Doesn't matter. Long as it's someplace quiet where we can be alone."

"Mmmm," she hummed. "Sounds wonderful. I want to stop at my place and change, though. Get out of these stockings."

"I'd love to see you out of those stockings, too," I teased.

"Play your cards right, kiddo, and you might get to."

"Tell you what," I said, putting my arms around her waist and pulling her even closer to me. "You go on home and change. I'll return this guy's call, run home and take a shower, unpack, and pick you up around eight. How's that?"

She brought her face close to mine, as close as she could get without touching.

"Don't make it any later."

"Don't worry," I said, my gut doing the anticipation flip-flops again.

I stared at the door as she closed it behind her on her way out. This had all happened so fast, and yet I wouldn't want a second of it to be any different. I sat there for what must have been a full couple of minutes before thinking of the telephone call.

The message was here someplace: there, a 347 exchange. Where was that? I tried to remember.

I dialed the number and listened to it ring about ten times before somebody answered.

"Hello," a voice said. Quick analysis: young, professional.

"This is Jack Lynch," I said. "I'm calling for Bob."

"You got him. Thanks for returning my call, Mr. Lynch."

"Sure, no problem. What's this all about?"

"I need to see you. I can't talk about this over the phone."

"All right," I said. "Why don't you come by my office tomorrow morning."

"No, I can't do that," the voice said, suddenly tense. "I can't do that at all."

"What's going on here?" I asked. "Why can't you talk over the phone?"

"I just need to see you," he said. "Tonight. Quickly."

"That's impossible," I said, tired. "I just got in off the road. I'm sweaty and tired and I have a dinner engagement in a couple of hours—"

"It's worth your while," he said, interrupting. "I promise you."

"What's this about?" I demanded. "Either tell me something now or leave me alone." I was in no mood for any of this.

"It's about Mr. Murphy and your investigation of him."

My heart clutched in my chest and I felt a cold chill down my back. A trickle of sweat ran down my side.

"How do you know about that?"

"Meet me in twenty minutes and I'll tell you. You know the Napoleon House, in the Quarter?"

"Yeah."

"Meet me in the back room there."

"How will I know you?"

"Don't worry," he said. "I'll know you."

There was a moment's silence as I tossed a few things around in my head.

"Okay." I sighed. "Twenty minutes."

Napoleon House, an artsy-intellectual hangout full of students and frustrated writers and tacky painters and tourists, had once been a favorite watering hole of mine and Katherine's.

I'd just bitten into the slice of cucumber in my Pimm's Cup when the guy walked up to my table and sat down without saying a word.

"Take your order, sir?" the elderly waiter asked.

"Just a Coke," he said.

I held my hand out across the table. The young man sitting across from me was in khakis, button-down oxford-cloth shirt, horn-rimmed glasses. Early twenties, maybe.

"Jack Lynch," I said.

"I know," he offered, shaking my hand. "Bob Sparks."

"Well, Mr. Sparks," I said, reaching for my pack of cigarettes, "what can I do for you?"

"You know Charlie McCorkle?" he asked.

Charlie was vice president of Data Processing at the bank. I'd known him nearly ten years, but never been very close to him. Just another guy at the bank.

"Sure, down in D.P.," I answered.

"He's my boss."

"You work at the bank?" I asked, surprised. "Why didn't you just come up to my office?"

Bob Sparks looked at me and smiled.

"Because," he said, "Charlie would *kill* me if he knew I was talking to you."

My patience with yuppies ran out about fifty years ago. I guess the expression on my face let him know that.

"Listen," he continued, "let me explain before you get weird on me."

"Okay," I said, lighting my cigarette, "I'm listening."

"A week or so ago, you sent down a request to get an S.O.A. on Sheriff Murphy's accounts."

"Yeah, a summary of activity."

"And Charlie gave it to me to handle. I'm a programmer/ analyst down there. In the basement, you know."

"Yeah, yeah, get to the point," I said.

"Anyway, I'm new down there. I just got out of school last spring. Just a few months on the job and I'm trying to impress Charlie. So I run the standard search string. I find Murphy's accounts. He's got savings, a couple CDs, and three checking accounts. Business, personal, household."

"Yeah, I know. I got those. So what?"

"So just kind of for shits and grins, you know, I put together a system-wide global search under company personnel lists, account numbers, social security numbers, the whole ball of wax, you know."

"And?" I said. He was beginning to get my interest.

"So I figure nothing will come of it, but I'm trying to impress Charlie, learn more about the database, whatever. So I'm being real creative in my search strings, running a global sort and merge, all that good stuff. I'm there till about ten-thirty one night."

"So what happened?" I asked, exasperated.

"I figure I'm not going to find anything," he said. "After all, the guy's not the head of Exxon, you know. How complicated can his life be? But bang, this guy winds up being connected to so many accounts with so much activity that I tie up main processor time for almost five minutes."

"Five minutes?" I asked. "What's the big deal?"

Bob Sparks smiled a condescending, somewhat arrogant smile at me.

"When processor time is measured in nanoseconds, five minutes is a very big, very expensive chunk of time."

"So what's this mean?"

"It means that this guy is involved in so many accounts with so much activity that it'll take me an hour or two on the high-speed Honeywells just to get you a printout."

I sat back and took a sip off the drink. What the hell did this all mean?

"So why didn't I get all this stuff?" I asked. "All I got from D.P. was a three-page summary on Murphy."

"That's the rub," Bob said. "I got all this stuff together, without printing it out, of course, because I can't tie up the printers for that long without authorization, and I go to Charlie. I figure he'll be impressed with my initiative, you know. I'm very aggressive."

"I can see that," I said.

"Well, instead of being impressed, you know, Charlie fucking threatens to fire me if I ever do anything like that again. I mean, he's busting my chops like a mad dog. 'All they wanted was the three pages,' he said. 'Don't ever tie up big box time like that again if you expect to make it here.' He really got on my case."

I sat back and thought of Charlie. Why? What's going on here?

"Anyway, I sat on it a week or so and figured maybe this was something you should know about, since you made the request. Only thing is, if Charlie ever finds out I went to you, he'll burn me right out the door."

"Don't worry, Bob," I said. "He won't find out. What kind of stuff was this?"

"You name it," he said. "Companies, dummy corporations, what looks like to me holding companies. EFTs out the yin-yang."

"Electronic fund transfers?"

"Yeah, all automatic. Some to the Caymans and the Bahamas. All untraceable. All we get are account numbers. All done very quietly, very quickly."

"Jesus." I sighed. "Can you get me the printouts?"

"You want it all?" he asked, incredulous. "That's a freaking lot of work."

"Yeah, Bob, I want it all. Can you do it? There'll be something good in it for you. I can guarantee you that."

He thought for a second.

"It'll take a while. The problem is I'll have to do it a little bit at a time, late at night. The programmers are on call twenty-four hours a day. We have round-the-clock access. The only thing is not to draw attention to yourself."

"Can you do it?"

"Can you give me a few days?"

"No longer," I said. "It's important."

Bob Sparks looked at me through his fashionable, yuppie glasses. I wondered if he really knew what I was asking.

"Yeah, sure. Can do," he said, smiling.

There was nothing else to do but continue on until my young programmer friend came through for me. The next step was to keep digging into Jimmy.

I wandered into the office late again the next morning. Jeez, after nights at Sally's I just couldn't get moving in the morning.

"Glad you could make it," she said snidely as I walked in. "You're late, even for you."

"I haven't been able to get to sleep at night lately," I said, teasing, as I took off my jacket and threw it onto the couch, "Too many distractions."

"Oh, distractions, eh? Maybe we can remove some of these distractions in the future."

"Do it and I'll bite you," I said sternly.

"Ooooh, and spank me, too," she cooed, raising her voice a couple of octaves.

"God, you're such a sex kitten," I said, offhandedly, as I walked into my office.

I poured myself a cup of coffee and got one for Sally as well. I walked back to her desk and put the coffee in front of her.

"Trying to get back in my good graces, huh?" she said.

"Only for the next hundred years or so."

"Hey, baby," she said. "Don't kid about stuff like that."

"Who's kidding? By the way, I'm going to be gone the rest of the morning."

"Yeah, where to?"

"Bankruptcy court. I've got to track down any records on Herbert's bankruptcy."

"If there is a bankruptcy . . ."

"Yeah, right."

As I left the office a few minutes later, I said, "Don't go to lunch without me."

The drive over to the courthouse was slow and tedious. The taste of stale coffee and cigarettes was in my mouth and my stomach was in a knot at being back in pursuit. It took twenty minutes to find a place to park.

By the time I walked up the massive concrete steps into the columned halls of the courthouse, I was tired, irritated and dripping with sweat. The high ceilings and the marble floors echoed my footsteps into a head-splitting clatter. A security guard behind an information desk looked at me, unsmiling.

"Excuse me," I said, approaching him.

"Yes, what can I do for you?"

"I'm looking for the office for the bankruptcy court."

"Records or archives?"

"I guess archives. I'm looking for a real old filing."

"It's in the basement, Room Fourteen. Take the stairs down, make a left, then go to the end of the hall."

The archives were kept in a mausoleum-like office at the end of a dank, dimly lit hallway. Good place to get mugged, I thought, even if it was the courthouse. I walked through a frosted-glass door and into a room that smelled of dust and aging, rotting paper. It was an enormous room, full of filing cabinets and shelves as far as the eye could see. Bare metal desks, massive ledgers, leather bindings rotting with age. A thin, middle-aged man wearing a frayed shirt and thin necktie, horn-rimmed glasses, and a pocket full of pencils homed in on me. Now here was a guy that hadn't seen much sunlight in the past few decades.

"May I help you?" he asked.

"Yes, how are bankruptcies filed?"

"First you have to see a lawyer," he commented, sounding strangely like he was trying to imitate Humphrey Bogart. Even his lip curled up a bit on the outer edge.

"No, that's not what I mean," I said, not eager to get in a tangle with this guy. "What I mean is how are they kept, how are they filed?"

"Alphabetical, by year," he answered, returning to his desk.

"Good. I need to see a bankruptcy that was filed in 1960."

He looked at me suspiciously. "Vat for?" Was that Conrad Veidt? I thought.

"It's a matter of public record, isn't it?"

"You still got to have a reason, Charlie," he said. No, it's that character back in 1940s radio who had the tag line "Vass you dere, Chollie?"

I looked at him for a real long moment.

"My name's not Charlie. It's Lynch, Jack Lynch. I'm a bank officer and one of our depositors has applied for a rather large loan and indicated on his application that he filed bankruptcy in 1960. As a matter of course, the bank always checks such matters out."

"Dat vass dumb," he said dryly.

"What do you mean?" I asked.

"I wouldn't admit to a bankruptcy that old. There's no way to check it out."

"Why can't you check it out?"

"Records that old aren't kept."

The man reached inside his desk drawer and pulled out an unfiltered Pall Mall, stuck it inside a long black plastic cigarette holder, and lit it. I pulled out my wallet and flashed my bank ID card.

"Don't do a thing for me, Charlie."

"Let me see your supervisor immediately," I ordered, flaring. "Either that or I'll have the bank's chief attorney call the clerk of courts to report your extreme lack of co-operation."

"Listen, Charlie," he said, breaking into a terrible Jimmy Cagney imitation, "for all I care, you can call the White House. We don't keep records that old. They're destroyed."

"Destroyed?"

The man became Walter Brennan now.

"Once the court releases you from bankruptcy, heh, heh, we can keep the records on file for either seven or eleven years, depending. Beyond that, we burn 'em. Don't have room to keep 'em. Too dadburn many people taking the easy way out these days, gawl-darnit."

"Great," I muttered. Damn.

"Sorry, Charlie," the man said, a wry smile crinkling up the corners of his dried face, then breaking into the lousiest Walter Cronkite imitation I'd ever heard. "And that's the way it is . . ."

"Excuse me, what did you say your name was?"

"Didn't. Name's Palmer," he said, chomping the cigarette holder between his teeth and holding it in a mouth salute, "Milton Palmer," in a not-half-bad Franklin Roosevelt.

"Well, Mr. Palmer," I said, turning to leave, "you need to have your medication adjusted."

Too many years with not enough sunlight. Severe vitamin deficiency, I'd guess. Mental scurvy.

"So that's it, huh?" Sally said, setting a coffee cup on my desk and taking a seat on the couch. I swung around in my chair, frustrated and itchy. I'd just described my brief sojourn into "The Twilight Zone" with Uncle Milty of the Many Voices.

"Sure looks like it. Records so old nobody even remembers destroying them."

"What are we going to do?" she asked. "The creek's rising fast."

"Time's running out," I said, rubbing my temples. "There's got to be a way. Got to. I can't believe we've come this far. We don't even know if there was a bankruptcy."

Sally laid her head back on the back of the couch and stared up at the ceiling. I fought the urge to go sit next to her, convinced for once that business took precedence. This would be the first time that I'd ever completely, miserably failed at doing anything the Old Man has asked me to do. I wondered how he'd react. Would he fire me? I did a quick mental audit of my bank account, savings, and meager stock portfolio to figure how long I could go without work. The situation wasn't as bad as I feared. I lived cheaply, as many dull bachelors do, and over the years I'd accumulated enough to live maybe even a year or two if I were careful.

It was the concept of failure that was really eating at me. This whole process had brought out an aspect of my personality I hadn't realized was so strong; this stubbornness, this inability to let things go, this compulsive need to be obsessed with something.

This need to be as good at something as he was . . .

Scenes of my past life with James Herbert played on one of my screens. A Derby Day party where I had too much to drink and flirted with one of Katherine's sorority sisters and Jimmy had to step in and make peace before we all made fools of ourselves. Our last Christmas together, made sad and sweet at the same time by everyone's unspoken perception that Katherine and I weren't going to make it. The way Jimmy talked to me and even put his arm around me as I cried one afternoon after Katherine was gone. He encouraged me to go to law school, said he'd help pay for it, if only I'd take the LSATs and go for it. The offer was still good, he told me once, even after the divorce.

Oh, hell. I'm glad the records are gone. I simply don't want to know.

But, dammit, I do. I do want to know. I need to know. It's important to know. The truth doesn't set you free. It's just the truth . . .

"This is driving me crazy," I snapped, hitting the desk. Sally jumped.

"Don't get your panties in a wad," she said. "We'll figure this out."

I put my thumb and index finger on the bridge of my nose, trying to rub some of the tension out.

"You know what this reminds me of?" Sally asked.

"What?"

"That time, God, how many years ago was it? When you first came to the paper? You were right out of college and Watergate was big then and you didn't realize you were working for the worst newspaper in the world." She laughed. "All you wanted to do was be Mr. Big Investigative Journalist, and you dug into that mess at the Superdome. That minority company that was accused of raking money off the top for maintenance services. What was it?"

"SOS," I answered. "Superdome Office Services."

"You worked day and night like a dog, and then when you turned the story in that toad Arnold who was city editor showed it to Mr. Jennings and he blew a fuse."

"Yeah." I laughed. "The Old Man turned out to be one of the chief backers of the company."

"I thought I'd have a heart attack that day," she said.

"But you stood up to him and I think that's why he didn't fire you."

"We never ran the damn story, but I got to keep my job."

Sally shook her head, her brown hair brushing over her shoulders.

"You were like a dog on that one. One of those little yappy dogs that won't ever let go. Too bad the newspaper was the wrong place to be."

"Oh, it was the right place to be," I said. "After all, I met you."

She smiled.

"Those were good days, Jack. We were all younger and poorer and dumber, but they were good."

"These days are better," I said. "I don't have as much trouble getting my expense forms by you."

She looked almost far away at that.

"We really had to watch the money then. Mr. Jennings would come down on us like a bear if everything didn't zero out at the end of each month. Some of the trouble I had collecting . . ."

And she drifted off here. Something erupted inside her, I felt, like a bubble of air floating up to the top.

"That's it," she said quietly, staring down at the floor, not looking at me. "It's right there in front of us. The whole time."

"What?"

"Bankruptcies. They're public record."

"I know that. But the records have been destroyed."

"No, no, no. You don't understand. Public records have to be really *public*. They have to be published!"

I'd forgotten. But Sally was right. The newspaper . . .

"Lawyers are required by law to publish in an established newspaper the names of bankrupts and a detailed list of all the assets and debts," she said. "So what do they do? They publish bankruptcies in places where they'll least likely be read!"

"Like our newspaper!" I almost shouted.

"Of course! You never dealt with it much because you were cityside, but ninety percent of my accounts receivable were from lawyers who owed us for space they bought to publish their clients' bankruptcies!"

"No," I said slowly, incredulously. "It can't be . . . It's too easy."

"It's so easy it's right under our faces. If James Herbert declared bankruptcy in 1960, then that narrows it down to two hundred and sixty issues it's got to be in. Five days a week, fifty-two weeks a year; the most unread newspaper in town turns out to have the most valuable stuff!"

Probably every town of any size in the country has got one; a daily newspaper that's largely unread and usually carrying a name like The *Daily Court Ledger* or some such that's nothing more than a cheap vehicle for public notices. Bankruptcies, marriages, divorces, incorporations; all were there to examine, if you just knew where to look.

"But, honey," I said. "The newspaper closed down almost ten years ago."

"I know, but there are records. I don't know where. But not everything was thrown away."

"Maybe Carlton would know where all that stuff is."

"Carlton probably doesn't, but his secretary might."

A couple of hours' worth of digging and a quick lunch later, we found the crypt. The dead and rotting bones of a once living, breathing newspaper were in the attic of the Commodities Exchange Building, one of the Old Man's older, more neglected holdings. A few blocks from the office, the five floors of the building were rented out to small business people, independent real estate hustlers, even an astrologer who charged his customers twenty-five bucks to come into the dusty office for a reading.

There wasn't even a building manager; Sally and I had to traipse over to Maintenance to get a key to the building. We got my car and weaved our way through the traffic and were lucky enough to find a space only a few car lengths away from the entrance.

I opened the trunk of my car and took out a flashlight. "We may need this."

"Boy, is this weird," Sally said as we walked into the building.

The Commodities Exchange Building had once been one of the most vibrant, busy buildings in the downtown area. Around the turn of the century, the entire fourth floor was taken up by the world's largest commodities exchange. Fortunes were made and lost daily as the hustlers, brokers, traders, and con men of the day struggled to outdo each other on the floor. Crumbling drywall and faded woodwork now cut the once thriving exchange into tiny, cheap, run-down offices. There was no security guard or elevator man here, only an empty lobby, an out-of-date building directory, and a couple of rumbling, grinding self-service elevators.

I pushed the button to call one of them and felt the wall shake as the car started moving somewhere above us.

"You think this is going to be okay?" she asked nervously.

"You want to walk?"

"Up five flights as hot as it is in here? You're crazy."

"So I'm told."

She smiled as the elevator came and we stepped in. There were five buttons with faded painted numbers; I pressed the button for the top floor and the door closed with a thump and a squeak.

"Alone at last," I said, pulling her to me. Sally came into my arms without protest and raised her head as I kissed her. We kissed through four floors without interruption; there wasn't much traffic in this old building nowadays.

The door opened on five and we stepped out. There

was a hallway that took a left around a series of unrented offices. The place was dusty and stale and hot, with a pervading, inescapable sense of age, disrepair, and decay.

"Can you believe the Old Man would actually let this building get in this shape?" I asked.

"He's probably forgotten he owns it."

"C'mon."

We wandered down the hall, wondering if there were any living things on this floor that didn't belong to the order Rodentia. Small piles of droppings, gnawed cords, and other evidence of tiny creatures with sharp teeth led us to believe not.

We came to the end of the hall, to a door beneath a red EXIT sign with a burned-out light.

"C'mon, let's go," I said, opening the door into a dark, musty stairwell.

"You first."

I flicked on the flashlight to guide the way. A bare light bulb burned with little penetration into the darkness. The stairs ran down into black. Above us, a half-flight above our heads, was the doorway to the attic.

"I don't like this a bit," Sally said behind me.

"C'mon."

"I'm wearing a new dress."

"We'll have it dry-cleaned."

"What a pain," she griped.

"So take it off."

"What?"

"Take it off. No one's around. I will if you will."

"You've lost your mind."

"Okay, later."

"Keep your mind on your work."

"Party pooper," I said, climbing the narrow gray stairs up to the door. I pulled the key out of my pocket, parked the flashlight on the step pointed up, and stuck the tarnished key into the lock. At first, it didn't want to move. It had probably been years since anyone had been here. Finally, by yanking on the door and twisting the knob a few times, I got the key to turn in the lock.

The door was stuck, but a couple of good hits with my left shoulder popped it open. There were cobwebs everywhere in the dark attic as far as I could see. It was unbearably hot and I could hear the scurrying around of little furry things.

I pushed the door fully open and pointed the beam into the room. The ceiling was low, but there was enough room to stand up. The attic was huge, taking up as much room as one of the floors below it. Only it was all open area, with no partitions dividing it up.

It was a crypt, opened and violated for the first time since heaven knew how long.

"Well, go on in," Sally said, placing a hand on my back pocket and giving me a gentle shove.

"Yeah, hold on," I said, turning the flashlight to look for a light switch. There was one on the wall to my right, covered by a thick coat of dust. I flicked it on and a bank of fluorescent tubes above me coughed and sputtered and flickered to life.

"Wow, look at this stuff," I said, walking in.

"This is probably the first time anybody's been up here since the paper closed down."

"I feel like an archaeologist opening up a mummy's tomb or something," I said.

We were both in the room now, with the light from the old tubes filtering down through the dust. I took the flashlight and plowed through a thick field of cobwebs.

"I can't believe I'm seeing all this stuff again," Sally said, almost gaily. "God, I spent some good years around all this junk. Look, over in the corner. I think that was my desk."

We padded across the floor to a corner of the room where about a dozen desks were strewn around haphazardly.

"Yes, that's it," she said. "I recognize those cigarette burns."

Several small brown marks marred the finish of one of the desks.

"And that's my chair over there," she added.

Some of the junk even looked familiar to me; battered old typewriters and seats with ripped cushions and padding falling out. It was all rotten and moldy and mildewed; a treasure chest for an allergist.

"Where do we start?" I asked.

"The first thing we have to do is find the bound copies. Every three months, we took a sample of each issue and sent them off to the binder."

"Great, that ought to make it even easier."

"Only once we find the right year," Sally said, looking up at me in the dim light. "This paper was started in the 1890s. Four bound volumes a year for ninety years . . ."

"Jeez, and you think they're all up here somewhere?"

"They'd better be, or we're in trouble."

So we began the horrible process of digging through all the junk, the filing cabinets, sealed boxes, all covered with a quarter-inch of lung-clogging dust, spiders, rodent droppings, and other things I refused to speculate on. All in the unair-conditioned attic of a five-story building in the middle of an August afternoon.

Within minutes, I'd stripped out of first my jacket, then my tie, finally my shirt, as I sweated like a coal miner in the awful heat. Sally rolled her sleeves up and unbuttoned her new dress all the way down to the waist. I watched in the dim light as the white satin of her slip slowly turned gray.

Huge streams of sweat rolled off both of us as we labored in the sweatbox. I found a two-wheeler and did the heavy work, moving one row of filing cabinets to get to another, one set of sealed brown boxes to get to the layers behind it. Sally ripped open the boxes with my knife and dug through the contents just long enough to identify it as something we didn't need.

An hour passed as we grunted and sweated and moaned and complained our way through this. We were gradually working our way around the room, digging, searching, probing.

"I may have to take a break soon," she said. "I think I'm about to pass out."

"Why don't you let me keep on and you go sit down on the steps for a minute or two."

"Okay, here's your knife."

I took the knife from her as she trailed out, her hair sopping wet and stringy, great wet blobs staining the armpits of her new dress.

There was a bank of boxes, each about three feet to the side, stacked two high and eight or nine deep behind a series of filing cabinets. I opened the filing cabinets, saw that they contained only rotting files, and began the task of moving the battered old green cabinets out of the way so I could get to the boxes. That took fifteen or twenty minutes and finally, soaking and exhausted, I pulled out my knife and slit the tape on top of the first box and pulled the top back.

Inside, I could see, were stacks of huge black volumes, each the size of an issue of the newspaper.

"I found them," I called to Sally.

I walked across the room and to the door. Sally was down a half a flight, sitting on a step, her head on her arms, which were folded across her knees.

"Hey, you okay?" I asked, going down the stairs and sitting behind her, putting my hands on her shoulder.

"Just hot, that's all."

She turned and looked at me and we both started laughing.

"You're filthy," I said.

"You look like Al Jolson after a bad rain."

"This is really above and beyond."

"So you found them?" she asked.

"C'mon, can you make it?"

"Yeah, I think so."

We got up and walked slowly back up the stairs and into the attic, which only seemed that much hotter for our having left it for a minute. The heat was like a wall.

"Yeah, these are it," she said, looking into one of the boxes with the flashlight. "The only thing we have to do now is find 1960."

"And these damn boxes aren't labeled."

"Yeah, I'm sure that when they packed up, they just threw them in boxes and sealed them up."

I wearily began taking the boxes down and slitting them open. Each box weighed a good seventy or eighty pounds. I got a nasty paper cut on one hand, and ripped the pants of my suit on the corner of a box as I lugged it down to the floor.

Sally tore the boxes open and looked in each of the black volumes to get a fix on the date. The oldest ones, which dated all the way back to the beginning, flaked apart in her hand. Red dust from dry-rotted leather filled the air, choking us.

"We need respirators for this shit," I wheezed.

"Shh, don't try to talk," she whispered.

The thirty-second box contained the beginning of 1959 to the first quarter of 1960.

"Here," I said, exhausted. "Take this volume out to the steps and go through it while I keep digging for the rest of the year."

"Okay," she said, putting her hand on my shoulder. "Thanks. Don't stay up here too long. You'll get sick."

"Go on, now. I'll bring the rest out."

I got lucky. There was some kind of basic, twisted order to it all. The rest of 1960 was in a single box only four over from its neighbor. Within fifteen minutes, I struggled out onto the flight of steps carrying the three huge, dusty, crumbling volumes.

"Anything yet?"

"So far, nothing."

"We have to be real careful not to miss anything. We're both tired," I said.

"I'm not tired," she answered. "I'm dead."

I spread out the second quarter of 1960 on the floor and sat down. The cool concrete felt good after the heat inside the attic, even though it was probably in the nineties here in this stinking stairwell.

"Nothing here," Sally said after a while. "I've been through it twice."

"Grab another," I said.

She wearily picked up another of the bound volumes, which were so big she could barely lift them under the best of circumstances.

"Nothing in the second quarter," I said. "Let me try the last one."

I picked up the one remaining volume and opened it. "July 1, 1960," the dateline read. Sally must have gotten the fourth quarter.

I began flipping through the pages one at a time, coming to each day's public notices and filings. It was dull, dreary, and at this point, physically painful work. I was tired and discouraged, with an almost overwhelming drive to climb into a hot bath with a scotch and soda and Sally.

Then like an artillery shell slamming into the side of a house, there it was: July 31, 1960. I was eight years old. Katherine was seven. Sally was five. Kennedy was running for president against Nixon. Khrushchev was raising hell with everybody. Castro was settling in for the long run after whipping the shit out of Batista.

"What's my limit?" I asked blankly.

She turned to me. "Limit?"

"Limit."

"Five thousand without a signature."

"Good," I muttered. "I need a check cut for Lubbock Powell."

And I slid down the wall, devastated.

Nine

team rose off the water as I settled into the bathtub. Tension as palpable and real as sludge flowed out and was gone in a moment.

The irony of connections was as blunt and ham-fisted as a longshoreman on the docks or a brutal pimp down in Iris. Jimmy in the summer of 1960 must have been a man on the edge of collapse. All the newspaper stories, the bravado, the conviction rates, the image as a crusading young prosecutor had all been a sham.

A lie. A terrible lie? I asked myself. A man declares bankruptcy; is that such a crime that nearly thirty years later he should have it dredged up like reopening an old, finally closed wound?

Little things came back to me. Near the end of her life, Jimmy had been the sole support of his mother. She had cancer, and died a long, ugly death.

An expensive proposition, even back then. Cash equals

health; cash equals life; cash equals making the pain stop. And the price can be high.

Over drinks he told me once he'd lost a bundle in some land deal. I never asked for details; he never provided them. I never thought of it again, until now.

"No scotch. White wine," Sally said, walking into the bathroom. "I'm not used to having a scotch drinker around here."

"That's okay," I answered from deep beneath the warmth of the bath water. "Wine's fine."

She held a tray with two glasses of white wine and a candle. She was wearing a blue satin bathrobe, tied tight at the waist, that ran all the way to the floor. Gray smudges, streaked with darker sweat stains, were smeared carelessly across her face. The ends of her brown hair were still matted and damp.

She set the tray down on the floor and lit the candle with her lighter, then sat on the edge of the bathtub. I watched her, so thin and wiry beneath the bathrobe, as she crossed her legs and held out a glass of wine to me. I sat up and took it from her hand. Little beads of cold water formed on the glass as the sides fogged up.

"This is wonderful," I said, relieved that she'd come back and stopped me for a moment from thinking about all this.

"To love," she said, clinking glasses with me. "And to truth."

I stared at her for a couple of seconds over the top of the glass before drinking. Love and Truth. Her throat danced as she leaned back and took a long drink.

"Confusion to our enemies," I said, finally raising my glass.

"Would you like some company in there?" she asked.

She set the glass on the flat edge of the bathtub and stood up. Reaching over, she turned off the bathroom light, leaving us in darkness except for the small orange circle of light that came from the candle on the floor. The mirror caught traces of the light and bounced it around the room like a demented Tinker Bell.

Sally untied the bathrobe and let it fall open. It draped over her shoulders, loosely over her arms, the deep blue against her pale skin. Her skin was tight and smooth, her stomach flat, her breasts small but . . .

Lord have mercy, I thought, she's driving me crazy. This flood of anticipation shot through me, my stomach knotting up like a sixteen-year-old looking through a hidden peephole in the girls' locker room.

The closed bathroom was silent except for the tiny splash of water against the sides of the tub and my own breathing, which was becoming deeper and more pronounced by the second.

I thought I'd never feel anything like this again.

She took off the robe—no, it seemed more to come off from its own power—and laid it on the counter. I looked straight ahead at her, at her long, muscular legs, and then my eyes slowly, deliciously climbed her, to the tiny brown triangle between her legs, up her waist, her arms, to the brown of her hair and eyes.

"Move over," she said.

I slid back as far as I could go. She raised one leg over the wall of the bathtub and stepped in between my legs. Then she brought the other leg over and settled down, my legs around her, both of us facing forward, my arms around her and my jaw in the crook of her neck. I pulled her close to me in the warm water. She moaned and turned to kiss me. We kissed, and then she turned forward and leaned back on me as if to finally rest after a dreadfully long and exhausting day.

"A penny for your thoughts," she whispered.

"Inflation's set in, my darling—"

"Yeah, I noticed," she interrupted.

"It'll cost you a lot more than a penny."

"Well," she said softly, turning slightly toward me, "I don't happen to have any cash on me right now. Perhaps there's some other way . . ."

Back in the office, I saw it didn't take a genius to get some sense of where it had all gone wrong. Expensive tastes in clothes, in cars, in homes. Huge medical bills, some land speculation to try and make up the losses, to grind your way back up through the green felt to break even.

But James Herbert had violated the gambler's first rule: he bet the rent money.

And here it was now, in humiliating detail, for anyone to see who happened to have a dime to pump in a little yellow machine and two hands to pull the paper out and two reasonably literate eyes to make sense of it all on a hot day in July all those years ago.

72-5342 JAMES M. HERBERT, 5613 Commission Ave, City.
Occupation: District Attorney   Attorney: John Silverman

SECURED LIABILITIES:
Warranty Mortagage Company	$38,111.00
231 S. Simmons Street, City	
First National Bank Auto Loan Dept.	3,080.00
345 Sixth Street, City	

UNSECURED LIABILITIES
Eastern Methodist Hospital	2,400.45
2400 Parkway Blvd., City	
Dr. William Cantrell	5,633.01
4300 Medical Plaza, City	
Dr. James Robertson	3,428.70
2564 East 38th St., New York, New York	
Radiology Clinic Associates	6,000.33
4300 Medical Plaza, City	
X-Ray Technicians, Inc.	2,530.45
Rm. 403, Wilson Medical Center, City	

Lab Services of America, Inc.	1,580.89
Rm. 200, Wilson Medical Center, City	
Ward Bank And Trust	10,350.00
Ward Building, City	
American Finance Company	5,000.00
231 South Street, City	
William Bonner Enterprises, Inc.	7,555.36
405 Sunset Ave., City	
Worldwide Benefit Insurance Co.	843.00
Pan Worldwide Building, City	
Land Use & Development Co.	1,680.00
239 LaCoya Bay Ave, Los Angeles, Calif.	
James Singler, Attorney-at-Law	750.00
444 9th Street, City	
Westgate Realty Co.	3,590.10
5423 Avenue DeVille, City	
International Bank & Trust	11,500.25
1 Banks Plaza, City	
Saks Fifth Avenue	348.00
Fifth Avenue, New York, New York	
Dalton & Presley	656.30
Broad Street & Canal, City	

ASSETS

Wearing Apparel and Personal Possessions	8,000.00
Household Goods	1,000.00
Property Claimed as Exempt	1,000.00

TOTAL LIABILITIES	105,037.84
TOTAL ASSETS	10,000.00

I stared down at the section of newspaper I held in my hand. Somehow it seemed so humiliating, so exposing, to have it all laid out there for anyone to see. What did Lily buy at Saks? How many times did his mother have radiation treatments?

These are things other people aren't supposed to know, unless you screw up real bad and, like a second grader being punished for talking too loud, you have to stand up in front of the class and publicly write your sins on the blackboard.

I put the yellowed newspaper clip down next to the stack of copies Sally'd made of it. I picked up another piece of newspaper, one dated only two weeks later and printed in very tiny type buried in the classified section:

NOTICE OF WITHDRAWAL OF VOLUNTARY PETITION
James M. Herbert, Petitioner

Therefore, petitioner and all listed creditors in said petition, having reached satisfactory agreement of said and listed debts, included in the petition and otherwise, the petitioner's motion to withdraw the voluntary petition of bankruptcy is ordered granted by this court.

Matthew M. Compas
PRESIDING JUDGE

Two weeks later. It was all over in two short weeks. One minute, the guy's in hock out the whazzoo; the next, he's free and clear. As much as I loved him, I didn't just fall off the freaking turnip truck.

Something happened. But what?

"It's pretty damned obvious, isn't it?" Sally said, reaching across my desk to take one of my smokes. "He declares bankruptcy, owes six figures, then ten days later he's out of it. Shortly thereafter, the case is dropped against a real bad guy. Put two and two together, Jack."

"And come up with what?"

"Jack, honey, you've got him."

"We haven't got anybody yet," I snapped. "If we were to make something like this public and it turns out not to be true, the next five generations will still be paying off the libel judgment."

"What else do you need, Jack?" she asked, walking around the back of my desk and placing her hands on my shoulder.

"I don't know."

"You don't want to believe it, do you?" she said gently. "You loved him a lot, didn't you?"

"My own feelings for him don't count," I said, trying to convince myself more than anyone else, and not fooling either one of us. "It's just that if we take this to the Old Man and he confronts Herbert with it, it goddamn well better be for real. Or else you and I can nuzzle up in the unemployment line."

In answer to that, she nuzzled down into my neck, next to my ear, with her soft hair rubbing against me like down.

"What's it going to take, baby? What's it going to take to make it real?"

"I don't know. Let's get out of this office. It's lunchtime." My head was spinning, aching. I had to get out of there before I went ape-shit screaming mad.

"Lunchtime?" She laughed. "It's barely eleven."

"Buzz Madge and tell her to grab the phones."

This place around the corner was already packed with light-suited businessmen having drunch, a term coined by guys whose concept of a midday meal consisted of the three-dollar-a-bucket lunchtime martini special. The place was raucous and electric. We waited for a table in the corner, where we sat as far away as possible from the early rowdy crowd.

"This is driving me crazy," I said to her, sipping a rare lunchtime drink. I usually don't drink during the day, but God, the way the last few days had gone . . . "You know what it's going to take to sew this up, don't you?"

"What?" she asked.

"We've got to get *proof*, dammit. Somebody, somewhere has to give us proof."

"How we going to find that? You think Herbert will admit it? Yeah, that's right, Mr. Jennings. I took a helluva bribe thirty years ago and there's nothing anybody can do about it now."

"We've got to find Big Al," I said.

"Find Zimmerman." She laughed. "Oh, honey, he's bound to be dead by now."

"I didn't see any mention of his death in the paper."

"You weren't looking for it, either."

"So I'll look for it. Shouldn't be hard."

"Maybe, maybe not," she said. "But what if you do find him? What makes you think he'll talk to you?"

"He's got nothing to lose. He couldn't be prosecuted by now. It's been too long."

"He's probably dead. And if he's not dead, you'll never find him. And if you do, he probably won't talk."

"Thanks a lot," I said, "for being so encouraging."

"Hey, you say to-may-to and I say to-mah-to."

"What worries me the most is time," I said.

"Yeah, it scares the hell out of me, too," Sally said, grinning.

"I mean the time we don't have to find Zimmerman."

"Jack?"

"Yeah?"

"I'm worried about you," she said, reaching across the table and taking my hand in hers. I looked into her eyes, knowing full well that my own eyes couldn't hide what was going on inside anymore.

"I'm worried about me, too," I whispered. "I'm worried about a lot of things."

Sally walked back to the office alone while I headed over to the main branch of the Public Library. I dug through the *New York Times* obituary index for every year since 1960. Nothing. I checked a couple of other places, flipping through a not very complete index for the local papers. Nothing.

I walked the long way back to the office in spite of the heat, past the bus station and the office buildings and the old hotels. What was it Powell had told me? About Zimmerman not being a citizen?

"Nothing," I answered in response to the question on Sally's face as I walked in. I breezed past her into my office just as the phone rang.

"Public Relations," I heard her say.

"Yes, may I ask who's calling please?"

"I'm sorry. Say again . . ." A long pause. "I'm sorry, sir, you'll have to let me know who you are before I can put you through to Mr. Lynch. It's company policy."

Bob Sparks, I thought. I stepped to the door and motioned as I mouthed, "I'll take it."

I picked up the phone.

"Jack Lynch here."

I fumbled to pull my jacket off and toss it across the room. My arm stopped in midair.

"Listen, asshole," a voice said.

"Who is this?" I interrupted.

"Never mind who this is. Consider me a friend."

I strained to recognize the voice.

"All this digging around shit is going to stop. Understand?"

"Who are you?" I demanded. My gut tightened into a hard knot; I felt sweat popping out on my forehead.

"If you don't want to wind up gator bait," the voice said, low, mean, a slight Cajun twinge to it. "You keep your nose out of where it don't belong."

He hung up. The dial tone blaring in my ear had a slightly unreal sound to it.

Jesus, what have I gotten myself into? For a moment, none of this sunk in. I punched three buttons on the phone: Carlton's office. His secretary put me through.

"Carlton?" I said.

"Yes, Jack."

"I need a favor. I was hoping you could help me."

"I'll try. What is it?"

I described my search for the lost Zimmerman. If there was anyone who'd have a contact in the government, the federal government, it would be Carlton. Maybe somebody in the Justice Department or Immigration and Naturalization . . .

"I have a few numbers I can call," Carlton said. "But it may take a while."

"Top priority, Carlton. Time's becoming a factor here."

"This *is* about Murphy's lawsuit, isn't it?"

"Yes," I answered. "But I can't give you the details just yet. I just need to find this guy bad."

"I'll get back to you as quickly as I can."

"Carlton?"

"Yes, Jack?"

"I just got a threatening phone call." I felt my own voice breaking.

There was a moment's silence on the line, then: "What did the caller say?"

"Some reference to my being gator bait if these little inquiries of mine don't stop."

"My God, boy," he said, his voice revealing for the first time any emotion. He sounded tired suddenly, drained. "This is getting nasty."

"No kidding."

"Right now, I don't know what to say. Just be careful. Maybe we should pull back a bit."

"The Old Man won't like that."

"Nobody wants to see anyone get hurt, Jack. This is getting ugly."

"I'll watch myself, Carlton. In the meantime, try to find Zimmerman for me."

For the time being, that was it. Nothing to do but wait for inspiration.

"Have any idea what you're going to say to Zimmerman if you find him?" Sally asked.

She was standing in the doorway to my office, leaning against the doorjamb with one foot crossed over the other. I searched her face for any sign she'd overheard the last half of my conversation with Carlton. If she had, she wasn't showing it.

"No," I answered. "I have a feeling that I'm not going to be able to bullshit him. I may just have to come out and ask him."

"Doesn't leave you a lot of out if he turns you down, does it?"

"There's not going to be much out anywhere in this mess, I'm afraid."

"What if he won't talk to you at all?"

"I'll worry about that when it happens, I guess."

My shock at the phone call wore off, and in a few minutes I found myself furious. Maybe I was out of my league here, and maybe not. There are lots of ways to play rough. Threatening phone calls are just one.

"Why can't I go with you?" Sally asked, in a mock-pouting voice.

"I promise you, when this is all over we'll take a trip somewhere. Just the two of us."

"I know, I'm just kidding. C'mon now, you'll miss your plane."

The second boarding call for Flight 231 had just been made. I grabbed the hanger bag off the back of the stool in the airport bar where Sally and I had just finished a drink and started walking. Fortunately, the gate wasn't too far past Security and there were no crowds in the airport for a midnight flight.

We picked up our pace a little as we walked down the carpeted, empty corridor toward Gate 9. The fluorescent lighting above us cast a blue pall over everything and our voices echoed down the hall.

"You're going to be in the office tomorrow, right?" I asked.

"Of course, where else would I be?" she said impatiently.

"I just wanted to make sure I could reach you."

"You can reach me anytime you like," she said.

I hiked the bag up over my shoulder, kissed Sally good-bye, and walked up the jetway to the airplane and past the somewhat sleepy flight attendants. There were no more than fifteen or twenty people on the red eye to Miami.

This was a sudden, rushed trip. It had taken Carlton two days to track down Zimmerman through a Department of Immigration connection. A friend dug out Zimmerman's file and found a last known address on him. I went back to the library just before it closed and looked through the phone book, but found he wasn't listed. I called information just to make sure. Nothing.

By Sunday, I'd decided, what the hell, wing it; pack a bag and fly down in the dark of the night.

The huge plane eased out onto the runway and took off. Below me, the bright lights of the city burned merci-lessly and somewhere, in that string of tiny lights all in a line down the highway, was Sally. I missed her already, still unable to understand why after so many years of getting along perfectly fine by myself, I was suddenly so dependent on someone else for any sense of peace in the world.

The flight attendant, tired, pretty, and bored, walked by with a cart full of drinks and gave me a scotch and soda. I lit a cigarette and savored the drink as the cool, filtered air of the plane blew down on me. I looked out the window again, to find that the lights of the city were far behind us. We were flying along the Gulf Coast, the dim lights of the oil rigs and the fishing boats flickering up at us weakly. It was a clear night, beautiful and still, and out off the wing I could see a thin sliver of moon and stars everywhere.

I had a second drink and drifted off into an uneasy sleep as the plane banked right cross Florida diagonally and headed down the Atlantic Coast toward Miami.

The flight attendant woke me up enough to raise my seat back and tighten my seat belt, but it was the thump of the wheels hitting the concrete that finally brought me back to full consciousness. I looked at my watch and saw that it was 3:30 in the morning, 4:30 Eastern Time. I'd missed a night's sleep for sure this time. It would be sunrise soon and my traveling wasn't over yet.

I got a cab to the hotel by the airport and checked into a room, leaving a wake-up call for 7:00. I dropped my clothes on the floor and fell down on the bed, asleep before my head sank all the way into the pillow. The call came what seemed like moments later and it took fifteen minutes under a colder-than-normal shower to bring me around.

The flight I needed to Freeport, to the Grand Bahamas Island where Zimmerman was hidden somewhere, wasn't until 1:30. I mulled it over for a minute or two and decided it was worth whatever it took to get there quicker. A cab driver who knew Miami International better than I knew my own apartment got me around to Page Avjet. I walked into the office and up to the man behind the counter. I'd shaved and put on a fresh suit, but my eyes were the blood-shot red of a binge victim and my skin felt like somebody shrink-wrapped my skull. He eyed me as I stood at the counter, waiting for him to finish going over some information on a clipboard.

"May I help you?" he asked coldly.

I pulled out my business card case and handed him one of the cards.

"I'd like to charter a plane."

"When?"

"Right now, if possible."

"I'm not sure if we have an aircraft available now."

"This is a corporate charter and we'll pay whatever's necessary to get me to Freeport International as quickly as possible."

"There are commercial flights into Freeport this afternoon."

"I'm in a hurry."

"It may cost a great deal more than a commercial flight."

I pulled my wallet out of my suit coat and opened it. A fanfold of credit cards dropped out like a spilled accordion file.

"What cards do you take?"

My array of credit cards seemed to get his attention. He took one of the gold ones, ran it through a machine to verify the account, and ten minutes later I was standing on the tarmac in front of the hangar by a new Piper Seneca. The twin-engined plane looked awfully small to fly across the ocean. I told the pilot that.

"Well, we're not exactly flying across the ocean," the red-haired man who looked altogether too young to be a pilot explained. "Freeport's only an hour or so away."

I strapped myself nervously into the small plane next to him. The concave door closing seemed to swallow us as we sat there shoulder to shoulder. I watched as the guy's fingers seemed to dance unconsciously across the controls and instrument panel, checking things I'd never heard of, didn't understand, and was becoming increasingly nervous about.

"You don't look too good," he commented.

"Didn't get much sleep last night. Haven't had much to eat today either, besides coffee."

"Barf bag's in the seat pocket behind you," he said.

I was beginning to regret my decision not to stay with the commercial flight. Somehow, being in a light plane 9,000 feet off the ocean floor is less comforting than being in something much bigger than your house five miles straight up.

The islands seemed to rise up out of the water below us, and within minutes of sighting them, we were on a final, steep approach to Freeport International.

A sleepy customs guard made a quick, easy inspection of my bag and I walked through the hot, somewhat seedy, terminal to the cab stand. A group of tourists milled around out front, just in off a charter. They waited impatiently for cabs to cart them off to the Princess for a few days of sunburn and slots.

There was a different line of cabs off to the right. I walked over to this muscular black man standing by a red Checker made dull by years in the sun.

"Sorry, mon, you got to stand in line for transfers," he said as I approached.

"I'm not with the charter," I said. "I've got a room booked at the Lucayen Beach Hotel. Can you take me?"

"Hey, mon, no problem," he said, reaching for my bag, pleased to have a cash fare.

The Lucayen Beach was one of the nicer hotels on the island and I figured after all this I deserved at least that. I checked in and went up to my room, ordered lunch from room service, and lay down on the bed to rest until it came.

The man downstairs had given me a map, but it was a tourist map that only showed the main highways on the part of the island frequented by the flocks of mainland visitors. I phoned down to the car rental desk and asked them to find me a complete map and to get my car ready.

Outside my window, the sand and palm trees spread out for miles. Off in the distance, a fire burned, clearing vegetation, and a thick column of smoke rose into the deep blue sky that lay above us unmarred by clouds. The sun was fierce, yet a gentle breeze blew across the island. People move very slowly here; it's easy to understand why.

And the end of the search was here, in an exclusive area on the eastern end of the island, in a place called Layman Cay.

The number for the Zimmerman estate was unlisted, unavailable, unknown. Not even a way to bribe somebody. Only the address that Carlton had dug up. I pulled out of the hotel parking lot in the rental car and started the long drive down past the Princess Complex, the cutoff to Xanadu Beach, past the tourists in their goofy clothes and cameras, the tanned, muscular Bahamian boys on the make for American girls, the locals with the British accents and the snooty air of long-time colonials. Driving on the left was awkward and uncomfortable at first, but it gradually became smoother and more natural as I went on.

I'd changed into my best blue pinstripes and unpacked my banker's briefcase. If I was going to bluff my way into Zimmerman's house, I'd better look the professional. Out past the dense part of the island, where the houses were farther apart and much more expensive, I began looking for Layman Cay. Occasionally, the road would pull near the beach and I'd get glimpses of sailboats, yachts, bronzed girls in string bikinis wandering the sand; a world I wouldn't know how to even begin to fit into.

I stopped at a small restaurant, had a cup of coffee and a smoke, and got directions to the Cay. A small, unmarked street off from the main highway led north to an exclusive area of estates, mansions. No tourist hotels here; no tourists allowed. Here was where the real wealth of the island hid.

No. 32 Prince Edward Drive was in a quiet, sandy little cul-de-sac far away from everything else. I parked the car on the side of the road and got out. A locked gate blocked the driveway. There was a button off to the left of the high stone wall. I pushed it, expecting to hear a voice over an intercom, only there was no speaker anywhere. After a minute or so, a teenaged boy of much lighter skin than the local Bahamians came to the gate, wearing a white butler's coat.

"May I help you?" he asked, in a heavily accented voice.

I took out one of my cards with my name, the bank's name, logo, and address on it, and handed it to him.

"My name is Jack Lynch," I said, "and I have some

important bank business to discuss with Mr. Zimmerman. I would have called in advance, but I was unable to find the phone number here."

The boy took my card through the gate, told me to wait there, and disappeared up a path leading to the side entrance of the house.

The house itself, I could see through the trees, was a large one, two stories high, of what appeared to be freshly painted brown stucco. Off to the right was a three-car garage, holding a really slick Turbo Carrera, a Mercedes sedan, and a four-wheel-drive Jeep Cherokee. The driveway was tile, lined by a curb of bricks that bordered the well-kept grounds. I could hear unseen parrots squawking in the trees. There was a child's swing under the limb of an immense tree. Nearby, a large greenhouse sat baking tropical plants probably worth a fortune. Way off to the left was a building that looked like it might have been servants' quarters.

The young boy walked back down the driveway and opened the gate.

"This way, please," he said, locking the gate after me and leading the way up the driveway. Off to the left, where I couldn't see before, was a chain-link pen with two fierce German shepherds locked inside. As soon as they saw me, the dogs began to bark madly. The chain-link fence shook as they slammed into it, trying to get to me. My stomach knotted up in a tight ball and my palms began to sweat.

The boy led me up a large porch and in the front entrance. It was dark inside; I had to squint to adjust my eyes. The house was full of antiques, mahogany cabinets filled with silver, oriental rugs on the floor. We went down a long hall and into a room off to the left, kind of an office. In it stood a man almost a foot taller than me. His hair was jet black and combed back on his head. He turned to look at me. I could see that he was well-built, perhaps in his early forties. He had the air of a well-educated, sophisticated man, yet one who also seemed tough as hell at the same time. He glared at me with a pair of probing, deep-brown eyes.

"That will be all, Joseph," he ordered. The boy exited the room. "I'm Mr. Zimmerman. You'll forgive me for being rude, but we're not at all fond of visitors here. I don't remember ever having had any business with you or your bank, either one. Kindly explain yourself."

"There must be some confusion here," I said. "My business is with Mr. Alton V. Zimmerman."

He looked at me suspiciously, with a hint of cold steel in his eyes.

"My father has been retired now for years," he said. "It's quite impossible that you could have had any business with my father. You've made a mistake, Mr. Lynch. I'm afraid I'm going to have to ask you to leave."

He leaned over against his desk and pushed a button up under it.

"Perhaps I can explain this a little better," I said, grabbing at something, anything, that would buy me time. "Some thirty years ago or so, your father had some business dealings with a man—business that now involves my employer. I'm here as his representative. I've come a long way and it's extremely important that I see him."

"That's impossible," he said, his voice deepening. Behind me, two large Bahama Papas stepped into the room. One was about my height, but maybe fifty pounds heavier. The other could've taken on the front four of the Pittsburgh Steelers. If these guys wanted to evict me, I decided in an instant, to hell with truth. I was going easy, not that I'd have much choice.

"My father is very ill and very tired. He's had two strokes and is quite unable to handle even the smallest strain on his nerves. He is in his nineties and confined to a wheelchair. He probably wouldn't remember who you're referring to anyway."

"Ask him," I said quickly. "As far as I've come and as much trouble as I've gone to, the least you can do is ask him if he remembers James Herbert. That's all, just ask him if he remembers James Herbert. I'm sure he'll want to talk to me then and we'll be glad to compensate you or him for your time."

The son's eyes softened as he laughed at me.

"We don't need your money, Mr. Lynch."

"I know that. I'm just desperate."

"You must be. All right, Mr. Lynch, if it will get you out of here any quicker and any easier, then I will ask him. I doubt if he'll remember, though, and if he doesn't, you go immediately."

"Okay, fair enough. Thanks."

I sat in a chair as he went out of the room, leaving the two goons wordlessly watching me. I looked up at them, smiled, and then settled back, staring at the wall, when they didn't exactly jump to return my grin. I craved a cigarette, but there were no ashtrays.

The desk phone chimed and the smaller of the two guys went over and picked it up. He listened silently, then placed the phone back in its cradle. He smiled at me, then made a motion to the other guy.

Suddenly, the two were on top of me. Each one grabbed an arm and I felt myself coming out of the chair effortlessly.

"Wait a minute, guys, what's going on?"

One of them grunted as I got half-carried, half-dragged out into the hall, then pulled in the general direction of the front door.

"Where's your boss, fellas?" I asked. "Let me talk to him."

They were moving faster now, with me dragging my feet and stumbling, trying to keep up with them and delay them at the same time. I tried to stifle a rising panic as I wondered what they were going to do with me. Was this just the bum's rush, or was I going to find myself out in the garden somewhere digging my own grave?

This is getting out of hand, I thought to myself. I'm really scared, terrified, and I'm getting this picture of Sally flashing before me and wondering if I'm ever going to see her again. I make up my mind then and there that if I get out of this alive, it's time for a career change. I'm taking Sally away with me, away from all this craziness and crap.

We rounded a corner and turned into another room, then through it into another. Wherever they were taking me, it wasn't the front gate. I got this clutching in my chest; it's real panic now. They're taking me toward the back of the house, and in a flash of something, terror, whatever, I decided to not go quietly.

"Dammit," I yelled, planting both feet on a rug as hard as I can and jerking my arms opposite the way they're pulling me. "Where are you taking me?"

The two stopped momentarily. The smaller one, the one that answered the phone, bared his teeth at me, just slightly but enough that I know what he's doing. Then the two of them continued on, with me like a stubborn puppy on a leash. There isn't a thing I can do; these two gorillas have got me.

And I'm scared as hell now.

We went into a room with glass doors on the opposite side from where we entered. The doors led out onto a deck that overlooks the ocean. And suddenly the thought that I'm really going to freaking die here hits home and I feel my bladder starting to let go. But I'm holding on, just barely, hoping that something . . .

The big one grabs my shoulders, spins me around, slams me into a wall. He jerked my arms up and slapped them on the wall, then began frisking me. His huge hands moved roughly, professionally, up and down. They do this shit well down here, in the sunny, peaceful Bahamas.

I heard steps behind me, and a voice. The big guy finished with me, then jerked me off the wall and turned me around again. The younger Zimmerman was standing there, angry, glaring at me, not in the mood.

"My father will see you," he said abruptly, any hospitality gone from his voice. "But only for a very short time. Let me warn you of something else, Mr. Lynch. If you do anything to excite or upset my father in any way, both you and the bank you work for will be very sorry.

"Excuse the imposition," he added, "but my father has made his share of enemies. It's only precaution."

Through the glass door, I saw a metal table with a large, crank-up beach umbrella opened above it. Zimmerman motioned for me to follow him. My legs were shaky; I had this fierce urge to urinate. I walked through the door behind him, with the two bodyguards behind us.

Under the shade of the umbrella was a wheelchair. In it sat an old man with his back to me. He was almost bald, with only a small shock of wispy white hair blowing in the breeze. He stared out at the ocean as we approached.

Zimmerman's son led the way over to the table and we stood in front of the man. He was emaciated, wrinkled, with folds of loose, translucent skin draped over his cheekbones and forehead. His drawn-up, paralyzed hands lay loose in his lap like claws. Only his eyes, deep brown and lucid, were clear. He was wearing a blue striped bathrobe and his legs were covered with a light blanket.

"Dad," the son said in a gentle tone that I wouldn't have imagined he was capable of, "here is the man who wanted to see you."

"All right, Vincent," the man rasped, his voice straining to make itself heard. "Let us alone now."

"Remember what I told you, Mr. Lynch," he warned as he walked away.

Right, Vinny, I thought. Go chill out somewhere.

"Sit down," the man said.

I pulled up a chair and sat in front of him.

"Hello, Mr. Zimmerman," I said. "I'm pleased to meet you."

"How do you know me?" he asked.

"I know who you are," I answered, as his eyes darted up and down, looking me over. "I know quite a bit about you."

"Do you now?" he commented. "And what of it?"

"Mr. Zimmerman," I said, edging close to him, "I have something very important to talk to you about. I've come a long way. I need your help."

"What did you say your name was?"

"Lynch," I answered. "Jack Lynch."

"What do you want, Mr. Lynch?"

"I want to explain this to you," I began slowly. "I work for a man who, like yourself, is very wealthy and powerful. He has many people who work for him, who depend on him for their livelihoods, and he's good to them. One of my boss's people is causing him trouble, though. He's filed a lawsuit against the man who got him his job. My boss. The lawsuit can hurt my boss very badly."

"People have no loyalty," Zimmerman rasped. "It's terrible."

"Yes, it's terrible," I agreed. "My boss wants the suit dropped and he doesn't want to ruin the man who brought it. He'll take care of that later, when the time is right. Right now, he just wants the lawsuit dropped. The man behind the lawsuit is a lawyer. We wants to get the lawyer to drop the suit. His name is James Herbert."

Zimmerman's eyes brightened a bit.

"James Herbert was once district attorney," I continued. "And he caused you a lot of trouble. Just like he's causing us trouble now. I've done a lot of research, Mr. Zimmerman, and it seems that Herbert was in a good deal of financial trouble. Right about the time you were indicted back in 1960. That time when things looked really bad. Then Herbert got out of his financial trouble. And a short time later, all the indictments against you were dropped."

I took a deep breath and sucked in my gut. The pain in my groin was matched now only by the pounding in my head. I felt as if I was against the wall, staring at the firing squad.

"I just wondered if there was any connection . . ."

I spoke directly at him, but not too loudly, to make sure he could hear me. He listened intently, then shifted a bit in his chair. I began to sweat in the heat, and grew just a little dizzy.

"So you think I paid him off," he said, the same abruptness in his strained voice that I'd heard earlier from his son.

"I don't know. That's what I want to find out. I think if you told me, it wouldn't make any difference to you. No one would bother you about it."

He laughed at me like his son had.

"Don't worry about that," he said. "No one can touch me here. I own this place."

"If it's true and you tell me, my employer will use the information to get Herbert to drop the lawsuit. Herbert will, of course, and nobody will ever see the information besides my boss and me and Herbert. It will never be public."

"Without the threat of going public," Zimmerman said, "you got nothing on him. He pushes you, you got to go public."

"It won't get that far. Believe me, I know Herbert."

"I'm tired," he said, his voice becoming weaker. "And I'm old as hell. I got out of the rackets a long time ago. I don't want no trouble."

"No trouble, Mr. Zimmerman," I said, edging closer to him. "Nobody will ever bother you about this."

"I don't want any trouble," he whispered.

I laid my hand on his arm, feeling the bone beneath the

cloth of the robe. He seemed a burnt-out shell of the man I imagined he once was.

"No trouble, Mr. Zimmerman. I promise you."

He stared at me. His clear brown eyes were the only part of his body that showed any life at all. Then he shifted a bit in his chair. I leaned in even closer, looking at him intensely. Finally, his thin voice spoke.

"That sonofabitch cost me two hundred thousand dollars," he said, slowly, clearly, deliberately. "I paid two hundred thousand for him. He was mine. Now he's yours."

Bull's-eye.

Ten

Big Al Valentine Zimmerman gave me two hours of his time, which was not exactly a commodity of which he had a great surplus.

I had it all: statements, descriptions, witnesses, most of whom were all dead, gone, or disappeared. But there was enough backup to lend the tale just the right amount of credibility to make it a bitch to dispute.

I'd won.

Mr. Freaking Goddamn Captain Avenger had done it. The truth was out there running from me, and I caught it and wrestled it down and hog-tied it until it was mine.

I should be feeling a helluva lot better than I do.

The late-afternoon crowds at the beach were too busy incubating their future melanomas to pay any attention to the guy walking through the sand in a suit; tie pulled down loosely, jacket over one shoulder, a disjointed, disoriented look on his face.

This was the emotional equivalent of surviving a terrorist bomb blast. You're walking down the street, going after groceries or some such harmless thing like that, and suddenly the building or the car or whatever next to you is blown all to hell. You're knocked down, stunned, but not physically hurt. It wasn't your car; you're okay, what's the big deal? But there's something inside you now that was never there before, some little thing that sits like a lump and you think about it and feel all around it, and suddenly you realize what it is that's lying there all charred and dead. It's your illusions, your ability to trust anything anymore. The feeling that you can safely walk down the street to pick up your groceries without fear is gone forever. Even though you weren't hurt, some part of you is dead, and you'll never quite feel comfortable in the world again.

That's the way it was for me when I knew without any doubt that James Herbert, the one man I looked up to and respected as a really straight guy, was a crook.

He wasn't just a crook; he was slime, pond scum, dog shit on the front lawn turning white in the sun.

I'd set out to prove to the Old Man that good still exists somewhere and its name was Jimmy Herbert. I'd set out to prove to myself that the man whose standards I couldn't measure up to had immeasurable standards.

Immeasurable standards, hell. The paradigm was just a bit frigging defective, wasn't it? How many innocent people got hurt because he didn't put Zimmerman away? This is, of course, assuming there are any innocent people left.

I'm not stupid. I didn't just step off the bus. In this day and age, you expect corruption to be as common as carcinogens in the drinking water. But somewhere in the back of my mind, I kept figuring there were still some good guys walking around somewhere. I know I'm not one of them; I know I don't work for one of them. But I also know there's almost a certain crazy nobility in admitting what you are and who you are. The people I know who are corrupt are up front about it. Hell, most of them are proud of it.

It only seemed to make it that much worse that for all these years, he'd been parading and crusading and playing it on the up and up, and it'd all been a lie.

He'd have made a helluva television evangelist.

Back at the hotel room, sipping a scotch and soda, I tried to take it all in. The curtains were pulled, the air-conditioning as cold as I could get it, the bed drawn.

I flipped on the television and stared at it, not paying much attention to the late-afternoon soap opera from Miami. It seemed like hours passed as I paced around the room, agitated, crazy, unable to sit still.

The electronic chatter of the phone bell brought me back. I picked up the phone; the Bahamian operator asked my name, then told me to hold for a call.

"Jack?"

"Yeah, Sally," I said, the sound of her voice the sweetest thing I'd heard all day.

"How's it going?"

"Fine, darling. I miss you. How are you?" I was squeezing the phone so hard my knuckles were turning white.

"Fine, I miss you, too. I just wanted to see if I could get you before I left the office. Did you find Zimmerman?"

"Yeah," I said, "I found him."

"And?"

"I'll have to tell you when I get back. But we hit—"

"Yeah?" she said, excited.

"Big time. This will all be settled very soon."

"Great. Are you all right?"

I thought for a second. My head was pounding and the scotch was churning in my stomach.

"I guess so. Been a long day."

"I'm sure it has. Listen, you hurry home. You coming back on the same flight?"

"Yeah, same one. I'll see you tomorrow night."

"Great. Everything else okay?"

"As well as it ever is," she said lightly. "Oh, I forgot to mention. We've had a little excitement here."

"Yeah? What's up?"

"One of the employees got killed last night. Murdered. Pretty horrible, from what the newspapers said. Some kind of pervert thing, the police think."

"Yeah? Who?"

"Some new kid down in Data Processing."

The breath I was drawing in locked up like a panic stop in a traffic jam.

"Sally," I snapped. "Who was it?"

"I don't know. I didn't know him."

"Have you still got the paper there?"

"Well, yes, it's in the wastebasket, but why—"

"Get it! Get me his name!"

"But, Jack."

"Dammit, Sally, do it now!"

There was a noise as she put the phone down, and I could hear the rustling of papers in the background. Please, let me be just paranoid. I'll settle for just paranoid . . .

"Here it is," she said, picking the phone back up. "Bob Sparks."

"Oh, Jesus." I sighed, my eyes clouding over, the pounding in my head an even 10 on the Richter Scale. "Goddamn."

"What is it, Jack? Jack? Are you there, dammit?"

"Yeah," I said, trying to pull myself together. I had a wild thought. "Listen, Sally, did a box come for me today? A package, maybe a stack of papers?"

"Yeah. It came this afternoon. It's on your desk."

"Jesus," I said, panicked, my knuckles turning even whiter around the telephone. "You gotta go in there and get it for me, and take it—"

"Jack?"

"No, for God's sake, don't take it out of the office. Somebody might be watching you. Lock it in the fireproof filing cabinet, okay?"

"Jack, what is going on here? What's this Bob Sparks got to do with you and that package?"

"Sally, I promise you I'll explain everything tomorrow. But for right now, you've got to do exactly what I'm asking you, honey. You got to."

"Jack, I don't like this." Pause. "Okay . . ."

"Lock the package in the filing cabinet. Then go home and pack a bag and get out of your house for tonight. Go to a motel, anywhere. Just get out. And whatever the hell you do, don't go to work tomorrow. Call in sick. Pick me up at the airport tomorrow, but make sure you're not followed. Is there anybody else there who knows what flight I'm coming in on?"

"No, I got the tickets through the travel agency myself."

"That doesn't mean anything, but we'll have to take a chance. This is all happening too fast."

"Jack Lynch, you're scaring the hell out of me. What is going on?" she demanded.

"I can't tell you over the office phone. We may have said too much already. Go home, pack a bag, get the hell out of your house, and meet me at the airport tomorrow."

"Jack, I—"

"Be careful, Sally," I interrupted. "And listen, I . . . I really love you."

"I love you, too," she said, calmer. "Come home safe to me."

"I intend to. You be careful."

Bob Sparks dead. Suddenly, it was as if a part of me went dead, too. I was swept over with this wave of exhaustion the likes of which I honestly believe I'd never felt. I didn't even know the kid. But he was dead because he tried to help me. As I sat there staring straight ahead, feeling every ounce of my weight, every second of my years, I thought to myself that we are dealing with some serious sons of bitches here.

I stripped off my clothes and lay back on the bed, the glass in one hand, a lit cigarette in the other. Room service was on the way up with a plate full of club sandwiches and another bottle of soda. There wasn't much chance I'd be able to eat.

Truthfully, I was swept over by the urge to do something really demented, but my demented, twisted days were long behind me and now here I was, a somewhat dull, almost middle-aged man stuck in a hotel room alone after a successful business trip. The only difference was that one of the by-products of my business had become a surprise corpse.

The food didn't help, what I could eat of it. Neither did more scotch, although after three or four more I was beginning to be anesthetized a bit. The mirror on the wall across the room, tilted at just the right angle for couples who felt like getting a bit kinky, reflected a face back at me that I hardly recognized.

Dark circles were embedded like tattoos under eyes that had the glazed-over look of the shell-shocked. My skin seemed to hang off my face. I realized I'd lost weight over the past few weeks. A body that was lean and tight only a few years ago now sagged and drooped over bones that once carried it like a sprinter, an athlete, a dancer. A prick that once stood up and danced at the whiff of an approaching female or the thought of an encounter now lay flabby and loose in my lap, unresponsive to fantasies it'd seen too many times before or the touch of a hand that no longer held any hidden thrill.

If this is getting old, this process of watching the body deteriorate and illusions evaporate, then it sucks.

I got tired of watching myself smoke, drink, and age in the mirror. I was itchy and restless and scared, and unable to sit in this damn hotel room any longer.

I showered, dressed, pulled myself together as well as possible under the circumstances, and went down to the casino.

One of the few consolations of aging is that you can do things you never would have been able to get away with as a kid. I walked up to the window, pulled out a credit card, and with a quick signature and a smile from the cutie behind the cage, I had a thousand cash in my fat little hand. I walked toward the action in the center of the enormous hall. To my right were banks and banks of slot machines, hundreds of them, gaily-colored, electric, loud. Little old ladies, tourists, bizarre characters of every type imaginable sat on stools in front of the hungry boogers, their fingers growing blacker as they pumped the dirty quarters in hour after hour. Paper cups that once held thousands in coins lay crumpled next to the machines, deserted by their owners after the ship, once again, failed to come in.

To my left were the crap tables and the roulette wheels, with a higher class of gambler. Men in tuxedos with women wearing formal gowns stood gathered around, betting money that would put your average joe into apoplexy. Beyond them were the blackjack tables, the intimate little gatherings of seven and a dealer that went on for hours and hours, the people at the tables often becoming dear and true friends as the night went on. Green felt is comforting under the fingertips of a true gambler; it's like wall-to-wall carpet in a fine home. If I ever buy a home, I thought through the haze, I want it covered in green felt. And I want noise, noise like this tonight, bells clanging, people whistling, yelling, hooting, the sounds of a twenty-four-hour-a-day party.

Like the night before the apocalypse.

The drink girl brings me a plastic glass; free drinks for

everybody at this party. I edge up to a blackjack table and take a seat at first base, the chair to the dealer's immediate left.

There was a hand under way. After it was over and the dealer paid off and scraped the cards off the table, I pushed five crisp, new hundred dollar bills across the felt. I looked up and noticed the dealer was a young, thin, freckled blonde. Her hair was cut short, nothing fancy, and she had the kind of long, thin fingers that made her a perfect dealer.

"Cashing in," she said out loud, in what sounded to me like a perfect educated British accent. "Five hundred."

She took the blade and shoved the money into the cash slot and counted out three stacks of black, red, and green chips. I pushed a black chip into the square and sat back to wait. The other six at the table looked at me oddly, and I realized I'd just bet a hundred dollars on my first hand at a five-dollar minimum table. The other players laid their one or two green chips down and waited for the deal.

Just don't bet the rent, I thought. Roll as high as you want to, as high as you can, but don't ever get caught. Because then you have to take help from people who'll own you body and soul forever and after. And somebody always finds out.

Always.

The pretty young dealer's hand flashed out of the shoe faster than I could follow. A black ten. Another flash and a red jack appeared.

"Blackjack," she called out. A lady in a green polyester blouse two chairs over applauded. The dealer laid another black chip and two reds down in my square. I handed one of the reds back to her.

"Thanks," she said sweetly, tapping the chip on the counter to alert the pit boss she was dropping a tip into the hopper.

I laid down another chip, then another, and the drinks came, and her pretty hands flashed and her eyes brightened and the chatter continued until it became a din, a stream of unrecognizable noise. I was going to drown it all out no matter what it took.

And always the dealer out there, looking better by the moment, chatting with me, dealing cards, taking my money, thanking me for my tips. It went on until the middle of the night, the pit boss shifting her around from table to table with me following her, as if we were old buddies in adventure. I could have lost my heart to her, but lost my ass to the casino instead.

I was a bit unsteady the next evening as I stepped out of the airplane onto the jetway and made my way down to the gate. A couple of scotches on the plane helped burr the rough edges, but dinner had been completely inedible. Blood sugar levels were dropping fast; another crash and burn was on its way.

Sally was there waiting for me at the gate, smiling but tight, so crisp and clean and lovely enough to bring an ache to my gut. As she stepped quickly through the crowd up to me and came into my arms with the easy grace of a dancer, I dropped my suit bag and briefcase and hugged her tightly for a long time. The rest of the disembarking passengers split to either side of us and stepped wearily on.

"I missed you terribly," she said.

"Me, too," I answered. "God, you look good."

"You look like hell. What did you do, lose ten pounds down there?"

"And a couple thousand dollars," I added.

"What?" she asked.

"Long story. I'll tell you about it later, over dinner. Some place cheap, though. My Visa's maxxed out."

"C'mon, let's get out of here."

She picked up the briefcase and carried it for me, which gave me the opportunity to put an arm around her shoulder. We walked slowly, side-by-side, down the crowded, bright concourse.

"Didn't they feed you on the plane?"

"They tried."

"I gather not too successfully."

"I know a little place on Airline Highway, right before you get to the Interstate," I said.

"Great. C'mon, let's get you fed. Then you can tell me what the hell's going on here."

The place down off the highway was a funky little barbecue joint that I discovered back when I was in school. I hadn't been there in years. It hadn't changed, though, like so many other things down here in the land that time forgot, or didn't give a shit about. Whatever.

We ordered barbecue and corn bread and huge bowls of salad. I ordered a beer.

"And you, ma'am?" the blue-jeaned waitress asked.

"Just coffee for me," Sally said.

"What, we're not drinking tonight?" I asked.

"No," she said, looking down. "Not in the mood. I want to keep my wits about me tonight."

"Is something the matter?"

"That's kind of a silly question, isn't it?" She waited for the waitress to walk away. "All right, you want to tell me what's in the package?"

I thought for a second, unsure if it was smart to tell her everything. Her stake in this was getting about as big as mine. That thought made the decision for me.

"That kid down in Data Processing was working for me."

"What do you mean, working for you?"

"That phone call I got a week or so ago, the one where the person wouldn't identify himself and I had to meet him after work. Real cloak and dagger stuff."

"Yeah?" she asked, her face darkening.

"He was on to something—and I don't know what yet

because I haven't seen the printouts he sent me—that may have put us right in the middle of whatever the hell it is that's going on with Murphy."

"Then somebody found out what the kid was doing . . ."

"Yeah."

Sally took in a deep breath and seemed to sway just a bit in her seat. "And they killed him for it? My God, Jack, what kind of people are we dealing with here?"

I looked at her, scared, not knowing exactly what to say. Suddenly, I was more terrified than I'd ever been in my entire life. Not so much for me. Hell, I've had times in my life when I could've cared less, but the thought of anything happening to her . . .

"My God," she said, in shock now, tears welling up in her eyes, "they killed that poor boy. Jack, the newspapers said it was horrible. He was mutilated. They—"

"Sshh," I whispered. "Don't." I reached across the table and took her hands in mine.

"Jack, what are we going to do?"

"Darling, we're in over our heads on this one. We don't have any choice. I've got to get that package to somebody in the police or the D.A.'s office, and then we'll get the hell out of town. This isn't a bank matter anymore."

"Who's that going to be? Who can you trust in this town? You just don't know who owns who in New Orleans, Jack. We could turn what we know over to the very people who started all this in the first place."

I thought of Fred Williams at the D.A.'s office. "There's one person I think we can trust. I'm not sure, but I think . . ."

We both hushed as the waitress brought our meal. Neither of us had much appetite. I picked for a while, then finally ordered another draft and lit a cigarette. I held the pack across the table to Sally. She took one, her hand shaking slightly as I lit it for her.

"Want a beer?"

She shook her head no, and looked down at the table.

Something was bothering her, something besides all this other craziness.

"What's the matter?" I asked.

"What do you mean?" she asked.

"C'mon, what's bothering you?"

"Does something have to be bothering me?" she said, irritated.

"Sally, what is it?" I asked gently. I leaned across the table and took her hands in mine once again. "Is it something I said, something I did?"

There was a long pause as she silently looked down at our hands. "I'm scared and confused and angry at myself," she whispered.

"Why angry at yourself?"

She stared at me hard, as if suddenly that anger had taken over and was not directed inwardly any longer.

"I've been thinking about us."

"What about us?"

"Jack, I love you. I'm *in* love with you. But I don't know how much of you I can take."

"I'm sorry for getting you in this mess," I said, suddenly feeling like she was about to tell me something I didn't want to hear. "But we'll be okay. We're getting out of town tonight. Just the two of us, together."

"Are we really going to be together?" she asked, an edge of tension in her voice. "Jack, I don't know you. You're affectionate, but it's mechanical. You're a wonderful lover, but you hold back. I can't go through life wondering what you're really feeling, what's really going on behind the wall. We're disconnected on some level and I don't know what to do about it. And if we can't fix it, I can't go on. I'm already too tied up in this. I feel too invested already. I can't risk being torn apart again. I think we ought to think about quitting this before we get in too deep."

Time stopped; flat, cold, dead in its freaking tracks, locked up with the brakes smoking. There was the longest moment of silence I'd endured in a long time. I had this surge of my own anger; like, goddammit, here the world is falling apart and she's doing that *communication* stuff again!

I thought she was different from the others.

Then the anger went away like the tide washing garbage out to sea and I was left drained, exhausted. My eyes swelled and hurt, like pressure behind them, like somebody inside trying to break out. I stared through a film of tears that made everything dance before my eyes.

Everything she said was right. And I was losing her.

"Don't just sit there," she said, exasperated. "Tell me what's going on inside!"

"I just don't know how much more I can take," I whispered.

"God forbid I should be another thing you have to get through. Let's go." She stood up, throwing her wadded-up paper napkin on the table.

She took a step. My arm shot out like a snake and grabbed her wrist. "Sit down."

Sally looked down at me. "Don't pull that macho shit on me, Jack."

I looked up at her, pleading. "Please."

She sat back down slowly, cautiously. "What do I have to do?" I asked, my voice still a whisper.

"This isn't another hoop you have to jump through." She reached across the table and took my hand. "I'm giving you parts of me nobody else has. I only want the same from you."

I pulled my hand up to wipe some of the wet off my face.

"I've never seen you cry before," she said. "We're lovers, friends, work around each other eight hours a day. And I've never seen you cry before."

"It's been a decade or two." After a moment, I added, "Let me try to explain this to you. This stuff has never been very easy for me."

"I know, but—"

"Let me finish," I said, cutting her off. "Over the past few weeks, I've found myself feeling things for you that I haven't felt for anyone in years. Maybe never. We've known each other all this time, and it's just now come to me how much I love you."

She smiled and nodded her head almost imperceptibly. "Me, too."

"I've just always been alone," I said. "When I was growing up. My father dead, my mother looney tunes. No brothers, no sisters. All the schools, the time away from what little family I had left. Even when I was married. Hell, Katherine and I were divorced from each other emotionally a long time before we actually went to court. Afterwards, I just went through the motions."

"Yeah," she said. "You did."

I looked down at the table, at the pack of cigarettes, the ashtray full of butts, the sweaty mug of beer, the empty paper plates.

"This was it, is what I thought. This is life. Do your do, go home, have a few drinks, watch some old movies, listen to some music, go to bed. Get up the next day, do the same shit all over again. It's safe, you see. And comfortable, when you get into the right mode."

"But it's not life. There's got to be more."

"I know that. But it's all come crashing down on me at once. First I found out the guy who was as close to being a real father as I'll ever get is a scumbag. And then that safe little insulated world I've created is blown all to hell by you."

"So what do you want, Jack? What do you want from me?"

"I want you," I said. "I want to have a life with you and I want to get out of this lousy business. I want to get married, and I want a family."

Her head jerked up like I'd slapped her or something. She looked away, dazed. "You surprise me."

"Yeah, well, you're full of surprises yourself."

"I don't know what to think of this."

"It scares the hell out of me, too."

"I don't know," she said, shaking her head. "I just don't know."

"So, you want to get married or what?"

"Married?" she asked, stunned. "Wow . . . This is going to have to soak in."

"Take all the time you need," I said. "I love you. Let's go somewhere and make babies. What the hell, consider it fate. I just don't want to lose you."

My eyes clouded over again, and I felt the wet on my cheeks, and the voice inside said, Don't do this. You're a tough guy, don't do this. And I did it anyway. I reached across the table and took her hands in mine and squeezed hard, and the tears kept coming, silently, painfully, but good, like lancing a boil.

Sally smiled at me, a faint glimmer of a smile that made me think at least she hadn't said no yet. Who knows, maybe she wouldn't even want to be married to me. She wouldn't be the first.

"C'mon," I said, scooting my chair back. "Let's get out of here."

"What are we going to do?"

"Escape, my dear. We're going back to the office, get that package, pack some bags, and hit the road. I'll call my friend in the D.A.'s office tomorrow, tell him everything we know. Then it's their sandbox. We'll phone our resignations in to the Old Man after that."

"Are you sure?" she asked.

"Yes," I said, taking her hand as we walked to the cashier. "I didn't bargain on being in the middle of people getting killed. That kind of shit's not in my contract. You and I are going away somewhere. We can practice making babies."

She yanked my hand and jerked us both to a stop. "Are you sure about that, too?"

I looked into her face and realized that this was the face I was going to wake up to every morning for the rest of my life. And that was just fine.

"Especially about that."

"Okay, then." She smiled. "Let's go."

It was September now, and almost as if someone had flicked a switch at midnight, August 31, it had become cooler. There was a slight wind blowing, a wind that was cool and damp and smelled of autumn. It was coming up on my favorite part of the year, when the heat breaks and before the cold dampness of winter sets in. It's time to start over again, to do something new, to take life off in a different direction.

A certain restlessness sets in after the heat-dulled senses of the summer come back to life; this year would be the one for me, for us.

We drove in on the busy Airline Highway, with the traffic and the lights and the craziness.

"So it's true?"

"So what's true?" I asked.

"About Herbert?"

Oh, yeah, I thought. Herbert.

"Yeah, it's all true."

"How much?"

"Couple a' hundred thou," I said.

She took a deep breath, almost a gasp, and I could feel her tighten next to me.

"Jeez." She sighed. "That's a lot of money even now. It was a fortune back then."

She reached across the seat and took my hand.

"God, Jack," she said. "I'm sorry."

"It's okay. Everything's going to be all right. I hate that it turned out this way"—my voice sounded detached again, far away even to me—"but it's going to be over soon."

"Murphy's beaten, isn't he?"

"If it turns out he had anything to do with Bob Sparks getting killed, he's going to lose a lot more than a lousy lawsuit. I wouldn't want to be in his shoes."

"And the Iris Project will go through?"

"Yeah, Iris," I said. "I'd almost forgotten what this was really about."

"Mr. Jennings will get a lot richer."

"Like he freaking needs it."

"And we can go away," she said, looking at me closely across the glow of the dashboard lights.

"I'd like that. I'd like that a lot."

"You really look tired, Jack," she said.

"I did a lot of thinking while I was down there."

"Yeah?"

"Yeah. A long time ago, I thought I knew the guy. I thought I knew Jimmy Herbert. I married his daughter and I thought I knew her. I admired him, respected him. Hell, I guess I even loved him. I felt like I was part of a family. Things just don't always work out."

"I know," she said. "But you have to have faith that they can."

"I don't exactly know what I'm trying to say here. It's just that finding out that Herbert's been lying all these years made me realize that I've been living a few lies myself. I actually thought about not saying anything to anyone. Just let it go and not tell anyone what I'd found out. Even you. But that would have been just one more lie . . ."

"It would have," she said gently, reaching across the seat to touch my arm.

"I'm babbling like a crazy man."

"You're not babbling," she said, "and you're not crazy."

She scooted over on the seat and put her hand on my leg.

"I want to stop by the office and get that package out of the filing cabinet and take it with us," I said.

"Are you sure that's safe?"

"I think it'll be a helluva lot safer late at night than it will be walking out of the building with it in broad daylight. Besides, I don't ever intend on going back after tonight."

"Yeah," she said. "Let's clean out our desks and get out."

We pulled off the highway and started driving through the almost deserted downtown streets. It was after ten now, and the offices were all quiet and the traffic was gone, and the concrete canyons of the Central Business District had an eerie, cold, empty feeling.

I drove up St. Charles Avenue, over the streetcar tracks, over to Carondelet, then down half a block and into the bank's parking lot. I pulled Sally's car into my own space and stopped the engine. The lot was empty except for a couple of parked cars. No security guard, no pedestrians. This part of the city closed down after dark.

"I'm going to run up real quick," I said. "You just want to sit here?"

"I don't know," she said, looking around. "It's kind of late."

"C'mon in with me, then," I said, reaching for the door handle.

Somewhere in back of me, I heard a car door slam.

I glanced up in the rear view mirror. Everything was dark. But I was tired, dammit, and off my guard, and wasn't thinking of anything except getting that package out of my office.

As I cracked the door to get out, I suddenly became aware of black forms coming at me in the night. No faces, no outlines. Just huge forms, yanking the car door open with my hand still on the inside latch.

Then hands were all over me, jerking me out of the car as if I were a throw pillow.

There were hands on the lapels of my jacket, pulling me up, slamming the car door behind me, then throwing me against the side of the car.

A fist came at me and caught me in the gut, full and

hard and with the impact of a cannonball. I doubled over in agony, every semblance of breath punched out of me. It was as if everything went into a bizarre kind of slow motion, as if time was suddenly broken down into components smaller than imaginable.

I heard Sally scream and tried to turn to her, when a knee came up off the pavement and caught me under the chin. My head snapped back; something, somebody, caught me in the ribs, and then there were hands all over me, pulling me five or six feet away and then slamming me into the side of the car head first.

Stars exploded in my head as Sally's disembodied, detached voice screamed my name.

And then there were hands under me again, lifting me to my feet. Something warm and liquid ran down the back of my head, under my shirt collar, down my back.

I looked up, and in the dim splatter of a streetlight, I saw that one of them had Sally off to my left, holding her from behind, with what looked like a massive arm around her neck in a choke hold. She was kicking at him, trying to scream.

"Let her alone," I said as loud as I could, then a fist came at me and the stars were back again, twinkling and sparkling behind my eyelids and everything was numb, tingling.

My mouth filled with blood and broken bits of my own teeth.

A huge head came down, two hands caught me under the armpits and lifted me up. Then the formless face was down in mine.

"Listen, asshole," this voice hissed. "Listen good." It was the same voice over the phone; I'd know that "Listen, asshole" anywhere.

Sally bit the guy holding her and he squalled, dropping his arm from in front of her mouth. She screamed like hell as I tried to raise my head to tell her to stop.

Stop screaming, dammit. If they were going to kill us, we'd already be dead.

"Shut that bitch up," the guy who had me growled. Somebody off to my right stepped over and blocked her from my sight. I heard the breathy grunts of her screams being muffled.

"Your little investigation is going to stop, right?" the guy who had me said, real low and real mean and right in my face.

"We don't want any more of this shit. You understand? Otherwise we might have to have another little talk. Like we had with that smart-assed punk. Understand?"

I shook my head yes and tried to stay standing up.

"Yeah," I said weakly, hoping not to pass out. "No problem. It's over."

"Good," the guy said, when the third one behind him yelped like a dog. I looked over just as Sally's foot came back down on the ground and he doubled over with his hands in his crotch. Dammit, Sally, I tried to yell, quit!

The guy behind her, the one she'd bitten, whipped her around to face him; my head dropped just as I saw him hit her. She made an awful noise and dropped, and then the one who had me let go with another right that caught me on the left side of my head and sent me to the pavement.

I could feel it slipping away from me and suddenly I realized there was no pain; I could feel no pain. Only a sense of being free from it all. A foot came down in my ribs, hard, like kicking a football, and there was only this pressure, only the feeling of not being able to breathe anymore.

I rolled over on the pavement, rocks and gravel digging into the side of my face like acid burns, and watched as the two hulking forms picked the third one up from where Sally'd kicked him in the balls. He dusted himself off, groaned, and then the three of them turned to look at us. Surveying the damage, I guess.

Then they walked over to their car, got calmly in, and drove off, leaving us there on the ground, in the terrible darkness and silence.

My brain was relaying signals like a bat out of hell, but my body was ignoring most of them. I came up on one elbow and started dragging myself over to where Sally lay on the hard pavement. Her dress was rumpled and bloody; she was very still. I pulled myself up to her and turned her head to me. Her eyes were closed; blood was streaming out of her nose, her breath coming in short gasps.

I tried to pull myself up, to get to my feet, but my legs were like useless slabs of dead weight hooked to the rest of me. I struggled like hell until it all gave way, and I settled back down on the parking lot pavement next to her. I pulled my hand up from under me, brought it over, and gently laid it across her.

Then something shifted, and the now sweet darkness slipped over me and took me away.

Eleven

If not for the pain, I would've bet anything I was dead. But nothing could be hurting this bad and not be alive.

I tried to put a coherent sentence or two together inside my brain; forget getting it out through my mouth. Just string a few words together that made sense, light up those synapses, send a flicker across those neurons. Just a tiny one. Anything.

I remember at one point trying to open my eyes. God, what a mistake. White flashing lights came at me everywhere, blinding white light, like peaking on acid, having an orgasm, and staring at the sun all rolled into one. Everything about me hurt. I breathed in through my nose; my chest ached and there was a sickening, awful smell that made me sick down to my bones. I shut my eyes and let the dark take me back over.

My arms wouldn't move. Neither would my legs or mouth. Was this it? Was I paralyzed?

And time drifted lazily by, the pain coming in whooshes;

with each contraction of my heart, torment. But between times, the pain would go away briefly, for a second or so, and I would breathe easier and find a moment's rest.

I was vaguely aware of voices around me constantly, and lots of activity, and the rustling of starched sheets.

A time later—how much time?—I opened my eyes and was able to keep them open. There was white above me, but not blazing white like the Great White Blinding Light. No, this was crisscrossed with lines and streaked with brown smudge.

Ceiling tiles.

I moved a bit and became aware of something holding me down. I moved my head, the bones in the back of my neck grating like broken glass being reduced to powder in a mortar. A long shiny pole was to my right, with tubes leading down to my arm. Suddenly, there was a face above mine, a pretty, young face and body, wearing white, smiling.

"Well," she said softly, the sweetness of her voice like waves over me at the beach, "welcome back to reality."

Reality? Oh, God, lady.

I felt my face tighten up in agony when I tried to talk.

"Don't talk," she said. "The doctor will be right here."

She walked off, leaving me there with only the awareness of my own body, and no memory of what happened to it. Not yet, anyway. But gradually, bits and pieces were beginning to come back together.

"Hello there, Mr. Lynch," a voice said. The doctor stood above me, balding, glasses, thin, with a silver metal clipboard in one arm and a pen in the other. "How are you feeling?"

I groaned.

"Yeah, that's to be expected. You're going to be kind of sore for a while. But I'm pleased to say that at least you'll be with us to be sore."

"What happened?" I croaked, my mouth dry, lips cracking as I moved them.

"Mmmm," the doctor hummed, "that looked like it hurt. Want a little water?"

I moved my head yes. He reached over and picked up a glass with a straw in it and held it down for me. The water was stale and tepid and the best thing I ever put in my mouth.

"We were kind of hoping *you* could tell *us* what happened," the doctor said as I sipped. My mouth relaxed and a dribble of water went down my chin. He put the glass down.

"How bad?" I whispered.

"Well, I think you're strong enough to hear the whole list," he said, opening the clipboard. "Let's see here . . . Four cracked ribs, a sprained arm, two badly swollen testicles, numerous abrasions, contusions, bruises, cuts. You're going to need a little dental work as well. In case you haven't noticed, you've got a few chipped and broken teeth. And then, of course, there was the concussion."

"Concussion?"

He closed the clipboard, studying me. "I'm going to be honest with you, Mr. Lynch. You've had about the worst bang on the head I've ever seen anyone survive. You've been asleep for almost four days."

"Headache," I said weakly.

"Yes," he answered, smiling, "headache. Bad headache. You'll have it another week or ten days anyway. Then intermittently for quite some time. Months, maybe longer."

Then he got down closer to my face. "And I want you to treasure that pain, Mr. Lynch. It means you're alive, and that you've survived something that probably would have killed anyone a bit less hardheaded."

"Give me something for it," I asked, my head pounding with each syllable.

"We can't give you much," he said. "Not until we're sure you're completely out of the woods. The swelling in your brain is going to be around a few more days. But you'll be all right. Each day will get a little easier."

I turned from him and stared off.

"Do you feel up to talking to anyone?" he asked. "Just briefly, mind you. But the police would like to speak to you."

"Police?"

"Yes, they'd like to hear what you can tell them about the assault. All I could tell them was that whoever did this to you was a consummate professional."

"Okay."

"Good, I'll phone them. They won't stay long." He turned to walk off.

"Doctor?" I asked, as loudly as I could.

"Yes," he said, turning back.

"Sally . . ."

"Sally?"

"Yeah, Sally. Where's Sally?"

The doctor opened the clipboard and looked into it.

"Oh, yes," he said, "Miss Bateman, your secretary. The woman that was with you."

"Yeah."

"I'm sorry, Mr. Lynch," he said, altogether too matter-of-factly, "she didn't make it. Cerebral hemorrhage. Whoever pushed you to the edge pushed her over it. She was brain dead by the time we got her in here. We unplugged her respirator two days ago, at the family's request and with their authorization."

Everything went red and I swung at the lying bastard.

Pieces of me exploded everywhere in pain; I saw the clear plastic tube of the I.V. go flying by and the smash of metal as the pole came across the bed.

I heard myself screaming.

His hands were on me everywhere, pushing me back down on the bed. I brought my leg up and planted it in his stomach and kicked as hard as I could. He went backwards, but so did I.

Ceiling tiles again. White everywhere, then red, then pain blasting through my chest.

I heard him yell something. The nurse, the pretty one, ran back in. I swung at her, hard.

He was up again, on me. I screamed again, and again, and then suddenly I couldn't stop howling. Something snapped in the back of my head and I heard a loud boom, a crash, and then they were all holding me down. I was yelling obscenities, things I'd never imagined could come out of a human mouth.

Sally . . .

A hand was above me, a pretty delicate hand, holding a syringe. It came down at me. I screamed for Jesus, for Sally, for my dead father, and then at the sharp fire in my thigh that faded to a glow and began diffusing through my body, toward my heart, my head.

They spread my arms on the bed; I fought them, but the glow was coming into my clenched fists now; my arms relaxed and this buzz came to my ears, and I let them crucify me on the bed. The strength was gone from every part of my body but my eyes, which were still trying to force themselves out of their sockets.

The two faces in white were above me again, with more behind them.

"What got into him?" the nurse yelled.

"I don't know," the man answered.

"I wish he'd quit that dreadful screaming!" she yelled.

What screaming? My mouth was open, but no sound would come out. What screaming?

"He'll stop in a second," the doctor-man said again. His face was the Old Man's now. "When the sedative hits."

The young woman above me was Sally. My mouth tried to—

"Who's Sally?" I heard the voice say.

"His secretary, the woman that was killed," the Old Man said.

"My God," Sally said.

And the choruses of voices coming at me began, lightly, sweetly: Sally's dead, Sally's dead, all is red, and Sally's dead. Only it was Sally singing, and then the buzzing in my ears drowned them all out and the lights started to dim.

The doctor was above me, staring through a wide-angle lens. "He'll be all right now. You're going to sleep a while, Mr. Lynch."

It was dark and they were coming at me again.

"Keep him sedated for the time being. Twenty every four hours until I make rounds tonight. Get that bloody I.V. started again."

God—

"Yes, doctor," the pretty girl said. He turned and faded away through the mist.

As the doctor walked off, one part of me got out of bed and stood there unseen, watching the other part of me twisting, pulling at the straps. Then I got still; tears formed in my eyes and rolled down onto the pillow.

An iciness came into my heart that had never been there before.

I don't remember much for days. Finally, they untied me and stopped giving me the shots.

I refused to see anyone, police included. Gradually, a more continuous state of consciousness forced itself on me. They started giving me a little something for the pain now, but none of it helped.

As the memory of the evening returned, all I could see was Sally laying there in that parking lot, so still and breathing so heavily, as if asleep. And each time I thought of her like that, I started to sob again, only the jolts from my broken ribs and smashed head made it look more like a convulsion than some grown man crying.

The police finally insisted on talking to me and I couldn't

put them off any longer. I'd turned it in my mind over and over; the three guys who did this to me and murdered Sally were pros, all right. No getting around that. They'd just slipped up with Sally, that's all. If they'd wanted us dead, we'd be long gone, maybe washing up on the opposite shore of Lake Pontchartrain by now, unrecognizable. Sally made the mistake of fighting them, that much I can remember, and when they finally had to hit her to shut her up, she fell and hit her head on the pavement.

Maybe Bob Sparks made the same mistake.

This was all my fault, dammit. I should have known that when I started digging up the real manure that sooner or later, somebody was going to take a notion to stop me. But I'd approached this all as a mental exercise, a freaking party game. Somebody decided I was getting a little too close to winning the big prize.

There was no way this was over. They might think it was over, but I had some news for them. I was behaving myself in the hospital now. It was important to me to get out. As quickly as possible.

I didn't tell any of this to the police. To begin with, I didn't think it would do any good. These guys were smart enough to cover up their tracks. Besides that, I wanted time to mend and get well before deciding what to do next. I could always go back to the police later, tell them I was too scared to talk, or couldn't remember, whatever.

I had options here. Not many, but a few.

The homicide detective who interviewed me was young, lean, hungry, with a thick New Orleans accent. He looked frustrated as I continued to stick to my story that I had no idea what had happened. Must have been a mugging gone sour.

"Yeah, sure, right," he said, exasperated. "There's something you holding out on me and I'm gonna find what it is."

"No," I said, not having to pretend too hard that it was causing me great pain to talk. "I don't know what you're talking about."

"Yeah, it just seems strange to me that suddenly I got two homicides and an attempted murder on employees of the same bank."

"Two?" I asked, not wanting him to know what I knew.

"Yeah," he said, getting down close in my face. "Two. Kid down in your computer department was found beaten to death in his apartment the night before. Guy named Sparks. He was raped, mutilated. Made it look like a kinky homosexual killing. They did some real nice stuff to him."

"My God," I muttered. My head sank down in the pillow and my vision blurred.

"You know him?"

I shook my head no. "Only who he was," I whispered. "Saw him at work a couple times."

"I want you to call me, Mr. Lynch," he said, standing back up, "if your memory gets any better. I don't need to tell you that you could get visited by these guys again any time."

I rang for a pain shot, and in a few minutes, I drifted back out again, glad to be away from it all for a while, somewhere deep down inside myself, where all these goddamn people couldn't get to me anymore.

I woke up to find the Old Man and Carlton standing above me. It was one of the few times I'd ever seen the Old Man with a gentle look on his face.

"How are you, boy?" he asked when he saw my eyes open.

"Sore as hell," I said quietly. "Other than that, couldn't be better."

"We're glad to see you, Jack," Carlton said kindly. "We hope you'll be back on your feet again soon."

The Old Man reached out and placed his hand on my

shoulder. "The police said you couldn't tell them anything about the guys that did this to you."

"Wasn't much to tell," I said. "It was too dark. Never got a look at them."

"We're going to find out who did this to you, son," he said, squeezing my shoulder just a bit, "and when we do, they're going to wish they'd never seen the light of day."

I already wished that for myself.

"Mr. Jennings and I are going up to Miss Bateman's funeral tomorrow," Carlton said.

My eyes started burning; I closed them quickly, before Carlton or the Old Man had a chance to read anything in them.

"Did she have any children, boy?" the Old Man asked.

Not yet, I thought, shaking my head no.

"The doctor says you'll be in here a week or so," Carlton said. "We'll be back to see you before you get out."

"And I want you to take a few days off," Mr. Jennings offered. "Then when you feel up to it, we'll get back into the fight and whip hell out of these bastards."

"We've gotten a continuance on Murphy's suit," Carlton said. "There's a little time, now. Not much, but a little."

"Yeah," the Old Man said, giving me a gentle shake, "but the important thing is for you not to worry. Get some rest and mend."

I nodded my head to him. He said something else, but by then I was beginning to drift in and out.

The Old Man and Carlton left me lying there with a tube in my arm and Demerol every three hours. But the Demerol couldn't dull the pain in my head and in my heart.

I wish the bastards had killed me as well.

Goddammit, I still couldn't figure it out. I lay there hour after hour, running around in circles mentally, trying to figure out what was so damned important about Iris that it was worth killing for.

About two in the morning, as I was still unable to sleep even after the sleeping pill and another hit of the Demerol, it suddenly came to me. The confusion, the grief, the thousand conflicting, fleeting, flashing thoughts had somehow convoluted the thought processes. And in one of those random flashes of insight that occur in the middle of the night, when it will slip away unnoticed if you're not real careful, I understood. It was enlightenment, satori, a moment of zen inspiration.

Greed. Greed on their part; wrong thinking on mine.

It was wrong thinking, that's what it was. All this time I'd been looking at Iris the wrong way. That night I drove through Iris, I'd been repulsed and frightened by the sleaze, the danger, the vice, the corruption, the inevitable decay and deterioration of an urban hellhole. I saw Iris as a chancre, an infected boil full of pus just waiting to be lanced and cleansed. Why would anyone want to stop its destruction, most of all Murphy, who stood to make a fortune off her demise?

There was only one answer, and I could've kicked myself for not seeing it sooner. But here it was now, the realization that Iris was not a diseased hellhole waiting to be wiped off the face of the earth.

Iris was a fucking cash machine.

Murphy didn't want the fortune he could make off the razing of Iris because there was bigger money to be made off of letting her sit there just as she was, had been for years, and could be for generations more. There's money to be made capitalizing off the poverty of countless thousands, just as the preacher makes a fortune off their desperate hope in Jesus and his promises for everlasting life, because there sure as hell ain't any hope for everlasting anything in Iris.

They're sheep to be sheared, and the only sin that counts is driving away the flock.

By God, I wanted those printouts. Whatever Bob Sparks had sent me would be the key that opened the door.

Ten days later, they let me go. I got a cab back to my apartment and paid the cabbie an extra ten to walk in with me. He thought I was still unsteady from the hospital; actually, there was no way I was going into the place alone.

The house was badly in need of a good cleaning, but I was too tired to attempt it. All I could think of was that package in the fireproof filing cabinet back at my office.

I lay down for a while, listened to some music, tried to get back into reality, which wasn't easy given my circumstances. Everything had changed for me; a few brief weeks of feeling alive had ended. The future was still in front of me, but it looked unendingly dreary.

The only spark now came from the prospect of nailing whoever the hell was responsible for all this.

There was no way I was going back down to the bank at night to get that package. It was just going to have to wait. If it was still in the cabinet, it would be okay there another night. If someone had gotten it, then it was too late anyway.

Moving stiffly the next morning, I struggled into my clothes and drove downtown. Maybe, I thought, I should've told the Old Man or Carlton about the package. But I wasn't sure what was in it, and I wasn't sure who to trust anymore, so I had simply decided to keep my own counsel.

My one concession to the new circumstances of my life was to dig through my closet until I found the .38 again. It hadn't been fired in years. But just having it with me meant something. I laid the pistol in my briefcase and closed the lid carefully, aware that this time I really might have to use it.

On the way to work, I stopped off at a gun shop in the 12th Ward. The place was a freaking arsenal; it's amazing what you can buy off the shelf. I could equip a small army for the credit balance on my MasterCard. The only small army I was interested in, though, was me.

I bought a box of .38 caliber Plus-P's, a light, high-velocity round. They wouldn't stop a tank, but they'd damn sure get somebody's attention. The nice man in the gun shop also sold me a leather holster that clipped on my belt and allowed me to wear the S&W on my hip. If I scooted it over my back pocket and kept my jacket buttoned, you couldn't tell it was there.

There was a secretary from upstairs installed in Sally's office to answer the phones and do the mail.

And maybe keep an eye on me.

"I'm Karen Dunne," she said. "I'm from the pool upstairs. I've been assigned to help you for the next few weeks, until you can decide who you want to get in permanently."

She was young, thin, rather pale and very blond.

"Okay, fine," I said. "Glad to meet you."

"Good," she answered. "I wanted to tell you, Mr. Lynch, how sorry I am about Miss Bateman and the accident you had."

"To begin with, Karen, call me Jack. And what happened to me and Miss Bateman was no accident."

I walked past her into my office, the first time I'd been there in two weeks. Neat stacks of opened mail were lined up in order of importance, with a stack of pink telephone messages off to the side.

"Is there anything I can do for you?" she asked, following me into my office.

"Yes," I said, reaching into my pocket for my wallet. "I promise you I won't make a habit out of this. I only ask because I'm still stiff and sore as hell. But would you run down to the newsstand and get me a pack of Marlboros, please."

"Sure." She smiled. "Glad to. Need anything else?"

"No, thanks, Karen. I appreciate it."

She turned and walked out. I came up out of the chair as fast as I could and walked into the outer office. To the left of Sally's desk, or what used to be Sally's desk, was the door into the supply room, where office supplies, some boxes, and the filing cabinets were kept.

I fumbled with the combination lock on the fireproof cabinet. It took three tries to get it open. I was nervous, agitated, plain damn frightened. Finally, I got the door open and pulled the drawers out.

There it was, tied up in a large, unwieldy bundle in brown shipping paper. It looked to be about three reams of computer printout; hundreds of pages, all holding a bit of the truth, the pot of gold at the end of the rainbow.

I pulled the package out, groaning as my ribs strained, and carried it into my office. I threw it under my desk and sat down just as Karen came back in with my smokes. She handed them across the desk to me and stood there for a moment.

"Thanks," I said, meaning it. "I appreciate it."

"Is there anything else?"

"No, not right now. I think I want to take some time and go through all this mail. Why don't you just cover the phones for the time being. Shut the door behind you, if you don't mind."

"I'll be out here if you need anything," she said.

The door closed and I carefully, so as not to make any noise, pulled the package out from under my desk. Then I opened my top drawer and laid the pistol just where I could get to it in a heartbeat if anyone came in on me.

I cut the strings and peeled the wrapping paper back. There they were, stacks of computer printout recording transaction after transaction, too many to count, too many to understand. This was going to take some time, but here it was. This was what Bob Sparks died for. I wondered, as I stared off for a second, if he was someplace where he could see and understand this, and if so, if it brought him any satisfaction to know he'd given me the guns on this one.

Probably not. This was damn small comfort to me; it would be even less for him.

The phone brought me out of my reverie like a horn going off next to my ear.

"Jack, there's a Mr. Fred Williams to see you."

"Just a second." I shoved the package back under the desk and closed the drawer that held the pistol. "Send him in."

Fred Williams opened the door and walked in. He looked fit, trim, as usual, and neatly dressed in his three-piece lawyer's costume.

"Hey, guy," he said, smiling. "Don't get up."

"Thanks," I answered, extending my hand. "I won't."

"Karen," I said, pushing the intercom button, "would you mind bringing Mr. Williams some coffee? How do you take it, Fred?"

"Black."

"Black," I said, leaning back. "Have a seat, fella."

Fred settled down in the chair across from my desk and relaxed.

"This business or pleasure?" I asked.

"What makes you think the D.A.'s office would take any interest?" he kidded. "Two murders and an attempted barely make a ripple in this town . . ."

I tried very hard to sit quietly and not let my face betray any of what I was feeling. I think it worked, but God it was hard.

"Doesn't matter, anyway," I said. "You probably ain't going to catch them."

"I know," he said, as Karen walked in with his coffee. She smiled at him, handed him the cup, and sauntered back out.

"Cute girl," Fred said. "Possibilities?"

"Not until my ribs mend. Right now, I couldn't stand the strain."

"Does this mean I'm not going to get that racquetball game?"

I laughed quietly. "Not for a while."

"Listen, Jack," he said, scooting forward and putting the coffee cup on the edge of my desk, "we're buddies, right? I'm here as much as your friend as anything else. You've gotten yourself in some deep fecal matter here."

"Fred—"

"No, wait, just listen. What happened to you and the girl out there in that parking lot was no damn mugging. You're out of your league here, boy. And I think the murder of that programmer is tied in with this, too. You think you're scared now, let me send you a copy of the coroner's report on him. It'll put you off your Wheaties for a few days."

"What do you want from me, Fred?" I asked, suddenly exhausted.

"I want you to tell me what the fuck is going on here."

"Is that official or personal?" I asked. "Just friends or what?"

"Let's say it's personal for now," he said.

"For now . . ."

"I could make it business. Haul your ass before the grand jury."

"I told the police everything I know," I said. "It's in their report."

He paused for a moment and stared right through me.

"I'm going to find out what's going on," he said. "One way or another. And if you're on the wrong side on this one, our friendship won't mean much. I'll nail your ass."

"Thanks for coming by, Fred," I said coldly. "But I've got an awful lot to catch up on."

He took a long swallow of coffee and put the cup down.

"Coffee's no better over here than the courthouse." He

stood up. "Watch yourself, Jack. I like you too much to see you wind up center stage at the coroner's office."

He walked over to the door and opened it, his back to me.

"Fred?"

He turned around. "Yeah?"

"Thanks, buddy. I appreciate your concern."

"Keep in touch, guy," he said, smiling.

Twelve

I left the office a few minutes later, walked painfully down to the mailroom on the third floor, and grabbed a shipping box and some strapping tape.

Back in my office, I tied the stacks of computer printout in a neat bundle. While Karen was out to lunch, I slipped out and returned to the mailroom by the backstairs. The two people who hadn't gone to lunch yet paid no attention to me as I hefted the box onto a table with a dozen others to be weighed, stamped, and placed into one of those huge canvas baskets that would be taken for mailing that afternoon.

Back out in the hall, I lit a cigarette and breathed a sigh of relief that soon the package would be entrusted to the care and safety of the U.S. Postal Service. Which gives you an idea of just how desperate I really felt at that point.

I went upstairs and locked myself in my office. Rolling a sheet of paper into my typewriter, I began typing my notes in an attempt to get all this under control. The pieces were falling together, painful bit by bit. The challenge now was to have them fall together before I fell apart.

The report was pretty easy to compile, considering how hard it had been to get together in the first place. The summary on Jimmy ran only a couple of pages. I included a copy of the bankruptcy notices out of the paper, plus summaries of my conversations with Lubbock Powell and Big Al down in the Bahamas.

Eight typed pages later, I had everything I knew up to that point summarized. I made two copies of the document, locked one in my filing cabinet, addressed the other to the same place Bob Sparks's printouts were going, and folded the other into an envelope and put it in my inside jacket pocket.

There was still a lot to figure out, but there would be no lawsuit. Whatever the hell that was worth. And by not killing me, whoever was really behind all this had unknowingly given me the advantage of time. Time was on my side now; I had the rest of my life. If that's how long it took, then fine. I had nothing to lose.

I decided to check in with the Old Man. As I entered the suite of offices on the twentieth floor, Madge looked up at me and rolled her eyes back. "Well," she kidded, "you don't look as bad as I thought you would."

"Good to see you, Madge."

"We're all going to miss Sally," she said, shaking her head. "God, this whole business is awful."

I tried once again not to let my face show anything.

The Old Man's door was open. He sat behind his desk, huddled over some blueprints with a middle-aged man in a blue suit. I tapped on the doorjamb; they both looked up.

The Old Man stood up slowly. Without saying a word, he pointed his left index finger at me, then jerked it toward a chair. I walked in and sat down.

"Get out," he ordered the architect. "And close the door behind you."

"Yessir, yessir," the man said nervously, grabbing a briefcase off the chair in front of him. He slammed the door as he stumbled over his own feet getting out.

"What are you doing in here?" he asked, angry. "I thought I told you to take some time off."

"I don't need any time off. All I'll do is sit at home and feel wretched. I'd just as soon feel wretched here where I can get paid for it."

He smiled. "What have you got for me?" he asked. "Something about the lawsuit?"

"There isn't going to be any lawsuit," I said, handing him the envelope. "Read this."

He ripped the flap loose. There was little change of expression until the end of the report. A wide grin came across his face and his eyes lit up like sparklers on the Fourth.

"By God!" he yelled. "We've got him! Jack, boy, this is great. Where did you get this?"

"It took some doing."

"How did you get Zimmerman to admit it?"

"It didn't matter to him anymore. He's out of the rackets altogether. He's also got one foot in the grave and the other on roller skates. Besides, why would he protect Herbert? He bribed Herbert; that don't mean he liked him."

"You did good, boy." He smiled. "But why didn't you let somebody else in on it sooner? Maybe we could have stopped those goons who worked you over in the parking lot."

"You said do whatever I had to do," I said. "This was the way I felt I had to do it. I knew once we had the stuff that's in the report, time didn't matter anymore. The truth removed the pressure of time. We could show that report to Herbert the morning before the lawsuit and that would be the end of it.

"I just never figured," I continued, "on anybody pushing it this far."

"That boy down in the computer room. What did he have to do with all this?"

"Nothing," I lied. "That apparently was just a coincidental thing."

"Yeah, mebbe," he said, rubbing the stubble on his jaw, "and mebbe not."

I sat silently for a moment as he tried to stare me down.

"I know when not to push you, though," he said. "You did good, boy. Real good."

"Thanks," I said. "My pleasure."

"We're going to pay Mr. Herbert a little visit after dinner tonight," the Old Man ordered. "You be here about nine. We'll take my car."

That ought to be interesting, I thought. Not much of a reaction, given the circumstances. But the truth was that Jimmy had become only a bit player in my life. He didn't matter anymore. I wanted the boys from the parking lot.

"Okay," I said, getting up to leave, "I'll see you later."

"You did good, boy!" he yelled again as I walked out the door. "I'm proud of you!"

I gritted my teeth and tried not to scream on the way back to my office.

I went to Ray's after leaving work. My usual waiter commented that he hadn't seen me in a while. In the dim light of the bar, the bruises on my face were hard to see. I explained that my work schedule had kept me away for a bit, and that I hoped my absence hadn't put too big a dent in their bottom line. I ordered a sandwich and a drink.

I felt that I'd be leaving this town soon.

I sensed this would be an ugly night, and while part of me wanted to miss it, to simply not show up, my curiosity wouldn't let me. I wondered what Jimmy would say, then realized that there was nothing he could say. What's done, as they say, is done, and the only thing left to do is end it by dropping the lawsuit. He had to do what the Old Man wanted. There was no other way.

As for Murphy; well, Murphy would be taken care of when the time was right.

The Old Man's chauffeur-driven Lincoln was sitting in the middle of the empty parking lot, motor running. I wheeled in and parked my car, then got out and walked over to the huge behemoth.

"I said nine o'clock, dammit," he growled as I eased into the backseat next to him. "Not five after."

"Sorry I'm late," I apologized in the most sincere voice I could muster. "Hi, Frank. Long time, no see."

"Hello, Mr. Lynch," he answered from the front seat. "Where to, Boss?"

"What's the address?" the Old Man demanded.

"5613 Commission Avenue."

Frank put the car in gear and the massive limousine silently jerked forward into the street. I settled back wordlessly in the padded leather seat and stretched out my legs as we began the long drive. No one spoke as we skirted in and out of traffic. I stared quietly at the passive, dark buildings, so empty and alone at night.

We left the business district and headed out toward the lake, to the exclusive part of town where Herbert sat safe and comfortable. When we came to the house, the Old Man had Frank park on the curb rather than the drive. We got out of the car and walked up the driveway. Lily's car wasn't in the driveway or the open garage.

Good, I thought. I don't want her here tonight.

"Mr. James Herbert lives pretty well," the Old Man commented as we approached the front porch. "For a man that was once a bankrupt."

I said nothing. He motioned for me to ring the doorbell as we stepped onto the porch. My stomach began to curdle; it was the same feeling I had when Katherine and I finally admitted a divorce was the only way, the same feeling I'd have when I told the Old Man I was quitting. It's that knot in the gut that comes from finally, inexorably cutting the ties to someone you love.

The door opened and Herbert stood there, wearing his smoking jacket, a pair of eyeglasses propped on his forehead. He smiled as he saw me.

"Hello, Jimmy," I said. "How are you?"

"Fine, Jack, fine," he said, opening the glass door and shaking my hand. The Old Man stepped out of the shadows behind me and Jimmy's smile disappeared.

"Hello, Mr. James Herbert," the boss said jovially, thrusting his hand forward. "I'm Bill Jennings."

I had never heard him call himself Bill before.

"I hope you don't mind this late-night unannounced visit," he continued. "But Jack and me were out for a late summer night's drive together. We do that occasionally, you see, and we got to thinking. I said to Jack, 'Jack,' I said, 'I've never had the pleasure of meeting this fellow James Herbert and since we're going to see each other in court, it might be nice to go by and meet this gentleman. Maybe get to know each other a little better. We might even see that we're not as far apart on things as we think we are.' Isn't that right, Jack, wasn't I saying just that?"

I looked from Herbert to the Old Man and back again.

"Yessir, Mr. Jennings. Just that."

"What other tricks do you do, Jack?" Herbert said, very softly, but with a knife's edge.

You bastard, I thought.

"Now, now," the Old Man said, "let's not argue on a beautiful night like tonight. You know, though, a late night's chill like this one'll give an old guy like me pneumonia. You wouldn't mind terribly if we came in and got out of the night air, would you? Just to sit and chew the fat for a while."

Herbert looked suspiciously at the both of us, thought for a second, then opened the door wider.

"I suppose not," he said, stepping back for us to enter.

"Where's Lily?" I asked, walking in.

"She and Katherine went to see a movie," he said coldly. "I expect her back around eleven-thirty."

"Boy, I tell you, this is something," the Old Man said, smiling broadly as he entered the house. "You really know how to live, Jim. This is real class. Jack, you should have told me about this place sooner. I feel like I've missed something not seeing it until now."

I didn't say anything.

"We can talk in the library," Jimmy said, leading the way back to the familiar old room. He walked in first and took the chair behind his desk, as if we were clients on a first consultation.

The Old Man walked in second and took a chair, with me behind him, taking the chair I'd sat in before.

"Would you like a drink?" Jimmy asked, more out of politeness, I guessed, than anything else.

"Aw, no," he answered, real homeylike. "I've found over the years that a man's better off to keep his wits about him. Alcohol dulls the senses, you know. Impairs the judgment."

The Old Man's East Texas accent had softened into a syrupy parody of itself. I'd heard him put on some acts before, but this one was driving me to the point of nausea. I wondered where he was headed with it.

"No, thanks," I said. Jimmy looked at me, then leaned back in his chair.

"I heard about the . . . incident, Jack," he said. "I'm terribly sorry."

"Accidents happen," I said, looking at him out of the corner of my eye.

"Well, gentlemen," Jimmy said formally, "if you've come

here to talk a deal, I can only say that Mr. Murphy has authorized me to tell you nothing short of full compensation and a cease and desist on the Iris Project as demanded under the terms of the suit will keep us out of court. Only then can we—"

"Naw," the Old Man interrupted in a forced drawl, "I never talk business after banking hours. It's one of the few advantages to being my age. A man don't have to work after the sun goes down anymore. No, like I said, I'm more interested in us getting to know each other a little better. After all, we're about to meet on the field of battle, what with your client and me having this unfortunate difference of opinion."

Jimmy looked as if he were about to say something and thought better of it.

"Yeah," Mr. Jennings continued, "I was even thinking that after all this is over you and me might get to be close friends. I've been thinking of redecorating my own little house and I sure could use your advice on it."

"Somehow, Mr. Jennings," Jimmy said sternly, "I don't think that's possible."

"Call me Bill," the Old Man said. "And I don't know, James, but that if you take a good look at me, you might find I'm not such a bad sort after all. Now, for instance, I'm not at all the uneducated goon people make me out to be. I'll bet you didn't know that I have almost a scholarly interest in history."

"History," Jimmy said.

"Yeah, history," the Old Man continued, his tone growing even friendlier. "Especially historical myths. Take the war, for instance. Several of my companies were big suppliers to the Allies during World War Two, and I had some friends in rather high places. You'd be amazed at what the difference between the truth and what the public believes can be sometimes."

"What's this all about?" Jimmy asked sharply.

"Calm down. This ain't really about anything. We's just jawing and swapping stories, like the two old plowhorses we are. Did you ever hear the story about the Battle of the Bulge?"

Jimmy rolled his eyes impatiently.

"During Christmas, 1944, the Nazis made their last big offensive of the war. Sort of one last shot at it. They surrounded this little town called Bastogne. The Allied commander was a guy named McAuliffe. On December 22, the German commander sent McAuliffe a note. 'The fortunes of war are changing,' he wrote. And he demanded surrender. The way the papers reported it, McAuliffe sent a one-word reply to the German commander."

"Nuts," Jimmy said, not to be outdone in the knowledge of history.

"That's what everybody *thinks* he said," the Old Man said. "In reality, McAuliffe, who was himself a student of history, stood on the historical precedent of a French commander under Napoleon at the Battle of Waterloo, who replied to a demand for surrender from the Prussian General Bulow with the one word reply 'Merde.' "

"I speak French," Jimmy said arrogantly. "Get to the point."

"The point is that the American press couldn't very well report to the American people that one of their commanders had replied to a formal demand for surrender by saying 'Shit.' Therein lies the myth. Appearance versus truth, nobility versus pragmatism. We have our eyes on heaven and our feet in the sewers, each and every one of us. Including you."

There was a long moment of the most awful, intense, deadly silence I had ever endured. The Old Man leaned back in his chair and put his hands behind his head. He'd gone for the jugular and gotten it, and was now sitting back to savor the kill.

Jimmy turned ashen gray, as pale as a heart attack. I shook as a trickle of sweat ran down my side from my armpit to my waist.

"On the long retreat from Waterloo, Napoleon was said to have dismounted and walked with his troops. He mourned the dead, and the fact that he had survived," the Old Man said.

"You're bluffing, Jennings," Jimmy finally said, in a strained voice that was barely a whisper.

"Oh, I never bluff, Jimmy," he said lightly. "If I ain't got the cards, I cut my losses and get out of the game."

The Old Man had all the cards this time.

"You can't prove anything," Jimmy said, staring ahead.

"Sure I can. You know I can. I wouldn't be here if I couldn't. You won't be prosecuted, of course, but think what this story will be like when it's splashed across the front page of Wednesday's newspaper."

"Under no circumstances," Jimmy said mechanically, "will I advise my client to drop his lawsuit."

"Yes, you will," the Old Man said, shooting forward in the chair like a leopard off a tree limb. "And you know why, Herbert? Because that worthless fat ass Murphy's not worth it to you. What's your wife going to think about when she opens up her morning paper over coffee and sees it on the front page? What's your daughter going to say? What will your law partners think? You won't go to jail, but how do you feel about being disbarred?"

He was pressing his advantage like a knife, up to the hilt and down deep in the marrow.

"You don't understand," Jimmy said, in a monotone that said shock more than anything else. "Murphy said the same thing to me when I refused to represent him."

"You leave Murphy to me," the Old Man said.

"The papers will never print it."

"Of course they will! You're not the D.A. anymore.

You're no sacred cow. This'll make good copy, damn good copy, and that's all the papers are after."

The Old Man was right and I could see Jimmy knew it.

"Under no circumstances will I advise my client to drop his lawsuit," Jimmy said again, one last salvo at his own personal Waterloo.

"Listen, Herbert. Everybody's got something they'd just as soon not have other people know about. It's a safe, common assumption about people and it makes a good basis for doing business. You cooperate with me; I'll cooperate with you. Murphy drops the lawsuit; we make a settlement. Quid pro quo. Everybody's happy. We forget everything. It's as simple as that."

The Old Man pulled a sealed envelope out of his jacket pocket and tossed it on the polished desktop. I assumed it was a copy of my report.

"Take a look at that," he said. "Everything in there we can back up. All of it."

Jimmy looked up and glared at both of us. There was pain and anger and betrayal in his face.

"You did good work, Jack."

"Why did you do it, Jimmy?" I asked. My voice was blank, hollow.

"Don't you dare condemn me, you self-righteous hypocritical—"

"Don't talk to me about self-righteous!" I snapped. "I've spent the better part of my adult life being compared to you, first by my wife, then by myself. Well, guess what, buddy? The comparison wasn't a good one and it wasn't me that came up short."

There was a short pause. It was a stalemate. "How did you think you could get away with it?" I asked.

Jimmy gazed back over the years, then spoke very quietly, very sadly: "I didn't have anything to lose. I was desperate. I told Zimmerman the charges against him could be reinstated at any time if he ever approached me about anything else. I never had contact with him again."

"And you don't ever have to have contact with us again," the Old Man spoke up.

"Just do what you ask," Jimmy said, still peering back over something I couldn't see.

"Simple enough."

"Again, Jack," Jimmy said. "I commend you on your work."

That's right, I thought, good work. I sat there silently, glaring at him. If he hadn't screwed up, there wouldn't have been any work for me to do. You can shoot the messenger, but it doesn't change the news.

"Get out of my house," he said, his voice the sound of grating metal.

"Yeah, I'll be glad to," the Old Man said, standing up. "It's getting late and the air's kind of stale in here. You call me at my office tomorrow, Herbert, after you talk to Murphy. Try to call early. Our court date's next Friday. I'll give you till five tomorrow afternoon."

"Get out of my house," he ordered again.

"C'mon, Jack, let's go."

We turned to walk out of the library, where Jimmy still sat staring at the floor.

"Jack," he said weakly. I turned to him. He looked as if I'd just shot his dog.

"You got nobody to blame but yourself," I said, ice in my veins and my voice.

"Good night, Mr. Herbert," the Old Man said, sounding a little tired himself. "I'll talk to you tomorrow."

We walked out the door and shut it behind us. My knees were shaking; I was sick at my stomach. My palms were sweaty and sticky. My shirt was plastered down my side. The Old Man had done himself a neat little piece of surgery.

We drove wordlessly back to the bank parking lot. As

Frank pulled up to my car, Mr. Jennings reached out and put his hand on my shoulder.

"You better go home, go to bed, son," he said. "You look a little peaked."

"I'm okay, just tired," I said wearily.

"You should be," he said. "We did us a good day's work today. And there'll be something in this for you. Just to show you how much I appreciate your good work. See you bright and early."

"Yeah, see you tomorrow," I said, feeling dull and leaden, and thinking only of the scotch and soda that was waiting for me at home.

I was in a sleep so deep it was black, void of dreams, void of thought, just a dense hole into which I dropped endlessly, still falling as if in death. In front of me was Sally's face, transparent, pained, grimacing.

At the end of the tunnel was a ringing that wouldn't go away. As I came up toward the sound, it became louder. I saw dim light and pulled the covers over my head, unsure of where and who I was, the heavy blanket of exhausted sleep over me like thick fog.

"Yeah," I groaned, fumbling for the phone and finally getting it somewhere close to what I hoped was my ear.

"Jack?"

"Yeah?"

"Carlton here," the voice said. "Did I wake you up?"

I looked over at the clock: 9:30.

"Yeah, I must have overslept."

I rubbed my eyes and squinted.

"Then you haven't heard . . ."

"Heard what?" I asked groggily.

"It was on the news this morning. On the radio. Jack, he shot himself last night."

"Who? Who shot himself?"

"Herbert. James Herbert shot himself."

I was awake instantly, as if someone had poured a bucket of ice water over my heart.

"Oh my God," I said. "Is he dead?"

"Yes. I fear, my friend, that we have a hell of a mess on our hands."

I sat up in bed and felt a quick tremor of pain through my chest.

"Jack, are you there?" the voice said over the handset.

"Yeah."

"You'd better get down here."

"Yeah?"

"Mr. Jennings is screaming for you. Apparently, the police found out Jennings was there last night. He wants you down here before the police get here to question him."

"Oh, shit, this is all screwed up."

"I'm afraid it's just starting. Get down here as quickly as you can."

I hung up the phone and stumbled into the bathroom. The image of Jimmy sitting in that chair, trying to justify himself, hung in front of me as I flipped on the light. My own face staring back at me in the mirror made me suddenly and violently nauseous, and like a freshman kid who's just discovered keg beer at his first frat party, I turned to the toilet and retched until I thought my ribs would splinter.

Thirteen

All I could think of was Lily. God, what's going to happen to Lily?

I cleaned myself up and brushed my teeth, although there was no way the acrid taste of bile in my throat was going to wash away.

It wasn't necessary; he didn't have to do that.

The cowardly bastard. Yeah, it takes great big brass ones to put the barrel in your mouth. But it takes bigger, brassier ones not to.

I dressed as fast as I could. *My fault, my fault*— I couldn't find my car keys. *I pulled the trigger.* The damn car won't start. *The sonofabitch, I loathe him*— The car finally starts. Traffic is everywhere, as thick as flies in an open Dumpster on a hot day. *Damn him*—

I pulled into the parking lot and jumped out of the car, then crossed the street. There were two squad cars and an unmarked car in front of the bank.

Jesus, I'd forgotten about the police. What are we going to tell the police?

"Mr. Lynch . . . Jack, you look awful," Karen said as I pushed open the office door.

"I look better than I feel. What happened? Any details?"

"Not much. It happened too late to make the morning papers. The television said his wife returned home from a late movie shortly before midnight and found him there. That's about all. There should be more in the afternoon paper."

"Have the police been here yet?" I walked into my office.

"Not here," she answered, following me in. "Madge called and said they were upstairs talking to Mr. Jennings now."

"How did they find out we were there?"

"Madge heard one of the cops say a nosy neighbor remembered the car and the license plate."

That's what the Old Man gets for having a vanity plate that reads FATCAT.

"I'll call upstairs and see if he wants me up there now," I said.

"Twentieth floor," Madge's crisp voice announced.

"Madge, Jack. Put me through to his office if you can."

"Good," she said. "He's been yelling for you."

She put me on hold for a moment.

"Yes," the Old Man yelled.

"Jack here. You want me up there now or should I wait until the cops leave?"

"Now," he barked, hanging up.

I started out the door, then remembered the gun. Maybe it's not such a good idea to walk into a room full of cops with a .38 on your hip. I locked the gun in my desk drawer, ran out, and grabbed the first elevator that stopped. I told the operator to skip his other calls and go straight to the twentieth floor. He growled, but he did it.

Madge glared at me, sticking a pencil she'd been chewing on behind her ear. She looked even more frazzled than usual. She motioned me past her. There were two plain-clothes officers in the Old Man's office, seated in the visitors' chairs.

"C'mon in, Jack," the Old Man ordered. "This is Lieutenant Briscole and Sergeant Marks. Gentlemen, Jack Lynch, my vice president of public relations. He was with me last night at Mr. Herbert's."

"Mr. Lynch," the Lieutenant said, "I want you to understand that this is just routine. The M.E.'s already classified this a suicide."

A suicide, I thought, how convenient.

"However," he continued, "we always like to follow up on any information that might be available to determine why Herbert shot himself. Mr. Jennings told us you and he visited Herbert last night. What was the purpose of this visit?"

The Old Man boomed. "I told you why we—"

"I'd like to hear it from him, if you don't mind," the lieutenant shot back harshly. Here was a man who obviously wasn't impressed.

The Old Man scowled and settled back in his chair.

"Well," I said nervously, "we had some business to discuss, the nature of which is somewhat confidential. Mr. Herbert was representing one of Mr. Jennings's associates in a legal matter and we needed to discuss some details involved, that's all."

"Nothing that would make Herbert want to do himself in?" the lieutenant asked while the sergeant took notes.

"Who knows what makes a man kill himself?"

The lieutenant lifted a bushy eyebrow and eyed me suspiciously. Carlton Smith appeared suddenly in the doorway. He walked in without waiting for an invitation and sat down on the couch next to me.

"Mr. Jennings," he said cautiously, "perhaps it would be appropriate if you were to have an attorney present at this time."

"Since this is just routine questioning and no one here is a suspect, I'm not even sure you have the right to an attorney here," the lieutenant commented. Carlton stared him down.

"There is *always* the right to an attorney."

"All right, Carlton," Mr. Jennings said. "If you want to stay, then stay. But sit down and keep quiet. Let's get this over with. We all have work to do."

"Mr. Lynch, our investigators found a pile of ashes in Mr. Herbert's fireplace. Freshly burned papers, we think. You wouldn't have any idea what those papers might be, would you?"

I looked at the Old Man. His face was a stone blank.

"No," I said, my stomach wrapping itself in knots again.

"There's not really much else, Mr. Jennings," the lieutenant said. "Like I said, pending the results of an autopsy, this case has been classified a suicide."

"Christ," I said, my ribs aching from suppressing the urge to heave, "why an autopsy?"

"It's SOP in a case like this," he said. "Just routine."

"If that's all you gentlemen have, then we'd like to get back to business," the Old Man said, not bothering to get up.

"Okay," the lieutenant answered, standing up to his full six-feet-three. "But I expect both of you to remain available for further questioning if necessary."

The two cops left. Carlton stood up and walked over to the front of the Old Man's desk.

"What happened last night, Bill?" he demanded. "Really."

"Aw, hell, Carlton. How were we to know the sumbitch was going to blow his head off the minute we walked out the door? All we did was make him a simple deal."

"A simple deal that could wind up causing us a lot more trouble than we bargained for."

"Bullshit," the Old Man said irritably. "There ain't going to be any trouble. Everybody just get back to work. One more thing, though. I expect to hear from Murphy or one of his flunkies any time now. I want both of you to stick around."

"Okay," I said.

"I'll be in my office," Carlton offered.

We got up and walked down the long hall, past Madge, and out to the elevators.

"This is ugly business, Jack," Carlton said.

"I know."

"We can't have people who tangle with us shooting themselves in the head. It's bad for the bank's reputation."

"Christ, Carlton! Is that all you're worried about? Reputation, hell! That's why Herbert's dead. He was worried about his goddamn reputation!"

"You're understandably upset, my boy," he said. His hand on my shoulder seemed to bleed the anger off like steam off a boiler. "But we must look at this objectively and try to save what's left of a very bad situation. No one can help Mr. Herbert now."

"Yeah," I said, after a moment. "There's nothing anybody can do for him."

"Exactly," Carlton answered, as we stepped into the elevator.

Karen was on the phone, talking rapidly and angrily with someone. Finally, she slammed the phone down.

"Damn reporters," she said.

"We can't talk to them," I warned.

"That's what I've been telling them. No comment!"

"Is the early afternoon edition out yet?"

"Want me to go check?"

"No, I'll do it." I was too restless to sit still anyway.

I took another elevator down to the lobby and walked

over to the newsstand by the main entrance. The early paper had just arrived. I grabbed one, flipped a quarter to the guy behind the counter, and headed back upstairs fast. I was afraid someone would stop and hassle me. It was a sure bet that what had happened was all over the company and that everyone knew the police had questioned me and the Old Man. Latrine-o-grams have a way of shooting through this place like lightning bolts.

Once safely behind my desk, I opened the paper and began reading. There weren't many details we didn't already know. There was a sidebar on his term as district attorney. Lily, the main story said, was resting quietly at home under a doctor's supervision. Katherine was quoted as saying she had no idea why her father would take his own life. An autopsy was scheduled for 10:00 A.M. Friday; the funeral would be held Sunday afternoon.

There was also a brief mention that Mr. William Jennings, prominent banker, industrialist, and financier, and an associate had visited Herbert the night of his death.

How much can you say? He killed himself. That's about it. I wish I'd never heard of Murphy or the Iris Project. None of this, not Iris, not every dollar the Old Man has, not Murphy, is worth one little damn bit of this.

I should call Lily, I thought. I don't know what to say to her, though.

"Karen," I called on the intercom, "do me a favor. Run down to the drugstore and find me a nice sympathy card, will you?"

Her voice sounded detached, like a robot's. "Certainly," she said. "Be right back."

Later that afternoon, I got called back up to the boss's office. I started to ask Madge what was going on, but her console started buzzing and I never got a chance. I walked back to the Old Man's office. The door was open. I could see him sitting behind his desk, smiling. Carlton was in a large plush chair off to one side. On a plain metal office chair that had been brought in just for him sat Murphy.

Murphy looked nervous and fidgety. The cheeks of his huge behind hung over both sides of the small chair and he was sweating hard enough to show through the armpits of his white suit coat. He turned quickly as I came in and looked at me as if he were the Thanksgiving turkey and I was the guy with the ax in my hand.

"I got here as fast as I could, Mr. Jennings," I said.

"No problem. No problem at all, Jack," the Old Man said in the same jovial tone he'd used with Herbert. I'd learned over the past few days that the friendlier he got, the more dangerous he became. "Have a seat. Over here in this chair."

I sat in another large, comfortably padded chair, in contrast to the suffering Murphy.

"I just didn't want you to miss the surprise that showed up here for us," he continued. "It seems that the bleak, gray halls of this building have been graced with a visit from the civil sheriff himself. What do you think about that, Jack?"

"My, oh, my," I said. "Life's full of surprises."

"Yeah, it certainly is. We haven't been honored like this in quite some time. Do you realize, Jack, that in addition to being the civil sheriff, Mr. Murphy is also a very powerful man politically?"

"Do tell," I drawled as Murphy squirmed.

"Yeah, and on top of that, Mr. Murphy is a large stockholder in this here bank."

"I'm impressed," I said.

"Yes, Jack," the Old Man said. "Mr. Murphy is a big man here and about town. A big man with a big mouth and a fat ass—"

"Now wait a minute, Bill," Murphy whined. "There's no call at all to go talking like that."

"Call me *Mister* Jennings," the Old Man shouted. "You useless tub of lard."

Carlton and I looked at each other uncomfortably.

"But . . ." Murphy blubbered, his massive jowls shaking and sweat pouring off his forehead.

"But nothing, you slob!" the Old Man yelled again, pounding his desk. "You know what hurts me most? Not the fact that you turned against me. I could almost expect that from somebody like you. What hurts is the way you bled me and took me for a fool all these years! You've been leeching off me twenty years now. What hurts me most is that I didn't have sense enough to shut you down back before you soaked off so much gravy! I must be slipping in my old age."

Murphy was beaten, and he knew it. It was the rule of the game; you throw your best against an opponent, and when your champion is whipped, the game's over. No lawyer with half a brain would take his case now, and the simpering hulk in front of us was just savvy enough to realize it. He could keep pursuing it, but it would only make things worse. Murphy's job now was to salvage whatever could be saved, what little bit he had left.

"Now, you know I wasn't trying to buck you, boss," Murphy pleaded. "That lawsuit was just to make things look good, so the press wouldn't raise hell with us. I was going to settle out of court with you, but Herbert wouldn't let me! Why, I—"

"Shut up, Murphy," the Old Man growled, as low and threatening as he could be. "I'm going to take a lot of pleasure in seeing you lose everything."

Murphy looked as if he were about to shrivel up and die. He seemed to shrink a size or two inside the six-hundred-dollar suit, as if someone had put a tire gauge to him and let out ten or fifteen pounds of air.

"We're going to make an out-of-court settlement, all right. It's going to be fair and decent, in line with what the suit was really worth in the first place. What would that be, Carlton?"

"We had originally proposed ten thousand to Murphy's office and another twenty-five to the community redevelopment fund. In view of the way things have turned out, though, I think nothing to the civil sheriff's office and perhaps five to the fund would be fair."

"Five thousand!" Murphy blurted. "How am I going to explain that to the Twelfth Ward Association?"

"You'll explain it, damn you," the Old Man snapped at him, "and you'll be happy with it. On top of that, I'm going to make sure not one cent of it finds its way into your pockets. And if you say one disagreeable word on this to anyone in this town, I'm going to personally see you broken down so far you have to look up to wipe your butt!"

I began to wonder just how much Murphy would take. I would have had less contempt for him if he'd jumped up and told us all to go to hell. But he couldn't. Of the four of us sitting in that office, Murphy and I were the only two who knew how much he stood to lose.

"Do you understand all this, Murphy?"

"Yes, sir," he said, looking more and more shell-shocked.

"I just talked to Sam Groves over at the Twelfth Ward Homeowners Association," the Old Man said matter-of-factly. "And if I were you, Murphy, I wouldn't be terribly surprised if I were voted out of the chairmanship at the next meeting."

Murphy's jaw dropped.

"No, boss," he whimpered. "Don't do that. Don't take the Twelfth away from me."

"Do what, Murphy? I didn't do anything."

Murphy groaned.

"You know what, Murphy?" he asked. "All this discussing has made me thirsty. Run down the hall and get me a glass of ice water."

"Do what?" Murphy asked in amazement.

"You heard me," the Old Man ordered. "Go down the hall and bring me a glass of ice water from the kitchen."

I thought for a moment that maybe he'd gone too far. Murphy's face reddened; it looked like it was coming for real this time. But I saw Murphy struggle with himself, and after a moment it subsided, almost as quickly as it came, and he stood up.

"Yes, sir," he said, rolling forward and out of the office.

"You were a bit hard on him, Bill," Carlton offered.

"Hell, he had it coming. He'll think twice the next time something like this happens. I'll let him stew in his own juices for a few weeks. Then if he's a good boy, I'll give him back the Twelfth."

"I just hope he'll be a good boy," I said.

"He will. I know his type well and it sickens me. If he had any guts at all, he would have jumped on me and punched the hell out of me. But he didn't. And he won't. He hasn't got the stones."

Murphy came back in and handed the Old Man a glass. He started to sit back down, but the boss motioned him to keep standing.

"That's real good, Murphy," he said, after a long sip. "You did good. We're finished with you now. You can go."

Murphy looked around at us, with the look of a whipped old dog in his eyes. It was as if he expected us to put in a good word for him, or to offer him some hope or comfort. We declined.

"Well, that's over with," the Old Man said after Murphy was gone. "Everything's back to normal."

"Yeah," I said. "I've got to run. I've got work to do."

"Good idea," he answered brightly. "Let's do something new and unusual. Let's go to work!"

I thought then of Sally and of Bob Sparks, and of Jimmy Herbert, and of all the wealth I'd seen. Even though I didn't know exactly what all those computer printouts said, I knew enough to see that the price of getting rich is a lot more than most people think.

* * *

I went through the rest of the week in a daze. All day Friday, I thought only of the autopsy. Instead of being in a courtroom cutting us to ribbons, Jimmy was lying on a stainless steel table in the morgue while the cold steel of the M.E.'s scalpel cut into him like carving up a side of beef.

The autopsy revealed that he'd died from a single bullet fired from a .32 caliber revolver, which entered his right temple and exited at a point just above his left ear. There was a low level of alcohol in his blood, but other than that, there were no indications of any drug usage. The coroner concluded positively that the wound was self-inflicted. There were traces of burnt powder on both his right hand and the wound itself.

That same morning the lawyer who replaced Jimmy on the case met with Carlton to draw up the settlement papers. That afternoon, the lawyers went before the judge to have the settlement outlined and the case dismissed.

We won.

All this time, the heat fought desperately to hang on a bit longer, but it was losing ground every day. People on the street seemed in less of a hurry to get out of the heat and into the icebox air-conditioned buildings. Tempers softened; the drivers' horns seemed less hair-trigger. At night, my dreams were of Sally and the faces of dead people coming up at me out of the dark.

I wrote a note on the sympathy card and sent it over to the funeral home by messenger, but didn't go over myself.

Each day, my body hurt a little less. Over the next few weeks, I'd make probably a half dozen trips to the dentist to get my teeth fixed. After everything else that had happened, having somebody drill on my jaw for several hours would be only a minor annoyance.

Everywhere I went, everything I saw, was a continual search for the guys in the parking lot. I'd only seen one of them, and then just barely in the subdued light. The other two were just a couple of black hulks shifting in the dark. I thought of every way possible to try and figure out how to find them, but nothing came of it. They were probably long gone. The night before Jimmy's funeral was a sleepless one; I drove down to the lot about 3:00 A.M. and just parked there, near the spot where it happened, hoping the killers would come back. But they didn't.

I started making plans for leaving, drawing up in my mind the imaginary scenarios of what the Old Man would say when I handed him my resignation. I thought about Murphy, and whether or not to tell the Old Man what had been going on in his bank without his knowledge. Part of me wanted to. Another part of me knew that would probably be signing my own death warrant. And a real big part of me didn't care one way or another.

I'd learned how to live again with Sally; now I had to learn how to live without her.

I spent a lot of time thinking about places to go, the most attractive idea of the moment being to simply sublet my apartment and drive for six or seven months. Maybe go back to the Bahamas and rent a place on the beach. I was fortunate in that money was not much of a problem. I could easily live a year or so on my savings. One could do an awful lot of recuperating in that amount of time, if the circumstances were right.

There was something else as well. Over the past few months, I'd felt for the first time in my life the almost imperceptible creep of age. It was frightening. The concept of mortality had been one I'd never dealt with before; now it was down on me like a swarm of crazed bats.

I wanted peace, and if it took hitting the road and driving myself to exhaustion to find it, then so be it. I'd better do it now, while I still had the energy and the inclination.

Before those goddamned bats get any closer . . .

Jimmy's funeral was Sunday, on a cloudy, humid afternoon that was appropriately depressing. I didn't go into the First Episcopal Church; besides the fact that I hate funerals, I really didn't know what to say to Lily or Katherine. I parked down the street and sat in my car so I could see when the ceremony was over. Then I followed the long procession out to the cemetery.

Some forty-odd cars slowly snaked through the city and out of the parish, to the suburban cemetery where Jimmy was to be buried. It was a newer cemetery, a fine one on higher ground, with proper drainage so they didn't have to bury you aboveground like in the older New Orleans graveyards.

A building stood in the center of the cemetery, with neat rows of markers surrounding it on all sides and seeming to stretch out for acres. A main paved boulevard cut right through the middle, with tiny paved streets stretching out like rays, each with names like Avenue of Heavenly Peace and Eternal Rest Drive.

The black hearse led the train into the cemetery, then turned left onto one of the smaller streets and parked. Behind it were two black limousines. The rest of the cars stopped anywhere they could find space, blocking the main road almost back to the entrance. I was near the end of the long line and left my car near the street.

I got out and walked slowly up a long, gently sloped hill to where, about fifty yards off and to the left, the dirt from a hole had been covered over with a carpet of artificial grass so that it didn't look like something quite so awful.

The pallbearers strained to pull the huge bronze casket out of the hearse, then march with it suspended between them toward the grave. A light drizzle began to fall, just a touch to cap off the day.

A large canopy protected the open hole. The line of men in dark suits carried the casket under the canopy and placed it onto the winch that would lower him into the ground forever. The place was covered with flowers and wreaths and what seemed like hundreds of somberly dressed people milling about. I approached the site cautiously, being careful to stay at the back of the crowd. I didn't want to be spotted. There was a tree just down the slope; I leaned against it and was able to hear most of what was going on without being seen.

Lily and Katherine, both dressed in black, with Lily's face covered by a veil, got out of the second limousine, followed by some other people in black that I'd never seen. Katherine was holding onto Lily's arm, as if to support her. They walked slowly over to where the pallbearers had laid the casket. Lily reached out and touched it. Then they all sat down.

I hate funerals, and cemeteries aren't a place of peaceful, eternal rest to me; they're a constant reminder of how frail and delicate and temporal we all are. The preacher in white robes, speaking of glory and judgment, provoked in me a rush of malicious anger. I could have throttled the man as he stood there droning on superciliously about God's wisdom and forgiveness.

I broke out in a sweat despite the intermittent cool drizzle, and longed for a cigarette. Why not? I thought. So I lit one and stood there under the tree, smoking and listening.

One of Jimmy's law partners got up to deliver the eulogy. He spoke of Jimmy's goodness and intelligence, his love for his family and his profession. He also spoke of Jimmy's service to the public and the society he lived in, mentioning specifically his term as district attorney. No one would ever understand, he said, why Jimmy had chosen to take his own life.

But I understood. This was the logical end to a process begun almost thirty years ago. Jimmy must have known that if he were found out, this would be the only answer for him. I wondered if that wisdom sickened him as it did me.

Yet these people don't know that. They don't know why they're here, I thought. They really don't get it. And they don't see the catalyst for this event. No one notices the agent, as he stands nervously under a tree, chain-smoking at a funeral, hoping his anonymity lasts.

Eventually it was over. Lily stood up unaided and gently dropped a flower into the hole where they'd lowered Jimmy. Katherine came behind her and tossed in another flower, followed by a tiny handful of dirt. People began milling about and chatting; the social part of the afternoon had begun. Some headed back to their cars. Others walked around as the drizzle let up. Katherine walked out from under the canopy and spied me standing by the tree at the base of the knoll, beneath the dried leaves and Spanish moss that hung down drearily in the afternoon's gloom.

I started to turn, but saw that she'd picked up her pace and was marching forcefully toward me. I dreaded seeing her, but I wasn't going to run.

Her hair was tied back tightly in a bun. A vicious, angry look clouded her face as her pale skin rippled over clenched jaw muscles.

"What the hell are you doing here?" she demanded.

"I'm sorry, Katherine. I'm terribly sorry."

"You're a damn fine person to be saying you're sorry," she whispered. "Sorry doesn't bring him back, does it?"

"No, Katherine, it doesn't," I said, lowering my eyes, unable to bear her glaring at me.

"You had to come back and look at the results of your handiwork, didn't you?"

"What do you mean?"

"You know damn well what I mean."

"Listen, Katherine. I don't know what you think happened—"

"I know what happened!" she interrupted. "I don't know how it happened. I don't why it happened. But I know you and your boss had something to do with it. What did you do to him, Jack? What was it?"

"Katherine," I said, struggling, forcing myself to lie to her like so many times before, "there was nothing. We didn't do anything to him. I don't know why he did it."

She paused a second, then started to let me have it again when she turned and saw Lily walking up to us.

"I just want you to do me one favor, Jack," Katherine said calmly. "I want you to tell your boss that I hope he's satisfied, and you, too, because you did your work well. By God, I just hope you're both satisfied."

"Katherine," I said helplessly.

"Hello, Jack," Lily said. Under the light veil, I could see her red, tired eyes. "I got your card. It was very sweet of you. I appreciate it. I'm glad you came. He would have wanted you here."

"Lily, I don't know what to say. I'm so sorry. If there's anything I can do . . ."

"There's nothing you can do," Katherine said abruptly. "You've done enough already."

"Katherine," Lily said, "don't be rude. Jack has gone out of his way to come here in a very uncomfortable situation. I appreciate him doing it. I'm very tired. I want to go home."

"Call me if you need anything, Lily," I said, leaning over and kissing her on the cheek as Katherine glared at me. I started to reach over to her, but she turned quickly and walked away.

I stood there a long time as the cemetery workers shoveled the dirt in on top of Jimmy. I thought of him lying

there, food for the worms. And as the afternoon sky darkened toward dusk, my anger subsided enough to where I
could hope that if there was anywhere in this universe that
one could go to find peace, Jimmy Herbert was on his way
there.

Fourteen

I t was one of those times when all you want to do is make it from one day to the next. You don't care where it leads to, where it comes from, you just want to get through it, hoping that enough time will pass that the rough edges will soften a bit, the ache in your gut will go away, and that finally you'll be able to sleep without dosing yourself with enough medication to stop a charging bull elephant with a serious testosterone problem.

I spent a long time on the phone with Sally's parents the night of Jimmy's funeral. I told them the truth about Sally and me, of our plans to get married, of how much she'd meant to me. Maybe this doesn't make any sense given the times and all the crap we swim in every day, but I wanted them to know their daughter wasn't just sleeping around. We were going to get married, dammit. We were going to do it right.

It was a difficult conversation for all of us. I offered to arrange to have the apartment cleaned out and her things sent home, but her father said he was going to come down in another week or so and take care of it. There are so many things to take care of when someone dies. We all accumulate so much baggage.

They asked me to stop by sometime if I was ever in their part of the state. I said I would.

I came to the office Monday morning determined to write out a resignation letter. My decisions had been made; I was getting out for good.

I strolled in around ten. Karen was at the desk, reading a magazine and watching the phones.

"What's up for today?" I asked, not really interested in the answer. I just wanted to know what I was up against.

"You've got that reporter coming in from the *Journal* who's going to profile Mr. Jennings. Carlton Smith wants to see you in his office as soon as possible. And next week the board's coming in and we've got to set up the caterers, get those brochures back from the typesetter, proof them, and get them off to the printer. I found Miss Bateman's files and called the typesetter this morning. The proofs are on their way over. Other than that, it looks like a pretty light day."

Oh, well, idle hands make the devil's work.

I decided to give my notice that afternoon, maybe catch the Old Man on his way out of the building. That way he can't spend the whole day screaming at me. He'll have overnight to adjust to the idea. I figured about two weeks' notice would be plenty of time.

I walked out of my office to refill my coffee cup, then stopped in front of the desk. For a moment, I thought I saw Sally leaning on the edge of the desk now, her back to me, wearing another bright new dress that was shorter than usual. Silk, very attractive, her hair pulled back, looking softer and fuller than ever before. I stared at her and my eyes blurred over for a moment; then I realized it was Karen.

She turned around quickly when she sensed me.

"Is there anything I can do for you, Mr. Lynch?" she asked, very professional, very smart.

No, I thought, there's nothing you can do for me.

"No, just getting coffee."

"If you need anything, let me know."

"Yeah," I answered in a daze. It would happen to me a lot over the next few months, I thought. I'd see her in the face of a stranger on the sidewalk, in a seat on the streetcar, across a cold glass in a bar somewhere. Would it ever quit? Did I ever want it to?

I started to say something when the phone buzzed. Karen reached to get it, but I interrupted her movement.

"I'll get it," I said, pushing the button on my desk set and lifting the receiver.

"Public Relations."

"Front desk, Mr. Lynch. There's someone here to see you. A Miss Katherine Herbert."

What in the hell did she want?

"Mr. Lynch?"

"Yeah," I said, after a moment. "Send her up." I sat there staring, holding my cup of coffee, thinking that in a moment or so, I was going to need a cigarette.

My throat tightened when I heard the front door open and Katherine step in. I heard her voice, cold and impersonal and professional, ask for me.

Karen led her into my office. I stood up as they walked in.

"Someone to see you, Mr. Lynch," she said.

"Yeah, c'mon in," I said,

Karen motioned for her to take a chair, then backed off a step.

"Call me if you need anything," she said.

"May we speak privately?" Katherine asked. "With the door closed?"

I looked at Karen and nodded. She turned and left my office, clicking the door shut behind her.

"She's cute, Jack. Is she your keeper these days?"

Katherine looked at me in a way that to anyone else would have appeared perfectly normal. I knew better, though; I'd lived with her too long.

She was dressed in a soft brown cotton dress with a wide belt and a silk scarf around her neck. Everything about her was immaculate. Her hair, that deep, rich auburn hair that attracted me to her in the first place, was brushed tastefully back. She sat there composed, proper, but wired like a burglar alarm. I ignored her remark about Karen.

"Would you like some coffee, Katherine?" I asked, as politely as possible.

She thought for a second.

"No, but I will smoke if you don't mind."

"What can I do for you?" I asked.

"I came to talk," she said.

"I'm not sure there's much we can talk about."

I reached across the desk and lit her cigarette. She inhaled deeply, then exhaled a thick cloud of smoke.

"I want to know, Jack. I want to know what happened that night."

"It's history, Katherine. Nothing happened."

"Don't lie to me," she said. "If we ever meant anything to each other, don't lie to me. I need to know what happened. To put this all behind me."

"Katherine, what went on between my boss and your father was something so private and personal that nobody else has a right to intrude. I was there only as a flunky, a—"

"It's not an intrusion, dammit!" she snapped. "He was my father!"

"And he was my friend," I said back to her. "I hated this, too."

"Then tell me what happened! Tell me so that we can both make peace with it and each other!"

"You don't want to know, Katherine. I guarantee you, you don't want to know."

"I have a right to know," she said calmly. "You have no right not to tell me."

In the straightforward simplicity and directness of what she said, I realized she was right. And I realized that I was sick of the lies, the lies that killed Jimmy, the lies that led to Sally's death. No matter what happened, I was through with lying. Maybe, I thought, the truth will set us all free.

So I told her, as quickly and succinctly as possible, without hiding anything, without softening it a bit. I told her the whole story of her father's dishonesty, his betrayal of trust, and of how the knowledge of his own crime had been inside him all these years, like a time bomb waiting to go off.

After I finished, she sat there unmoved, stiff, as cold as an empress. She held the cigarette between the first two fingers of her left hand as it slowly burned down.

"You're lying," she said, after a moment's silence. "You always were a liar."

I almost laughed, but held it back.

"If it's not true, then why did your father kill himself?" I asked. In the simplicity and directness of what I said, there was truth she could not escape.

"My father was murdered," she said.

"Your father was not murdered. Your father killed himself."

She stared at me through the glazed eyes of a shock victim. But the truth would bore in on her, I thought, until finally it became the truth for her as well as everyone else. In time, she would face it and make peace with it, and get on with her life just like the rest of us.

"My father was murdered," she said quietly, her voice trailing off as she stood up. Her dress was unwrinkled and draped perfectly over her as she stood there. She moved slowly, as if in fog, toward my door. I came out from behind the desk and walked over to her. I reached out and, for the first time, touched her.

"Katherine, this has been horrible for everybody. But your father has found peace. Why don't we try to do the same?"

Her eyes narrowed as she looked first at me, then over at my hand on her shoulder. I brought my hand down, as her eyes had instructed.

"Good-bye, Jack," she said. "Take care."

That afternoon, I did it. A long lunch, a long talk with myself, and then about 4:30 that afternoon, a simple little typed note:

Dear Mr. Jennings,
   Effective two weeks from today I resign my position as Vice President for Public Relations for the First Interstate Bank of Louisiana.

Respectfully,
Jack Lynch.

I signed my name above the typed line and breathed a deep, penetrating sigh. I was glad to see this chapter of my life end. That little bit of ink washed ten years of crap off me. I picked up the phone and punched three numbers.

"Twentieth floor," Madge said.

"Madge, Jack."

"What's up?"

"Is the Old Man working late tonight?"

"If he is, he hasn't said anything up here. And he usually lets us know. He's probably leaving on time. Around five-thirty."

"Good, I've got something I wanted to talk to him about, but it's no big deal. I'll catch him on the way out."

"Okay. Later. Got another call."

About an hour. In an hour, I'd catch him in the hall and walk out with him. Yeah, that's it. I'd hand him the envelope, tell him what it was, and then back off quickly. He'd stew about it overnight and be mostly calm by the time he walked in the next morning.

"Make me a couple of copies of this, can you?" I asked, handing the letter to Karen. She looked at it and couldn't help seeing what it said.

"Short and sweet," she commented. "I'll be sorry to see you go, Mr. Lynch."

"I wish you'd call me Jack," I said. "Especially since I won't be your boss much longer."

"I'm sorry about that," she said. "I think we would have worked well together."

She walked out after a moment to make my copies. I sat down in my chair, lit a smoke, and waited.

Around quarter after five, I called and Madge told me the Old Man was just getting ready to leave. I caught the elevator up to his floor, the resignation letter folded neatly in my coat pocket.

I walked through the heavy glass doors and into the reception area.

"Has he left yet?" I asked Madge.

She shook her head and nodded toward his office. I heard him walking down the hall, muttering to himself and struggling with his briefcase and coat. He walked into the reception area and saw me.

"What are you doing out here?" he demanded, looking at me.

"I just needed to talk to you about something," I said. "But I thought I'd just wait and catch you as you left."

"Why didn't you come back to the office?" he asked gruffly.

"Didn't want to disturb you. Thought you might be busy."

"Well," he said, laughing as we walked toward the elevator, "actually I was. Did you hear about what happened in court last Friday?"

"Yes," I said, pushing the elevator call button. "Carlton told me a little about it."

"Carlton went to court that afternoon," the Old Man continued, obviously enjoying the story. "And, of course, Murphy was there with some young punk lawyer I guess was from Herbert's office or something. When Carlton explained the settlement to the judge, he said the man's eyes lit up like a neon sign."

The elevator came. I was glad the Old Man had started talking. It gave me an extra minute or two before I had to give him the letter. I felt the envelope in my pocket just to make sure it was still there.

"Nonstop," the Old Man said to the operator.

"Yessir." We began dropping past the floors where the other people were waiting impatiently to get home to dinner and happy hour.

"Anyway," he continued, "the judge wants to know what the hell is going on here. Carlton said Murphy started sputtering like a flooded lawn mower, got all red in the face, then told the judge that he decided to reconsider and accept a lower amount. Then Carlton said the judge started pumping Murphy's ass like a butter churn for wasting the court's time and the taxpayers' money in a lawsuit he didn't intend to pursue. It must have been great! God, I wish now I'd been there."

The door to the elevator opened and we stepped out into the lobby. Most of the people had cleared out by now, with only a small crowd left. Over to our right, stationed at the massive glass doors that were the entrance to the bank, I saw Billy Patterson standing, his cap pulled low over his wrinkled forehead, a great clump of white hair showing in the back. I smiled at the old security guard and thought, for a second or so, that I really would miss his battered, old smiling face. I grinned at him; he grinned back and tipped his hand to the bill of his cap.

"What did you want to talk to me about?" the Old Man asked.

"Well," I said slowly, the lump in my stomach doing jumping jacks all over my insides, "I've been doing a lot of thinking lately—"

It was then that I saw her, standing off to our left and across the room from Billy.

At first I didn't recognize her. She'd changed clothes. She wore a short blue dress now, with a leather bag slung over her shoulder. Her hair was still brushed neatly, beautifully back.

She stepped out of the shadows toward us, perhaps ten feet away.

Her hand came out of the purse with a glint of metal in it.

I heard a loud popping, then another. The sounds ricocheted off the walls, echoing into silence.

Everything moved in slow motion, as if nanoseconds had become decades.

Someone screamed. The Old Man grabbed my arm, moaned, and then I heard the sound of a briefcase falling at my feet.

My jaw dropped and I stood there like a dumb ass with my mouth open.

I looked up quickly to see her staring at me, coldly, directly. The gun was moving around toward me. She was raising it again, to draw a bead on me. I was frozen, mindless, absolutely stark staring freaking petrified.

My gun! I thought. *My gun's still in my desk!*

There was an excruciating sound; the roar of a cannon, a *boom* that banged off the walls and physically hurt like a nail through my eardrum.

My heart stopped.

I thought I was dead. But I wasn't. I felt a thump in my chest, but it was only my heart beating again.

The gun flipped out of her hand and clattered lightly, delicately to the floor. Her head jerked crazily to the side and she was lifted completely off her feet, shaking, convulsing, a slight grimace on her face as she went up. She seemed to hang in midair, as if undecided as to whether to complete the fall, and at the apex of her leap, like a deer trying to escape over a fence, she relaxed.

The grimace was gone now, and the woman I'd once thought I loved more than breath in my own body collapsed on the floor and lay there motionless.

To my right, Billy stood, the smoking cannon in his right hand, frozen in fear, terror, his perfect quick-draw the only thing between me and that gun Katherine had pointed at my heart.

The world went instantly out of control.

People screamed and ran about madly. Absolute, bloody, crazed pandemonium. I felt a tug on my arm as the Old Man slid slowly down to the floor, pulling me down beside him. I leaned over him, then dropped to one knee. His eyes were open. There were two small red dots on the front of his white shirt. I felt him squeeze my hand.

"What happened?" he asked weakly, my concentration on his voice the only thing that made it audible over the screaming.

I put my hand to his forehead; he was going quickly into a cold, clammy sweat.

"Somebody go for a doctor," I said blankly to the crowd of people gathering around us. "Call an ambulance."

"Jack, what happened?" he asked.

"Try not to talk," I said, holding onto his hand. "Somebody's going for help."

"It hurts, Jack. It hurts like hell," he said, the color draining rapidly out of his face.

I took out my handkerchief and unbuttoned his shirt.

There were two small holes that, strangely enough, didn't look that bad. One was on his left side, just above his nipple; the other down below, in his gut, just above an appendectomy scar. He'll be okay if we can just get him to the hospital.

I took the handkerchief and pressed against the hole in his chest.

Billy pushed through the crowd and dropped down beside us.

"I got her, Mistuh Jennings," he blubbered, in a strained, high-pitched tone, his head bobbing up and down. "I got her. She won't shoot you no more. Nawsuh, she won't shoot you no more."

He was crying now, tears running down the wrinkles in his face like floods cascading down a gully. I reached over and put my hand on his shoulder.

"Hold on to him, Billy," I said. "I'll be right back."

"I got her, Mistuh Jennings," he babbled. "I got her."

I stood up and pushed through the crowd. People saw the blood on me and backed away quickly, not wanting to touch me. I waded over to where Katherine lay, her arms sprawled out crazily. Her dress was hiked up to her waist, her legs cocked at an awkward, obscene angle.

I reached over numbly and pulled her dress down to cover her up, then lifted her arm. There was no pulse and she was growing cold. Her auburn hair, that I'd loved so much, was now a twisted ugly matted clump soaked in blood.

I started to lift her head and a piece of it came off in my hand. I gagged and staggered to my feet. People turned their heads and walked away, the revulsion of the living for the dead painted boorishly on their faces.

I felt someone grab my arm and turned to see Karen.

"What's happened?" she demanded, in a choked voice. I didn't answer her. "Jack, who is that?"

"It's Katherine," I answered softly.

Karen looked harder to try and bring her into focus.

"The woman who came to see you today," she gasped. "For the love of God, Jack, cover her up."

I took off my coat. Kneeling beside her, I gently laid it over her head. Somehow it seemed so undignified for her to lie there like that so horribly mangled; my Katherine who had always been so meticulous and fastidious about every part of her appearance.

Karen put her hand on my shoulder and gingerly tugged me to my feet. She turned me toward her and looked at me.

"Are you all right?" she asked.

"No, dammit," I said, looking at her. "I am not all right. I am not one little bit all right."

Then my eyes blurred over again and I felt myself collapsing on the inside as well. Something inside of me broke, and I began crying like a six-year-old.

I don't know how long I stood there. The next thing I remember were sirens, the screeching of brakes and tires slamming to a stop outside.

I shoved my way back through the crowd around the Old Man. Billy was sitting on the floor beside him, holding his hand and sobbing. He had taken off his security guard's coat and folded it under the Old Man's head.

"How's he doing, Billy?" I asked, squatting down next to him.

"He says it don't hurt so much no more. I put my coat under his head."

"Good, Billy, good."

The Old Man looked real pale. He looked like he hadn't bled much, though, and I hoped that was a good sign.

"How do you feel?" I asked, taking his other hand. He squeezed mine back, a little weak, perhaps, but with traces of the strength he'd carried all his life.

"A little better," he said. "I'm tired."

"You'll be okay," I said.

"Yeah, Mistuh Jennings, you'll be okay."

"Why, Jack?" he asked. "Why did she do this to me? I don't even know who she is."

"Don't talk now. Just rest," I said.

Two men in paramedic jackets pushed their way through the crowd pulling a large metal gurney behind them. They shoved me and Billy out of the way, knelt down, whipped on surgical gloves, and started working on the Old Man. One loosened his clothes while the other strapped a sphyg on him and examined the wounds.

"How is he?" I asked.

"Who are you?" one of the medics demanded.

"I'm Jack Lynch. I was with him when it happened."

"Were you hit?" he asked, seeing the blood on my shirt.

"No."

Two other men were loading Katherine on another gurney. They didn't seem to be in quite the same hurry.

"He's shocky," the paramedic who was working on the boss said. "We got to get him stable and then to the hospital."

Suddenly, it seemed as if there were people pulling at me everywhere. The lobby was full of police, witnesses, hysterical customers, employees, bystanders, gapers, gawkers. People shoved and yelled, cops barked orders, Billy sobbed. Karen's face stood out, shocked, from the rest of the crowd.

The two paramedics lifted the Old Man up and placed him carefully on the gurney. As they wheeled him out of the bank, I followed.

"I'll see you at the hospital. Don't worry. Everything'll be okay," I said to him. Just before the attendant slammed the back door of the ambulance, the Old Man smiled at me.

"Where are you taking him?" I asked.

The driver glanced back at me as he ran to the door of the ambulance. "Charity Hospital," he yelled. "Best E.R. in the city."

He jerked the ambulance into gear and squealed the

tires as he pulled away, siren screaming, horn blaring, trying to clear a way through the traffic.

Karen came out behind me as I stood on the sidewalk.

"Where are they going to take him?" she asked.

"Charity."

"Charity Hospital?" she asked, surprised.

"Yeah," I said. "You mind going back up to the office for a while? I'll call you from the hospital. We'll have some phone calls to answer, I'm afraid."

She nodded and stepped back, then looked up at me, into my eyes.

"Are you sure you should go?" she asked.

"I don't know. I want to get to the hospital. Go on, now."

I trotted back to the parking lot to get my car. I thought, pulling into traffic, of the bizarre irony of someone worth $350 million being carted away to Charity Hospital. In the madness, it almost seemed worth a good laugh.

Fifteen

I hung over the edge of the counter as the E.R. nurse shuffled through papers with the speed of a snail.

"Oh, yes," she said. "He's already been moved up to X-ray."

"Who's his doctor?" I demanded.

She looked down casually. "Dr. Thompson."

"Where's X-ray?"

"Third floor," she answered. "Elevator down the hall."

I felt lightheaded and nauseous as I headed upstairs in a daze. It had all exploded within the space of a few seconds, but as so often happens in moments of terror and violence, time sense is twisted so far out of reality that it takes on the aura of the surreal. Katherine's death leap became a pirouette executed in a divinely inspired ballet. The Old Man sliding down to the floor became the crescendo of some grand opera.

I knew she was really dead, but it hadn't hit. I didn't

know when it would, only that when it did I was in for a rough time.

I walked off the elevator and across the hall to the nurse's station. The nurse said she'd call Dr. Thompson as soon as he was available. I sat down, nervously smoking, my eyes fixed-focused on some invisible point far in front of me.

I called Karen back at the office. Carlton, she said, was taking care of things, handling the police and the press, and would be down to the hospital as soon as possible.

"Someone told him you'd been hit," she said. "There was so much hysteria down there, and the way you disappeared. He thought you got it, too."

Her voice was tight over the phone, the strain clearly showing.

"I was afraid she had hurt you," she said.

"She was going to," I answered blankly.

"I'm glad Billy was there," she said. "You were very lucky."

Right, I thought.

Karen promised to sit by the phone as long as she was needed. There was a click as we hung up. I sat in a hard plastic chair, waiting for some word on the Old Man.

Over and over in my head, I kept telling myself that he hadn't bled much, that he was as strong as a racehorse, even at his age. He was slim and tight and still walked with a light, hurried spring in his step. Surely to God he'd be all right.

All my desperate thoughts stopped cold. I thought of him helpless and bleeding on the hard polished floor of the bank. The look on his face, the pain in his eyes; I realized at the moment Jimmy Herbert had not been my only real father. The Old Man had to live. I needed him.

I sat there for the longest hour of my life before a tall, middle-aged man with a pale complexion and flecks of gray in his hair walked slowly down the hallway. He came to the nurse's station first. They huddled together for a minute and the nurse pointed me out. The man squinted down the hall. He looked worn out. I jumped up from the chair and met him halfway.

"I'm Dr. Thompson," he said, shaking my outstretched hand. "I understand you're a friend of Mr. Jennings."

"Yes, I work for him," I said. "I'm Jack Lynch. How's he doing?"

Dr. Thompson sat down and rubbed his forehead. He smelled of rubbing alcohol and hospital corridors. I sat down next to him.

"We've got him stable and he's being prepped for surgery right now," he began. "We've called in Dr. Redmond, who's one of the best thoracic surgeons in the city. Mr. Jennings's wounds are very serious, but he has a couple of things going for him. It appears that the first bullet entered his chest below the collarbone, above the nipple, but without hitting any major vessels. There's some lung damage, pretty serious tissue damage throughout. The second bullet entered the right abdominal area. This is the one we're less sure about."

"What do you mean?"

"The X-rays are telling us the bullet is not where it should be in relation to the entrance wound. When soft, small-caliber bullets enter tissue like the abdomen, they scurry around inside tearing all sorts of things up before they stop. We won't know how much damage has been done until we get in there and probe around."

"Do you have to operate?"

"Oh, yes. No doubt. The bullets have to come out and we've got to get him sewed up inside. There's been considerable internal bleeding. Some pretty serious shock involved. But we've got him stable. It could be worse."

"When are you going to do it?" I asked.

"Within the hour," the doctor answered.

"How long will he be in there?"

"At least five or six hours. He's got a rough row to hoe ahead of him, but I think he'll make it. He's remarkably strong and healthy for a man his age."

"Yeah, I know," I said.

"I've been told we've got a problem downstairs with the press. I had no idea Mr. Jennings was such a prominent person. I'm going to keep them downstairs, with only family members coming up."

"As far as I know, he's got no close family. At least not in the city."

"All right," he said. "Then we'll let company people up if they're kept to a minimum and don't disrupt anything. He won't have any visitors, of course. But you can stay to find out how he is."

"What are his chances, doctor?"

"It's hard to say. Because of his age and the nature of his wounds, I've had him placed on the critical list. As I said, though, he's a very strong man. We'll know more when we get him out of surgery."

"Where can I wait?"

"There's an O.R. waiting room on the fifth floor," he said. "You can get some coffee and a bite to eat up there as well. Which reminds me, do you know what he had for lunch today?"

"No," I answered. "He usually ate light."

"I hope so," Dr. Thompson said. "I hate cleaning a big meal out of somebody's gut."

He stood up, then walked away. I went up to the waiting room, got some coffee, and sat down on one of the couches and stared at the television. The local news came on, with the shooting as the lead story. I sat there smoking and sipping coffee. You could see the blood on my shirt in the news tape.

The police came up and took my statement. They were pretty sympathetic, not too demanding. But they did tell me I'd be required to testify at the coroner's inquest and to stick real close to town for the next couple of weeks.

Carlton came shortly thereafter. He didn't stay long. With the Old Man in the hospital for who knew how long, Carlton was going to be very busy. He left a phone number where he could be reached and told me to call him as soon as I heard anything.

A couple of reporters showed up. Fortunately, they didn't recognize me and the nurse on duty was savvy enough not to tell them who I was. Then she called security and had them escorted off the floor.

After a while, I went down to the hospital cafeteria and got a cold sandwich that tasted like sponge. Finally, I gave it up and went back to the waiting room, sat on the couch, and stared wordlessly at the television, exhausted. I looked at the clock on the wall; it was nearly ten.

This morning in my office, she said nothing mattered anymore.

I sat staring at the television, until the ten o'clock news came on and led off once again with the shooting. Funeral arrangements for Katherine had been made; Lily was in seclusion under a doctor's care. There was a lot of speculation going around as to what the tie was between James Herbert's death and what the reporters were now calling an "attempted assassination."

I slipped off a bit myself, sinking in and out of a troubled light sleep. I was the only one in the waiting room now; the lights were turned low in the halls. The night shift was on.

Katherine was staring at me with the gun in her hand again. I moaned and shifted uneasily as I felt someone shaking me.

I opened my eyes, squinted and tried like hell to remember where I was. The clock on the wall read 12:20. Dr. Thompson stood over me, looking like he'd been run over by a truck.

"Hi." I stood up. "What happened?"

"He's in recovery now." His voice as well as his face showed the strain. "As expected, we didn't have too much trouble with the upper chest area bullet. The abdomen was a different story, though."

"How bad?"

Dr. Thompson scratched absentmindedly at the stubble on his jaw. "He's scrambled pretty bad, but we managed to get him cleaned up. There was some liver, upper intestinal, and pancreatic damage. We had to remove his spleen. He's in for a very long recovery period, I'm afraid. But it could have been worse. Offhand, I'd say Mr. Jennings has the luck of the Irish. Another inch or two either way and he'd be in the morgue rather than recovery."

"He's always been a gambler," I said. "He'll make it."

"He won't be eating any T-bone steaks or pizza for a while."

"When can I see him?"

"Not until late tomorrow at the earliest. After recovery room, he'll be in intensive care until we can do a complete evaluation of his condition. If he holds up well by tomorrow night, I'll bump him off critical."

"Great," I said, relieved.

"In the meantime, I'm going home to bed. I'm not a twenty-eight-year-old resident anymore. These late nights wear me out. I suggest you get some rest as well."

"Listen, thanks," I said.

"My pleasure," he said over his shoulder, as he trudged wearily out.

I called the office from the pay phone in the hall, thinking that surely Karen must have gone home. But the night phone line rang, bypassing the closed main switchboard, and in a moment I heard her voice answer.

"I can't believe you're still there," I said.

"You sound terrible."

"Yeah, well. You sound kind of tired yourself."

"Little . . . It's been a long day. How's Mr. Jennings?"

"In recovery. The doctor says he's going to make it."

"Good. Jack, why don't you go home, get some sleep?"

"You, too. You need anything? A ride?"

"No, but thanks. My boyfriend's going to pick me up. Be careful."

"Okay, bye."

We hung up and I stood there for a second, dreading going back to my empty apartment. What I really wanted to do was go over to Sally's, fix a couple of drinks, and climb into bed next to her.

Only that wasn't going to happen anymore. I stood there alone in the hospital corridor, shaking, and wondered how much more of this shit I could stand.

It was three days before they got the Old Man out of intensive care. They took him to a private room on the eighth floor, with a private nurse and a security guard outside his door at all times. He was too weak to be moved to a better class of hospital, so Carlton arranged to have an outside team of specialists called in, as well as a private nursing staff. The regular hospital staff didn't like it very much, but Carlton insisted, made a few phone calls, and the next thing we knew, their objections were overruled.

The Old Man was on restricted visitation, but Dr. Thompson was kind enough to make sure my name was on the list. We could go in one at a time, once a day, and have five minutes with him.

His room was huge, one of a small group of suites held in reserve at the decaying hospital just for patients deemed to be special. A window looked out over the medical complex, but the curtains were pulled and the room was always very dark. He had all kinds of tubes running out of him: I.V.s, drainage tubes from the wounds, a catheter. He'd gone off the respirator, though, so he could talk, which had always been one of his priorities.

The first day they let me in, he was propped up in bed

slightly, very gray and tired-looking, and much thinner than I expected. He lifted a hand and motioned the nurse out; she warned me not to excite him as she left.

"Well," I said, standing at the foot of the bed, "how're you feeling today?"

His face was drawn, but his eyes were as bright and vivid as ever. He seemed to be thinking of a thousand things at once, his eyes darting back and forth across the room.

"I feel fine, dammit," he said, voice strained but not as weak as it could have been. "I need some things from the office—"

"Wait a minute. You're not asking me to bring you work, are you? Because if you are, I'm not going to do it."

"The hell you say," he wheezed. "I want you to get those papers I dropped in the lobby. There was a prospectus on a development down in Lafayette I was going over. Also the merger documents between American Mortgage and Warranty and United Title."

"Stop it," I said, smiling. "If I brought it here, they wouldn't let me give it to you."

"That's why you've got to sneak it in. I need to go over those papers before the board meeting."

"You think you'll be out of here by then? In case you forgot, you've just returned from a triumphant, all-star, six-hour engagement in the operating theater. Something tells me Dr. Thompson won't appreciate you not sticking around to find how this all works out."

"Who the hell are you working for?" he demanded, unable to scream at me like he really wanted. "Me or these idiot doctors?"

"These idiot doctors kept you off a cement slab in the morgue."

He went kind of quiet for a second, then settled back into his pillow and stared up at the ceiling.

"What happened to the girl?" he asked after a moment.

"The girl?"

"The girl that shot me, you nincompoop," he snapped.

"Billy shot her. She's dead."

"That's too bad," he said softly. "I hate that."

"Me, too."

"Who was she, Jack? Why'd she want to shoot me?"

I came around the edge of the bed to stand by his side. He rolled his head over to look at me with the question still on his face.

"It was Herbert's daughter."

"Jesus." He sighed. "And your ex-wife . . . God, I'm sorry."

"Me, too. Iris wasn't worth it."

"I'm sorry I got you into this." His voice trailed off.

"Yeah, well. You didn't know it was going to happen this way." I reached out on impulse and placed my hand on his shoulder. He was hot beneath the hospital gown, as if he were running a fever. I squeezed him gently and he smiled up at me, two old survivors who'd just pulled through one more battle.

"I hate this place," he said. "People always poking around you, sticking things in you. I hate these flowers, too. Makes the place look like a damn funeral home. See what you can do about getting them out of here, will you, Jack? Give them to the other patients. I hate 'em."

"I'll take care of it for you," I said. "I can tell you're starting to feel a little better. You're getting grumpy again."

"Go to hell."

"The doctor said you'll feel pretty bad for a while, but that you'll be back on your feet sooner than you think. If you do what you're told, that is."

"I've never done what I was told," he grumbled.

"Might be a good time to start."

The nurse came in, telling me my five minutes was up. I squeezed his shoulder one last time, then turned to leave.

"Jack?"

"Yeah?"

"Don't forget these damn flowers," he said. "And get those contracts up here."

"Yeah, if the doc says it's okay."

He growled something as I walked out the door. I took the elevator down to the first floor where a nurse located Dr. Thompson. He said he'd see the flowers were taken out, but work was taboo for now.

"Do me a favor," I said. "Tell him yourself. I'm not up for it."

I had to appear at the coroner's inquest the next day. Billy was there, too, in his uniform and still shaken up. No charges were brought against him, though. He was doing his job. I spent about twenty minutes answering questions once I finally got called. There just wasn't that much to say. Every witness told the same story. It was all over by lunchtime.

Katherine's funeral was that afternoon and I felt compelled to go, even though I might not be welcome. The weather had turned ugly, raining hard most of the past two days. It was dark, with a constant rumbling in the sky overhead.

There wasn't going to be a church service, just a brief graveside eulogy. I went straight to the cemetery and waited for the hearse to arrive from the funeral home. Visitation had been limited to family. The casket had been closed.

It started to spit rain, a little harder than at Jimmy's funeral. I sat in my car with the top up, smoking and waiting. There was an open pit next to Jimmy's grave, which was itself covered over with fresh sod that hadn't taken root yet.

A canopy covered the pit, with folding metal chairs set up in neat rows. Lily got out of the black limousine behind the hearse. She was in black and supported by a large woman who was taller and looked older than she was. They sat down in chairs under the canopy, next to where the pallbearers had just eased the casket onto a platform over the hole.

A million things flashed through me at once, all images of what my life with Katherine had been like, back when things had still been good. The moments when we giggled like schoolchildren, made love like thoroughbreds. Katherine never wanted children; she was afraid it would make her fat. Once we got so caught up with each other, she pulled me on top of her without bothering to put the diaphragm in first. For weeks, she was terrified she was pregnant. I secretly, and silently, hoped she was. Perhaps if she had been, none of this would have happened.

Now she was dead. She'd been taken from me a long time before this, but she was still with me, still inside me, still, in her own way, on me every day. I wondered if she'd still be with me after this, if she'd still be a part of me.

Do the dead really live in our memories, or is that simply another lie to make things a little easier for us?

The service was short. I sat in the back. Some cried throughout the brief ceremony. When it was over, most people got up and left immediately. This one was so bad that no one even wanted to socialize.

I walked over to Lily. The woman holding her arm glared at me, but I ignored her. Lily's eyes were watery, as if she'd cried herself out so many times but there were still more tears in there somewhere.

She looked at me for a second as if she wasn't sure it was really me. It took her a moment, but she reached over and touched my hand.

"I'm sorry, Lily," I said, trying to hold myself together. "I know that doesn't help much, but I am."

"I know, Jack," she said. More than anything else, she sounded just plain exhausted. "You couldn't help what happened. She loved her father very much. She just couldn't stand it. I don't know how I shall bear this."

"Sister," the woman next to her said, "the Lord doesn't give you any more than you can stand. And if he does, he also gives you the strength to bear it."

"Jack, this is my sister from Memphis. Lois, this is Jack Lynch. He and Katherine were married once."

"Hello," she said. "I'm pleased to meet you."

"Yes, ma'am," I said. "Pleased to meet you."

"Come on, sister," Lois said. "We need to get you home."

"Oh, God, Jack." Lily sighed, starting to cry once again. "I'm going to miss her so much."

"I know, I know." And I leaned over and hugged her tightly for what seemed like a long time.

Then Lily's sister took her arm and they began the walk back to the limousine. After a while, there was no one else there. The two men on the grave crew had pulled up their backhoe and shoved the last of the dirt in on top of her. I walked over as the men drove off. The bronze plaque that would mark her grave had already been placed. Like Jimmy's, all it had on it were her name and two dates. That's good, I thought. Years from now, no one will know. There had to be some comfort in there somewhere, although I wasn't sure where.

I pulled a rose from a wreath near the grave and laid it down on the bare dirt just below the plaque. The rain had started again, a slow, drizzling rain that would soon pick up speed and be a real soaker. I could tell; I could feel it. After years in this part of the country, you knew these things.

I stood up, my hair plastered down on my head, my dark suit coat heavy and cold on me.

"Good-bye, Katherine," I said out loud. Then I turned away from her for the last time and walked down the hill toward my car.

The last thing I wanted was to go back to the office. I pulled into a gas station and called Karen to see if anything was going on.

"Thank God you called, Jack!" she said breathlessly.

"Why? What happened?"

"Carlton told me to find you. The doctor just called. It's Mr. Jennings. He's hemorrhaging."

Sixteen

The Old Man managed to hang on for almost two days. The night of the first day, he slipped into an uneasy coma. He weakened so quickly there was no way they could go back and clean up the mess inside him.

Dr. Thompson said if he'd have been a younger man, they would have risked it. But at his age, there was simply nothing that anyone could do for him. Having worked for him all these years, and seen him on a day-to-day basis wearing out people half his age, it never occurred to me that he was really old.

He didn't have any family, at least none that anybody knew. There were probably a couple of illegitimate children running around somewhere, but nobody knew where. He never married. Carlton was his executor.

Mr. Jennings was cremated the afternoon of the second day. On the third day, the company plane flew his ashes out over the East Texas oil fields, where the Old Man started out, and scattered them to the wind. That seemed to me to be more comforting than being shoved into a hole in the ground; at least he was back where he came from and what was left of him was free to go anywhere the wind took it.

I went to Ray's near my house that night and had a bite to eat, a few drinks, and thought over some of the old times. My own private wake for all the dead. The Old Man never approved much of drinking, but I suspected he'd approve even less of a bunch of teary-eyed bastards sitting around crying over him, while at the same time plotting to see who was going to wind up in his corner office on the twentieth floor.

There wasn't much for me to do at work. I retyped the resignation letter with "Dear Carlton" at the top, made copies, put one in my coat pocket, and locked the others in a file cabinet. I was determined to turn it in to Carlton as soon as the transition was made. The board of directors would meet tomorrow to name an interim president of the bank.

Karen was at her desk first thing when I got in around nine, which was pretty early for me.

"Good morning," she said, very sweetly.

"Hi," I answered. I poured a cup of coffee and walked into my office. She followed, with a telephone message slip in her hand.

"The top floor called," she said. "Madge wanted me to have you check in with her as soon as you came in."

I took the message and held it as she left my office. Then I dialed O on the interoffice line.

"President's office," Madge's cool voice said.

"Hi, Madge. Jack—"

"Carlton Smith asked me to call you. The board of directors meeting will be over in another half hour. He'd like for you to stand by for a meeting in Mr. Jennings's office sometime after eleven. He'll call you."

"To prepare the press release, right?"

"That and some other things, I think."

"What's going on up there, Madge? C'mon, you can tell me."

"A real barn-burner, I'm afraid."

About 11:15, my phone rang again. It was Carlton, who sounded like he'd just stepped out of the ring after a ten-man tag team match.

"Come on upstairs, Jack. There have been some interesting developments over the past few hours."

"On my way."

Madge looked like she'd done some crying over the past few days as well.

"Are they all in there?"

"Yeah. And brace yourself."

"What's going on?" I asked.

"Just go on in," she said. "You'll find out."

I started to turn away.

"Jack?" she asked. "Were you with him the night he died?"

"No," I answered. "He was alone. But the doctor said it was real easy. Just like falling asleep."

"I would have felt better if he'd had somebody with him."

"Yeah, I know." Madge had been with the Old Man a long time.

I walked back to his office. Carlton was there, in a couch off to the side, with a dozen or so bank officers from the various departments sitting around in chairs.

Murphy was there, too, in dark pinstripes, surrounded by a haze of blue cigar smoke.

He was sitting in the Old Man's chair.

His suit coat opened to reveal a flashy diamond tie pin holding his necktie down on his fat stomach. Behind Murphy's chair stood a big guy with slicked-back black hair. He had huge hands and shoulders that didn't need the padding that had been stuffed into the three-piece set of pinstripes.

The kind of guy you wouldn't want to run into in a dark alley.

"C'mon in, Jack," Carlton said. "We're waiting for a couple more people, but we can go ahead and start. We've called you all here to announce to the bank's upper management that the board of directors has asked Mr. Murphy to assume the presidency of the bank."

The people crowded into the room erupted into a rumble of murmurings, surprised gasps, even a whistle from the far corner.

"Holy shit," Charlie McCorkle, the Vice President for Data Processing, and Bob Sparks's boss, muttered to me. "How in the hell did that happen?"

As if you didn't know, you freaking slimebag.

"Beats the shit out of me," I whispered.

"Mr. Murphy is taking over immediately and will want to meet with each department head as soon as possible to go over status reports and to discuss possible changes," Carlton continued. So far, Murphy hadn't said a word. He just sat there with a big cigar stuffed between his yellowed teeth. "Each department head will be responsible for announcing to his own people Mr. Murphy's appointment."

The meeting went on in that vein for about fifteen minutes. Then Carlton dismissed everybody and the army of lieutenants was quickly ushered out of the general's tent. Carlton walked over to me, though, and asked me to stay. They wanted to discuss how the media was going to be handled in all this.

Carlton sat back on the couch, looking exhausted. Murphy was smiling behind the Old Man's desk, with the goon standing at parade rest behind him. This was going to be a fun place to work over the next few months; I was glad to be getting out.

"You guys will excuse my surprise," I said. "But the newspapers are going to want to know how this happened. I don't blame them."

Murphy eased forward in his chair and laid the cigar down in a huge ashtray on the desk.

"This has been an interesting morning," he said. "At the board of directors meeting, a coalition of minority stockholders presented the board with enough proxies to cause a real fight if they wanted one. Mr. Jennings's shares are, for the moment, tied up in probate."

"Which is why you moved so fast, if I make my guess," I said. Murphy smiled at me.

"Yeah, on target again. As usual, Jack. Mr. Kramer, Mr. Scott, Mr. Frazier, Mr. Perrin, and myself held enough shares between us to control the voting."

Frazier and Kramer were on the board already, which meant Murphy went in with not only a ton of proxies, but two of the eight directors in his pocket. I wondered how he'd gotten them, or maybe it was gotten *to* them.

Like a corporate blitzkrieg, Murphy swooped in and took over everything before anyone had a chance to muster their forces. We were horse cavalry against tanks, civilians against storm troopers.

"I'll say this much for you, Murphy. You sure don't waste any time."

"From now on out, Jack," he said, smiling at me, "It's *Mr.* Murphy."

"How about you, Carlton?" I asked, turning in my seat. "You in on this, too?"

"Jack," he said wearily, "like the rest of us, I am simply an officer of this bank. Whatever the board votes, I am bound by the rules to follow. We must abide by the board's decision and simply continue to do our jobs."

"Mr. Jennings isn't here to run things anymore," Murphy said.

"You know something, Murphy?" I asked, turning around to face him again. "You disgust me."

The gorilla behind him snapped to attention and moved toward me. "Listen," he growled.

Murphy held up a hand to stop him.

There was a moment of silence as what I'd said sunk in on him. I couldn't, for a second, believe I'd said it myself.

"You can't talk to me that way anymore," he said, as calmly as if we'd been discussing the stock market or the results of the latest Saints' game. "We want you to stay because you're the best at what you do and, believe me, I'll be needing more of your services in the future. But you cannot talk to me that way. Whether you like it or not, Jack, you're working for me now."

I felt the red rising from my waist to my shoulders and neck and finally to my face. All the crap, the pain, the craziness of the past couple of months welled up inside me like the swelling of hot metal in the sun until the point right before the rupture, the explosion. And if I'd let it go like I felt like doing, I would have taken Murphy and Carlton and the pin-striped slab of beef with me like a flash fire. I could have incinerated the sonofabitch. I would have gladly gone out the window of the twentieth floor with my hands wrapped around Murphy's fat neck, and grinned at him the whole way down, as we both dropped to the sidewalk below and splattered like blood-filled water balloons.

I could have rested then, been easy at last and found peace.

And in that moment's thought, I saw Sally lying once again in that parking lot in the darkness, with the life seeping out of her and me helpless to do anything about it. As the pressure inside me grew and the bright colored spangles formed in the sides of my vision and closed in toward the center, blocking everything out before me, and my breath came in short little gulps, I hammered it all back down.

Sally was on the asphalt there in front of me, and the pain and hate and anger inside me grew cold, even colder than it had that night in the hospital, and I knew that killing Murphy wasn't the answer. Killing the bastard would have been too quick and easy. No, that wasn't the answer.

My eyes closed for a second as I struggled to regain control. Gradually, my heart slowed down to a locomotive's pace and my vision came back . . .

If Murphy wanted to think he'd broken me, then let him think it. I'd play along, whatever it took. I'd do *anything* to get him, and get him right.

"Okay, Mr. Murphy," I said quietly. "I'll cooperate any way I can."

I glanced sideways at Carlton sitting there with his mouth open. He watched me, stunned, as I let Murphy dress me down like an errant buck private. The guy behind him grinned meanly, with a look on his face that called me an anatomical part I didn't have.

"And another thing," Murphy said, his voice a little tighter now. "We're not going to have any more of this coming and going as you please shit around here. From now on out, mister, you're in your office at eight in the morning and you don't leave before five in the afternoon!"

"Yessir," I said.

"And lunch hour doesn't mean leave at eleven and stroll back in at two. I want your ass back in that office chair in sixty minutes. You understand?"

"Yessir, I understand." Murphy sat back and enjoyed himself immensely. This was turning into a good show for one and all.

"Now run down the hall and get me a cup of coffee. Black, two sugars."

Carlton audibly gasped. Something deep inside my gut contracted, hard, but none of them noticed. I slowly turned around and walked out of the office.

Down the hall, in the break room, I grabbed a coffee cup and filled it from the pot. Two sugars.

Over in the corner, Madge sat with her back to me. But her shoulders shook, and I could tell she was crying.

I thought a moment, then walked over to her.

"Madge, you okay?" I asked, very softly.

There was a moment of silence as she raised her head and sniffled. She wiped her nose with a tissue and stared straight ahead.

"Go away," she said.

"Madge, what happened?"

She turned around and looked at me. The lines in her face were suddenly deeper, and her eyes were as tired as time itself.

"He fired me," she said. My heart did a big cramp and it was my turn to stand there with my mouth open. "Twenty-two years of service to this company, and he fired me. No notice. No severance. Today's my last day."

"Oh, Jesus, Madge," I said, putting my hand on her shoulder.

"I was due to retire in three years," she said. "He didn't even have the guts to tell me to my face!"

"Is there anything I can do?" I asked, after a few seconds.

"Not unless you want to go in there and shoot Murphy."

"I left my gun in my office," I said, very sadly, very truthfully. Maybe I should go get it.

She smiled up at me.

"That's what I'm gonna miss about you, Jack. You're such a kidder."

"Yeah, a freaking laugh riot."

I took the cup of coffee and walked down the hall to what was now Mr. Murphy's office. I saw in my mind again the grin on Murphy's bodyguard's face as he stood there looking at me; the grin of a child sadist stuffing a lit firecracker up a cat's back end. I smiled in spite of myself, though, when I thought of how I'd set him off, the way he'd jumped and almost come after me and then stopped on command from Murphy, that growling voice saying, "Listen . . ."

"Listen . . ."

I stopped dead in the hall. A ripple of hot coffee sloshed

over my hand, the scalding burn of the liquid barely perceptible. I rewound the tape in my head and played it again.

"Listen . . ."

Where had I heard that before?

"Listen . . ."

The kind of guy you wouldn't want to run into in a dark alley—

"Listen . . ."

My head pounded, and I was suddenly as dizzy as if I'd stepped off a roller coaster. I'd heard that voice twice before; once on the phone, the other time face to face.

"Listen . . ."

I could still feel his huge hands on me.

"Listen . . ."

I leaned against the wall, terrified, and I knew then what I had to do. I set the plastic cup of coffee down on a table in the hallway and walked out to the reception area and through the double doors. An elevator was just opening. I stepped in.

"Sixth floor."

"Yessir," the operator said. Anybody coming out of the twentieth floor got himself called "sir."

All trace of feeling and tension evaporated as I walked into my office. Karen said something to me. It didn't register. I mumbled something back, then closed the door to my office.

The .38 was still in my desk drawer, holstered and loaded. I clipped the gun onto the back of my belt and pulled my coat around to make sure it was hidden.

"Jack, are you okay?" Karen asked, concerned, as I walked past her. I said nothing.

The cup of coffee was still on the table when I got back up there. I picked it up, then walked down the hall to Mr. Murphy's office and opened the door.

"What took you so long?" he demanded when I walked in. The weight of the gun felt like a lump on my hip.

"The pot was empty," I said, in a robot monotone. "Had to make a fresh pot."

I set the cup down on his desk, then backed off two steps. The goon was still behind him, only now he was half-sitting, half-leaning on the Old Man's credenza.

"Thanks, boy," Murphy said. "I appreciate it. I appreciate your attitude, too, boy. You know, good things are in store for you if you do your job and keep your nose clean. I might even say great things are in store for you."

"Thanks, Mr. Murphy," I said. "I'll try to do a good job for you."

My hand was drawing almost imperceptibly behind me. The pistol felt heavy and cold against my back.

"Well, you can go now, Jack," Murphy commented. "We'll call you when we need you."

My hand, under the coat, touched the hard plastic of the pistol grip.

"Go on, you can go now," Murphy said. My hand shook. The dizziness came back. Sparkles of light were coming in from both sides of my vision, first red, then silver, then bright, tingly multicolored spangles. Sweat broke out on my forehead; I was as cold as death itself.

"Mr. Murphy said go," the goon snarled. My heart double-somersaulted in my chest; I suppressed a yell as my hand touched the cold metal of the gun. Damn you! I screamed inside my head.

No!

I couldn't do it. Not this way.

I walked down the long hall I'd seen so many times before. Taking Madge's place, struggling with a stack of instruction manuals, was a young woman with bleached blond hair, too much makeup, and a chest like the front bumper of a '55 Cadillac. One of Murphy's babes. As I passed, she looked up at me and sighed in frustration, as she tried to figure out how to work the console.

And I took a lot of comfort in the great things that were in store for me. Hell was real, and I had found it.

A madness gripped me the likes of which I'd never felt. A lifetime's worth of anger and pain and frustration was crystallized in time in that one sublime, glorious, apocryphal moment. I went to work the next day, after a sleepless night.

Phone call No. 1: "Carlton?" "Yes?" "Just out of curiosity, who was that guy in Murphy's office?" "Mr. Murphy's driver, I believe. He was introduced as Mr. Robichaux. Jack, are you sure you're all—" "I can't talk now, Carlton. Later."

Phone call No. 2: "Security." "Billy, this is Jack Lynch." "Hello, Mr. Lynch. What can I do for you?" "Billy, I want you to tell me when Mr. Murphy's limo is brought around front this evening to pick him up. Okay?" "Sure, Mr. Lynch. I'll call your office. Sure is a shame the way things going 'round here—" "Thanks, Billy. Talk to you later."

Billy called at 4:20 that afternoon. Mr. Murphy's driver/bodyguard had pulled the limo around to the front of the bank and was waiting. I picked up my briefcase and threw on my coat, then dashed out of the office to Karen's "Where are you going? When will you be back?"

I'd never be back.

Downstairs, the tellers were wrapping up their daily reports as the first-floor officers, the lower-level grunts that actually had to meet the public, finished up paperwork. I walked quickly through the busy crowds, out the revolving front door, and down the sidewalk fast, hoping Mr. Robichaux wouldn't see me as he sat there in the big black Cadillac with the motor running.

My own car could wait in the lot. It was too easily recognizable. A block or so down Carondelet was parked the common pastel sedan I needed.

Sally's car.

A half-dozen parking tickets were tucked under the

windshield wipers; I'd parked the car there the night before. I dropped them in the gutter; this was a stack that wasn't going to get paid.

I jerked the car out into traffic just as the Cadillac was pulling away from the front door of the bank. I settled back two or three cars behind, and we began slogging our way through the dense downtown parade.

The limo crossed Canal and headed into the Quarter. It was common knowledge Murphy kept a little hideaway somewhere in the Quarter for entertaining his teenage girl-friends. It looked like I was going to find out where it was.

They turned left on Bienville, then down a couple of blocks to Burgundy. Then down Burgundy for what seemed like forever in the choking traffic, and a right on St. Philip. Two more blocks, and the limo stopped.

Murphy got out by himself, then leaned back in and said something to the driver. He looked in both directions, up and down the sidewalk, and disappeared up an ornate wrought-iron staircase to an upper apartment. The limo pulled slowly back out into traffic.

Mr. Murphy wouldn't be going home tonight. Mrs. M was sure to be disappointed.

I drove on past the building. Murphy could have his fun tonight. In fact, I hoped he had himself a memorable evening in the sack. If things worked out like I planned, it would be one of his last.

Two hours later, I was crouched down in Sally's car, smoking cigarettes, listening quietly to the radio, and watching one of the buildings in an apartment complex in Metairie. It was an apartment complex like any other in America. There was nothing whatsoever to distinguish it from a thousand others just like it, except for one thing:

The man who killed Sally lived there.

It was dark now, and I could see into the second-floor apartment through the sliding glass door that led out onto the balcony. A woman from two buildings over had walked through the parking lot and up into his apartment about an hour earlier. I watched them embrace and heard music from the stereo through an open window. Darkness fell, the music stopped, and I saw them walk out of the living room to my left. A moment later, a light came on in another room and I saw the silhouette of the man pulling a shirt over his head.

I sat there thinking. Now that I had him, I really didn't know what to do with him. Madness under the right circumstances, though, can kick the imagination into high gear. I did what any other self-respecting crazy person would have done under the circumstances.

I drove to the K-Mart.

A quick scamper through the hardware section, then the pharmacy, and a stop in luggage. Pay for it all in cash, and back to the apartment complex.

Now here I am, back in the parking lot. It's late, the lights are beginning to pop off in other apartments. But not in his. No, he must be a real thoroughbred. I've got the AM radio on, flipping around the dial listening to the late-night crazies from all over the country: Apostle Johnny Washington from the Tabernacle of Truth in Jamaica, Queens, New York; the Right Reverend Roosevelt Franklin screamin' about how you, too, can have that mink coat! God *wants* you to have that new mink coat! God *put* that mink coat here for you to wear! And for a five-dollar love offering, we'll send you the Roosevelt Franklin Prayer Cloth blessed with Holy Water and the Blood of the—

The bedroom lights go out.

A half-minute later, two forms silhouette in the living room. The two become one big shadowy blob for a moment, then separate. The building door opens; the babe with the beehive hairdo comes out wearing a jogging suit. She walks down the steps, up the sidewalk, passing right in front of me.

She disappears into her apartment. I'm out of the car

in a second with a bag over my shoulder and the revolver in my right hand. Up the stairs, I feel my heart racing like a locomotive gone wild, a million loose cannons on the deck in a Force 10 gale.

God, I'm scared. I've never done anything like this before. Didn't know I could. But I still keep seeing Sally on that pavement; keep hearing her breathing. And those black forms in the night all over me, all over her.

I stop at the door, just for a second, then tap on the door lightly, casually. I hear a laugh from inside.

The door opens. "Okay, honey, what'd you forget this—"

My foot's in the door, the revolver in his face, the hammer cocked fully back. Either of us hiccups and this guy's face is spaghetti sauce.

"Inside. Now."

"What the fuck?" he growls. No more "Okay, honey."

"Now," I warn. For the last time.

He backs in, a step or two at a time. His eyes flicker left, then right. I see in his face that he left his piece somewhere he can't get to it. Too bad. I shut the door behind me.

"Step back." He does.

"What the fuck is going on here?" he says, cocky, sure of himself.

"You talk like that in front of your mother? Turn around."

He hesitates, but just for a second.

I jam the gun into his lower back, hoping I don't accidentally set it off. But what the hell . . .

I pull his wallet. Robichaux. First name, Alistair.

"We're going to talk, Alistair. And if you make nice with me, you just might live to see another evening with that little cutie in the jogging suit."

"Mr. Murphy's gonna have your ass on a platter, Lynch. You little shit."

I jam the gun a little harder. "This thing might go off

by accident, you misbehave, now. Move to the middle of the living room."

He takes a couple of steps over in front of the coffee table.

"Down on your stomach. Put your hands behind you. We gonna talk, I don't want to have to worry about you coming after me."

"Oh, I'm coming after you, you little punk. You count on that," he growls. But he gets down on the floor and folds his hands behind him. After all, what are his options?

I'm shaking inside, but my hands are unexplainably steady. I open the bag and pull out an inch-and-a-half roll of duct tape, the silver kind that'll hold just about anything. I'm on top of him, now, with a knee in his back and the gun still in my hand, using my free hand to wrap him up tight enough it'll take an hour to get him out. Then I tape his ankles together.

Alistair's mine now. I uncock the gun and lay it on the counter that divides the kitchen from the living room, then roll him over, grab him under the armpits, and yank him into a sitting position. He's uncomfortable, with his back against the wall, but he's not hurting. And he's sure as hell not going anywhere.

"What do you want, cocksucker?" he snapped.

"Oh, your mouth," I said lightly, easing myself into the soft cushions of the sofa across from him. "If we're going to talk tonight, you're going to have to watch your language. Wimps like me offend easily." I smiled at him, wondering if he knew how much trouble he was really in.

"I got nothing to say to you," he said darkly, looking away from me.

"You've got plenty to say to me." I let just the slightest trace of a threat come into my voice for the first time. "And before the evening's over, you're going to talk to me."

"What are you going to do? Beat it out of me, you pussy?"

I shook my head. "No, not my style. Probably not very effective in your case."

He grinned meanly. "But you are going to talk," I added.

He said nothing.

"I want to know what's going on with Murphy and Iris. Why he filed that lawsuit. Why he had that programmer killed, and why he had you and those two other gorillas beat the hell out of me in that parking lot."

"You're fucking crazy," he spat. "You going to wind up a can of Alpo, you know that?"

"Beef-flavored chunks, right?" I laughed. "Now listen, Alistair, I know your buddies didn't mean to kill the girl. If you'd meant to kill me, I'd be long gone by now."

"Damn straight."

"So somebody screwed up. I want to know who those other two guys are. You're going to give them to me. And you're going to give me Murphy."

"Fuck you," he muttered. But I noticed a tremor in his voice, and I couldn't help but see the line of sweat that had broken out across his upper lip. His white T-shirt was crumpled up on his chest and his pants were twisted around uncomfortably. Mr. Bad Guy was getting worried.

"Alistair, you've brought out aspects of me that I didn't know existed," I commented, getting up from the couch. "I always considered myself a civilized man of reasonable intellect, a man in control of his feelings. You've driven me to lose that control."

"You're fucking crazy," Alistair said.

"That's right. And guess who's going to suffer for it?"

"What are you talking about?" A little false bravado there. Yep, no mistaking it. "I'm going to kick your ass up between your shoulder blades."

"Is that any way to talk to a man who's brought you presents?" I asked, kneeling down in front of him with the bag next to me.

"What the hell are you talking about?"

"We are going to have to do something about that mouth of yours," I said. "Now look, Alistair, I've brought you gifts. I'm going to bribe you, not beat you."

And I leaned down and unbuckled his belt.

"What are you doing?"

I pulled the belt apart, then unbuttoned his trousers and unzipped his fly.

"Now, listen, asshole."

My eyes closed tightly and every muscle in my body clamped shut. There he goes with that again. My head pounded and I suppressed a scream; suppressed is not the right word. I stifled the urge to strangle him with my bare hands. Then I got it all back together.

"Alistair, the first time we ever talked, you called me that. Remember? That day when you made the threatening phone call to my office?"

"I'm going to give you one last chance to get out of here," he said. "You leave now, I'll talk Mr. Murphy into not having you killed."

I smiled at him, then yanked his pants down to his ankles so hard he slid partly down the wall. He wasn't wearing any underwear. Cute.

He yelped like a smacked dog.

"No noise, Alistair, or I'll have to tape your mouth shut with that duct tape. And that'll hurt bad."

"What are you going to do?" he asked, scared now.

I sat down cross-legged next to him with the bag to my side.

"Now why don't you tell me what all that stuff with Iris is about? See, what you guys don't know is that before you killed that kid, he got me all the records of Murphy's accounts. *All* of them. I know that Murphy is filtering, laundering, money through the bank. I know where it's going. I just don't know where the money's coming from, and why. You're going to tell me that."

The goon's eyes got bigger. That hit home with him, I thought. "You *are* dead meat," he growled.

"Now I ask you again, is that any way to talk to a man who's brought you so many nice presents? I went to the K-Mart, Alistair. You know the K-Mart? Your one-stop shopping place?"

I pulled out a half-pound tub of petroleum jelly and set it on the floor next to him. His eyes got a little bigger.

"Now let's see what else is in here." I dug around in the bag. "Oh, look, an extension cord," I announced.

"What are you doing?" he demanded.

I pulled out the last item in the bag.

A soldering iron.

Alistair's Adam's apple bounced as he swallowed. The sweat line on his upper lip extended upwards now to his forehead.

"Talk, Alistair. You know how hot these things get?"

"Fuck you!"

I stood up, grabbed his ankles, and yanked him out away from the wall so hard he bounced off the floor when he hit. He made a dreadful thump, then groaned. I grabbed his left arm and flipped him over on his stomach like the losing side in a calf-roping competition.

I sat back down on the floor next to him, grabbed a handful of hair, and jerked his head around so he was looking up at me.

"Talk, Alistair. Now. Tell me about Iris. Tell me about Murphy!"

He remained silent for just a moment too long. I flipped the top off the petroleum jelly and dipped the soldering iron in it about three inches, then pulled it back out with a mound of the greasy yellow goop hanging off of it.

"Time's-a-wastin', old sport," I said. "Talk."

For the first time, I got the sense Alistair was really scared.

"I can't. Murphy'll kill me."

"Murphy's not your worry right now, buddy!" I was down about a half-inch from his face. "*I'm* your problem right now!"

"Go to hell," he whispered.

I got up on my knees next to him. His bare bottom was raised up in the air like two white hairy mounds. God help my poor demented, damned soul.

The goopy soldering iron touched him. He flinched, then clamped shut.

"Loosen up, Alistair," I said calmly. "You'll only make it hurt worse this way."

He moaned. I found the right place, then slowly—because, jeez, I didn't want to cut the guy or anything—buried the soldering iron inside him to the hilt. He was shaking now, sweat pouring off him. But he hadn't said a word. He really was a tough guy, I had to give him that.

I reached for the roll of duct tape and tore off about six strips. I criss-crossed the tape over his bottom, taping the soldering iron in so that it wasn't going anywhere. No way he was going to shake it loose.

It looked like a long, skinny tail with a plug on the end. I held back a snicker.

"Okay, Alistair, down to business," I said. I got up, picked up the extension cord, plugged it into a wall socket about six feet away and twisted it in the wall. "This is one of those expensive extension cords, Alistair. The kind that locks in the wall when you turn it. You can't pull it out unless you untwist it. Which is kind of tough when your hands are tied, right?"

"This is crazy," he said. "You can't do this."

I sat down next to him, cross-legged again, with the extension cord socket in my left hand and the soldering iron plug in my right.

"Now, first things first. Tell me about Iris."

"Please, Lynch, they'll kill us both," he said. Please, I thought. Nice touch. I think I'm reaching him.

"Let's go, Alistair, talk to me."

Nothing. I jammed the soldering iron plug into the extension cord socket. His eyes lit up like Christmas tree lights. He started shaking.

"Be still, Alistair, you're only going to hurt yourself."

"Jesus," he squeaked.

"Better start talking fast," I said. "These things take a while to heat up, but when they do, oh boy . . ."

He lay there for a moment, eyes gyrating madly, sweat pouring off of him.

"I hope you don't have to go to the bathroom anytime soon," I said lightly. "That's really going to hurt for the next couple of months. Try a low fiber diet."

He vibrated for about another ten seconds, then a huge gulp of air shot out of him.

"Okay! Okay, goddammit! Unplug it, please, unplug it! It hurts already!"

That's interesting, I thought. I pulled the plugs apart. His tears ran onto the carpet.

"It's the cash," he blubbered. "The cash. Murphy's got the biggest money-laundering operation in the city."

"But where does the money come from?"

He hesitated. My hands moved closer together, still holding the ends of the two cords.

"Drugs! It's all drug money, street sales. Most of it from Iris."

"C'mon," I said. "You expect me to believe that much cash comes in from a bunch of five- and ten-dollar street sales?"

Alistair looked up at me as if I were not only crazy, but stupid as well.

"Those five- and ten-dollar hits bring in six figures a day. Every day. Murphy's been in it for years. There's millions involved, most of it coming out of Iris. You kill Iris, you kill the cash flow.

"It's just business," he added. "You name it, Iris's got it. Crack, Ecstasy, MDA, Horse, Choo-Choo. It's all there. We get white kids from Metairie, Kenner, all over, driving into Iris. Murphy's got a reputation for being a straight shooter. He works for the Colombians, the niggers, the dagos. He launders the cash, takes twenty-five points off the top, and it winds up in clean accounts in the Caymans, Bahamas, wherever you want it. Safe, tax-free. He's fair, dependable, reliable. Just business."

"An equal opportunity scumbag," I said, thinking of my trip through Iris that long-ago night. "Now he's really going to get rich, isn't he? He's in charge."

"Yeah," Alistair said, shaking his head. "And you, too. There's plenty there for all of us. I'll fix it with him."

"What about Bob Sparks? The kid?"

"Charlie McCorkle iced him. Murphy told him to take care of him; he didn't necessarily mean that way. Just shut him up, fire him, get him out of town. But Charlie's got a thing for young boys, you know. It's common knowledge. He partied on the kid, messed him up real bad. He had to waste him."

Alistair was talking a mile a minute now. You'd need a stenographer to take it all down. I'd talk too if I had a soldering iron taped up my ass.

"Who were the two guys with you that night in the parking lot?"

He was quiet for a second. My hands brought the two plugs closer. "No, wait," he said. "This is going to sound crazy, but believe it or not, Murphy likes you. He says you're damn good at what you do. He wants you in on this. Figures he can trust you. He had one of the guys following you. Knew you were seeing the woman. He sent us to scare you, not hurt you bad. He was real pissed when the broad got killed."

"Where are they, Alistair? Where are the two guys that screwed up?"

He looked up at me from the floor. "I think maybe they're somewhere down around Grand Isle. Depends on how the tide's been running."

And so I had it all now. I understood. It all made sense, in its own twisted, perverse way. I stared off to where I couldn't even see the man next to me anymore, and a wave of something almost resembling peace came over me. I knew the truth now, and I knew what I had to do.

"Are you telling me the truth, Alistair?" He shook his head violently. "Oh yeah, yeah, the truth. All of it!"

Sure he was. Despite appearances, he was human, and no human could lie under these circumstances. Not with this kind of fear. Not holding on to this kind of hope.

"I believe you, Alistair. And it's been nice talking to you." I stood up, walked over to the pistol, and holstered it. Then I tore off about a six-inch strip of duct tape.

"What are you going to do?" he begged. "What are—"

I taped his mouth shut. "Just keeping you quiet, old buddy."

Then I tore off another length of tape, plugged the soldering iron into the extension cord, and taped the two cords together.

Alistair screamed, but it came out only as a muffled, guttural squeak.

"That's for Sally, Alistair," I said, patting him on the back. "Have a nice day."

I walked to the door, then turned. Alistair was still on his stomach, screaming through the tape and flopping around on the floor like a freshly landed, ten-pound large-mouth.

I closed the door behind me. My hand shook as I lit a cigarette. I drew deeply off it, then exhaled a lung full. Reaching inside my left coat pocket, I pulled out the mini-corder that had been silently whirring away and flicked it off. I pulled the tape out and snapped off the write-protect tab. Nobody was going to tape over this sucker.

I laughed to myself. It would take Alistair Robichaux about twenty minutes to realize I'd cut one of the wires at the base of the soldering iron. Boy, was it ever going to sting when the cops ripped that duct tape off.

Seventeen

It was nearly midnight when I pulled into the parking lot of the all-night convenience store. A carload of redneck kids was parked next to me, drinking beer, radio blaring, great clouds of dope smoke wafting out of the windows. The harsh streetlights glared off the slick oil spots on the asphalt. Typical night in the suburbs.

I pumped a quarter into an outside pay phone and fumbled with the piece of paper in my pocket. Dialing the number, I felt my heart crunch in my chest. Finally, after what seemed like a week, a woman's voice answered.

"Hello," she said, sleepy.

"Is he there?"

"Who is this?"

"I have to talk to him. Tell him it's Jack Lynch and it's an emergency."

There was a sharp thump as she laid the phone down. I stuck a cigarette between my lips, but didn't light it. The inside of my mouth felt like I'd been munching cottonballs. Another scraping sound in the phone, then his voice:

"Jack, what is it?"

"I've got to see you."

"Now? Hey, buddy, it's the middle of the night. Can't it wait till tomorrow?"

"No, it can't. This one's hot. I guarantee you, it'll be worth your while to hear me out."

"Where are you, a party? You drunk, guy?"

"I'm just next to a car full of loud kids. You want to hear this or not?"

"Okay, I'm listening."

"Not over the phone. To tell you the truth, I'm scared right now. Real bad."

"Okay, fella, calm down. Where you want to meet?"

"There's a place in Algiers, across the river. Way the hell out past the Harvey Tunnel." I gave him the address. "Think you can find it?"

"Yeah, I think so. Although that part of town's not my usual stomping grounds. What is this place?"

"Little dive called the Keyhole Lounge. You'll love it. Door's shaped like a keyhole. Don't bump your head."

"My wife's not going to like this."

"It's business. Believe me."

"Okay, buddy. Keyhole Lounge. Give me an hour or so."

"Also, you need to get somebody out to an apartment complex in Metairie. The Chateau Bienville. I don't know the address, but it's in the book. Apartment G-202. There's a guy there trussed up like a Christmas turkey. Take him into custody and hold him. But don't use the city police. Use your own people."

"What am I supposed to charge him with?" the tired voice asked.

"I'm no lawyer, dammit. Make something up. Conspiracy to commit murder; that'll do for starters. His name's

Robichaux and he's going to have a lot to say before this is over."

"This better be good, fella."

"It is. I'm not crazy, I just sound that way."

"Okay. An hour."

The phone went dead in my hand. I stared at it for a second, as if expecting it to come back to life and dance in front of me. The rednecks were hooting and hollering now, one of them pouring a Pabst Blue Ribbon on the other. I stared at them for a second, until they started staring back. Then I figured it was time to get the hell out of there.

I hope it wasn't stupid trusting Fred Williams. If he was one of the bad guys, then I was a dead man for sure. But at this point, I wasn't convinced that would be so bad.

There was barely time for me to get everything done before Fred made it to the Keyhole. I got in one of the long lines of traffic on I-10 and headed toward Canal Street and the Greater Mississippi River Bridge. The bridge led across to the other suburbs of New Orleans, to Gretna and Algiers, the older parts that didn't have quite the style or character of the French Quarter. It's too bad, really; the tourists didn't know what they were missing. But if the tourists wanted the real thing, they wouldn't go to Disneyland now, would they? They want the fake, the manufactured, the aura of memory and myth rather than the mean reality of a living, breathing place full of people.

You got to be crazy to want the truth. I wanted the truth; look what it got me. The truth doesn't set you free. It makes you crazy.

I thought about all these things, and a thousand others, as I struggled in the traffic, thick and choking even at this hour. The AM radio played and the preachers screamed out at me again, promising salvation for a five-dollar Love Offering or a ten-dollar Fellowship Offering, or for twenty-five bucks I could have a Lifetime Partnership Salvation

Contract. The promise of everlasting life for the price of dinner and drinks in a two-star restaurant.

Screw it, I thought. Not worth it.

I wasn't sure how this was going to turn out; I only knew the fat lady hadn't sung yet.

Soon, I was in faster moving traffic on a four-lane concrete highway running into the Harvey Tunnel. I took the first left and drove into an obscure little neighborhood filled with shotgun row houses and creeping Spanish moss hanging from oaks that heard cannonfire back in the Civil War. Rusting cars up on cinderblocks were giant black turtles in the moonlight. Another left, two miles down, another right, and there it was.

The U.S. Post Office. I was glad I'd rented one of the large boxes, and I was equally glad I'd never told anyone, even Sally, about it.

It was one of my little secrets.

I opened the door and walked into the area where the boxes were, a place that was open all the time, looking behind me in my ever-increasing paranoia to make sure I wasn't followed. I opened my box and saw the package there, with the envelope on top of it. The post office boys had beat the package up a little bit, but they hadn't destroyed it. Bob Sparks didn't die for nothing.

I threw the stuff onto the passenger seat and hauled ass out of there. I took a bunch of winding turns, around neighborhoods, backtracking, hell, probably getting lost, and finally came to a park. I drove in, found a secluded spot, and parked the sedan under a large tree with plenty of overhang to hide me.

The air was sweet and heavy and filled with the scent of night. I had maybe ten minutes before meeting Fred. I sat there calmly, opened the package, and read as much as I could in the dim light. I lit a cigarette as I read, and while it would take an accountant and a bank auditor to nail it all down, I saw the pattern and I saw the truth. I understood now why Iris was worth killing for.

Five minutes later, I pulled into the gravel parking lot of the Keyhole Lounge, a cajun dance hall. I'd discovered it years ago, back when I was a student and obsessed with finding absolutely as much lowlife as I could get my hands on. In the lowlife category, the Keyhole was a gold mine. In the lot were battered pickup trucks and four-wheel drive things with enormous tires and painted names like Stomper and Mama's Little Ass-Kicker.

If you had nothing better to do, the Keyhole was a good place to go get shot on a Saturday night.

Even though it was open until four, most of the action had already died down. After all, it was a school night, although I'm damned if I can remember which one. A country band with an accordion and a couple of horns and a slide guitar player was packing up its equipment. Over in the corner, nursing a Dixie beer, with his shirtsleeves rolled up and his jacket and tie off, sat my old buddy Fred Williams from the D.A.'s office.

I smiled at him as I approached the table.

"Dixie?" I asked. "Is that the best you could do?"

"Hey, made from pure Mississippi River water," he drawled.

"You know you'll be shitting green in the morning, don't you?" I said, sitting down at the table. "Thanks for finding us a dark corner."

"You sounded like you were going to need it," he said. "What the hell is this all about? The assault?"

"Partly," I said. "But it's a lot bigger than that."

"So get a brew and talk to me, guy."

I ordered a pitcher and a bowl of pretzels and asked the waitress to bring me another pack of Marlboros.

"This is going to take a while," I said. "You hungry? Want a sandwich? I'm buying."

"Jesus, Jack, breakfast is in a couple of hours."

"Sorry about all this," I said. "Hope your wife's not mad at you."

"She's used to it. I'm just worried about you. What the hell's going on?"

So I started at the beginning, back to what seemed like years ago. The lawsuit, the Old Man's reaction, his instructions to me, and everything I did, including the sleazy, the intrusive, and the ultimately deadly. I told Fred about my trip to the Bahamas, the bankruptcy, our late-night visit to Herbert's house, and the real reason for his suicide. And I told him about Katherine, and why she killed the Old Man and tried to kill me.

I stopped for a second to gather my thoughts and light another cigarette. I heard him sigh deeply.

"This is pretty damn bizarre, fella," he said.

"The best part's yet to come," I said, lighting one. "The real motive behind all this, Murphy's lawsuit, the killings, all the crazy bullshit that's gone down in the past few weeks, started to come to me in the hospital, although I really couldn't connect it all. I didn't know all the truth. I know it now."

"Yeah?" he said.

"What's the biggest thing going down every day in Iris?"

He whistled. "Crime, big guy, vice and dirty money."

"Dirty money," I said. "What do you do with dirty money?"

He paused for a second. "Launder it?"

"You just said the secret word and won a hundred dollars," I said. "What do you need to launder large, incredibly large amounts of cash?"

"An incredibly large washing machine." He smiled. "Like a bank."

"And somebody on the inside to work with you, to funnel the dirty cash into the mainstream of clean cash, then put it where you want as inconspicuously as possible."

"Murphy?"

"Yeah. He'd never get his hands dirty by actually having anything to do with drugs. It's not that he has scruples, you understand, it's just that he's a cowardly piece of shit and afraid of getting caught. But funnelling cash for the boys on the streets and taking your cut can be mighty lucrative and relatively safe."

Fred looked down at his can of Dixie and seemed to fade away for a second.

"Jack," he said. "Can you prove any of this?"

"All of it," I said. "That programmer who was killed, Bob Sparks. He came to me with stacks of printout detailing every transaction made by any person, group, or company that looked suspicious for the last year. And they all led one place—Murphy. All of it can be traced back to him."

"Jesus." Fred sighed. "The civil sheriff."

"Charlie McCorkle, the vice president for Data Processing, is in on it, too. He was the one who designed the computer architecture that enabled the transactions to be buried so deeply. Charlie's also the one that killed the programmer. Seems Charlie has a taste for young boys and got a little carried away one night."

"How much money, Jack? Could you get a handle on it?"

"It's going to take a team of accountants to figure it out. But think about it. Six figures or so a day, every day, year round, for who knows how many years—"

"All in twenty- and thirty-dollar deals."

"You take one junkie with a five-hundred-a-day habit and multiply him by the total junkie population."

"Looking at some pretty good demographics there."

"Millions. Millions of dollars in the past year alone. And God knows how long it's been going on."

"You really think Mr. Jennings didn't know anything about this?"

"The one thing I know about him more than anything else is that he was the last one in the world to want money bad enough to get it that way. It's just too freaking sleazy.

Besides, why would he have fought Murphy and tried to bulldoze Iris if he was in on the Iris cash machine?"

He looked away for a second. "He wouldn't have."

"I don't think Carlton Smith knew either. It was Murphy, and Charlie McCorkle, and a few others, I'm sure. But it was mostly Murphy's doing. All his fault."

"This is amazing," Fred said. "Will you testify on this?"

"Absolutely."

"Now what about this guy at the apartment complex in Metairie?"

"His name's Alistair Robichaux. He's Murphy's 'driver,' one of his boys. He and two other guys were the ones that jumped me and Sally Bateman that night in the parking lot. Only they didn't mean to kill us. While Robichaux was working me over, the other two accidentally killed Sally trying to shut her up."

"How'd you find this out?" Fred asked, amazed.

"I had a conversation with Mr. Robichaux. I had to get a little . . . persuasive with him. It's all here, though." I reached into my jacket pocket and pulled out the tape. "Take good care of this. It's the only copy."

Fred took the tape from my hand.

"I think you can turn Robichaux," I said. "Maybe McCorkle, too, although you let him go without hard time I may pop him myself. The two guys who killed Sally wound up as fish bait for screwing up. Murphy's orders. It's all on the tape. The rest is out in the car."

Fred was real quiet for a few moments, staring down at the tape in his hand, as if he couldn't believe what had just been laid on him.

"Just tell me one thing, buddy, will you?"

"Sure," I answered.

"You're a public relations executive, Jack. What in the hell drove you to get mixed up in this mess in the first place? If everything you've told me is true, you get the Nobel Prize for having the biggest balls in the history of P.R."

I looked for an answer somewhere back in the past few weeks, the past few years.

"I didn't know when I started out that the stakes would be this high," I said. "It just seemed at every step of the way, somebody was throwing up something in front of me that didn't make sense. I kept having to make sense out of it, to put the world back in some kind of order. That was it in the beginning. Then they killed Sally."

"Sally?"

"Fred," I said, my voice starting to choke, "we were going to be married."

He brought his hand up to his face, shook his head, and closed his eyes as if he couldn't bear to look at me. "Jesus, Jack." He sighed. "I had no idea. Man, this is awful."

"I'm in P.R., Fred. None of this stuff's in my contract. I can't believe I've done some of the things I've done, but I have. And I have to live with that. I want him, Fred. It was all that sonofabitch Murphy's fault, and I want him."

"You're sure you want to testify on this? All the way to the limit?"

"Yes. Hell, yes."

"It might get a bit hairy for you," he said. "I'd hate to see anything happen to you. You still owe me a racquetball game."

"I'll be careful. I want Murphy's hide flapping in the breeze. Whatever it takes."

We talked on a bit longer, then paid the tab and walked out into the dark parking lot.

"What are you going to do first?" I asked.

"First thing is wake up my boss," he answered. "We got to move fast here. When Mr. Robichaux doesn't show up for work tomorrow, Murphy may start covering his ass."

"*Will* start," I corrected.

"If my boss okays it, which he will, I think we'd better go wake up Judge Gesell and get a restraining order barring the bank from opening. I'll have a warrant sworn out on Murphy. We'll take him into custody first thing. I'll have to notify the U.S. attorney and we'll have to get the Feds in here."

"You're going to have a long night," I said.

"Yeah, we both are. You want me to take you into protective custody?"

"Do you have to?"

"No."

"Then let's pass on that for the time being. I'll lay low."

I opened the passenger door on Sally's car and lugged out the folder and the huge printout. It was all there, my one and only copy. I was turning everything over to him, taking a bigger chance than I was comfortable taking.

"One thing, Fred," I said, as he locked it in the trunk of his car. "I came to you because the D.A.'s office is the last bunch I knew of with no ties to either Murphy or the Old Man. I heard scuttlebutt that the Old Man even had the U.S. attorney in his pocket, which means Murphy may have inherited him."

"Okay," he said.

"If you sit on this and don't nail that fat sonofabitch, or I find out he owns you, too . . ." I said, pausing.

"Yeah?" he asked.

"I'll fucking kill you."

I hadn't slept at all in about forty-eight hours, and not much the week or two before that. I should have been exhausted, but there was no way I was going to get any sleep this night. I drove the long way back into town, into the empty Central Business District, and parked across the street from the bank about 4:00 A.M.

The .38 was on the seat next to me, along with a pack of smokes. I lit one after the other and kept listening to the middle of the night preachers promising me I could still find peace, if I'd only send in a small donation. I hoped they were right. I might even send in a few bucks just to see if it works.

It was deathly quiet downtown this time of night. The streetcar rolled by, with only a couple of tired faces in the windows, every forty-five minutes or so. A few drunks, the normal contingent of homeless, displaced, disoriented, but mostly the streets were empty. I sat in the car and stared, my mind going blank with fatigue, until the sun started to peek over the tops of the buildings, slowly casting shadows, lighting the city up. Bringing it back to life. ı

The traffic picked up. The streetcars and buses began to be filled with suits and pin-striped skirts and high heels with briefcases instead of the sleepless with their bottles hidden in wrinkled paper sacks. I looked at my watch; it was nearly seven. Billy would be along soon, to take his place at the front door in his uniform, greeting people as he had for years. I hated that it was all about to be taken away from him. But it was only one regret of many.

At five minutes to seven, a line of cars came racing down the street, locking up brakes and squealing to a stop in front of the bank. About a dozen guys in suits piled out. Behind them came a gray armored car. The back door to the armored car popped open and another five guys hopped out in combat gear. They wore blue flak jackets with FBI on the back in huge yellow letters and pump-action shotguns cradled in their arms.

The raid was on.

One of the suits banged on the front door to the bank. The night security guard came to the glass door and shook his head. The suit waved a piece of paper and yelled, "Open up, district attorney's office!"

The night guard looked a little confused, then scared as he saw the FBI guys with the guns. He fumbled with his keys and opened the door.

I sat low in the front seat, watching. The stream of guys

poured into the bank, taking it over like an army invading a castle. It was all over in about ten minutes. The night security crew and the night staff of computer operators were all brought out in handcuffs, loaded into cars, and taken downtown for what I assumed would be a pretty thorough question-and-answer session. I didn't figure they'd know much; it was more a matter of having to scare the hell out of a lot of people as quickly as possible.

The regular staff started showing up around 7:15, and one by one, they were taken into the bank. The best one for me was when I saw Charlie McCorkle's car pull into the parking lot, then suddenly squeal tires as he saw what was going on. Before he could take a deep breath, a dozen guys with pistols and shotguns had his car surrounded. He came out quietly and was thrown across the hood of his car.

Twenty minutes later, a cab pulled up and Murphy got out. Robichaux didn't show up to pick him up at his hideaway in the Quarter and Murphy, probably aggravated as hell, grabbed a cab to get to work. Big mistake.

They took him out front and had the handcuffs on him in a New York minute. He yelled and puffed and screamed and threatened and it didn't do him a damn bit of good. I smiled on the inside as they stuffed his fat bulk into the back of one of the unmarked cars.

Suddenly, there was a tap on the window behind me. I whipped around with the pistol in my hand.

"Hey, easy!" Fred yelled through the glass. "Put that damn thing down before you get hurt!"

I reached across and opened the door. Fred slid in next to me.

"I wondered if you'd be here," he said.

"Wouldn't miss it for the world," I said dryly.

"Jack, Jack, Jack." He shook his head, smiling. "A soldering iron? I'm shocked."

"So was I. At least it wasn't a *working* soldering iron."

"Small comfort to Al Robichaux. You said he was trussed

up like a Christmas turkey; you didn't tell me he was the kind with the pop-up thermometer already in."

"Was he done?"

"My investigators said he was a babbling idiot by the time they got there. But he's talking."

"What's going on in there, Fred?"

"Murphy's office is sealed, the computer room is sealed. Our resident computer whiz has disconnected their modems. We've taken McCorkle and Murphy into custody. The Orleans Parish grand jury convenes in two hours. The U.S. attorney is bringing it to the federal grand jury this afternoon and going after him under the RICO statutes. We're going to try to get them all held without bond as flight risks. The biggest hassle is who's going to get him first."

"Good," I whispered. "That's good."

"What are you going to do, Jack?"

"I don't know, Fred. Maybe go home and try to get some sleep."

He put his hand on my shoulder. "Good idea, buddy. You look like you need it. If you don't mind, I think I'll have a cop stationed outside your house for a while. Okay?"

"Sure, whatever," I said. Fred, I'd decided, could be trusted.

All that was six months ago. And like a river's cascade wearing down the rocks, time has taken some of the rough edges off.

I testified before both the Orleans Parish grand jury and the federal grand jury. Once it started to cave in on them, it went down like a house of cards. The D.A.'s office turned Charlie McCorkle faster than a pretty boy in the joint. He started talking and they couldn't shut him up; the more he talked, the tighter the noose got around Murph. Charlie took immunity on the money-laundering operation and copped to voluntary manslaughter on the Sparks killing.

He'll be out in less than five. A bunch of other low-level staffers at the bank talked; most got off pretty light.

Alistair Robichaux went witness protection. He's probably in a condo in Phoenix somewhere, courtesy of the U.S. taxpayers.

The state bank examiners seized all the noncriminal records and closed the bank down until they could bring in their own people to handle the depositors' routine transactions. The First Interstate Bank of Louisiana, for all intents and purposes, ceased to exist the day of the raid. It opened up later, managed by the Feds. Murphy's trough, where he'd been stuffing his face for years, was suddenly and irrevocably shut down. The party was over.

Murphy was indicted shortly thereafter. The U.S. attorney's office let it be known that when the local D.A. finished with him, they wanted a piece of the action. The I.R.S. is also on Murphy like a real bad rash. Last week, his vacation home, his cars, his bank account, and his stock portfolio were all seized pending the very long series of audits coming up. Between the RICO seizures and the Zero Tolerance policy, Murphy was lucky to have a pot to spit in.

And to top it all off, they yanked his passport. Not that he'd ever have a chance to use it, you understand.

God, I'm howling. I love it.

Eventually, even his lawyers recommended he cop to the best deal he could get. The D.A.'s office, with Fred Williams as the head of the new Commission on Organized Crime, pushed him to testify against the guys who were actually running the street operations. Murphy cooperated, but even then wound up with twenty-five to life. He's in administrative segregation now at the state penitentiary up in Angola. He won't last, though. If his cholesterol count doesn't get him, somebody up there will score a few points with the bosses by cancelling his ticket.

The executors of the Old Man's estate had no interest

in the Iris Project. Iris survives to this day, the streets still alive with the loud voices hustling every prescription known, the only drug not available being the one that can cure human despair.

As for me, whoever eventually wound up running the bank sure wasn't going to want my bony little ass sticking around. So I turned in my resignation, packed my car, and hit the road. I went out west for a while, holing up in little out of the way places, picking up the New Orleans papers when I could find them just to keep in touch. We even made the national news a few times; this was corruption on a grand scale even for Louisiana. A lot of silver-haired politicians swelled with pride, I thought, at the prospect.

Ultimately, I made my way back to the state, stopping off for a few days to see Sally's parents. I went to the cemetery as well, for the first time, and sat there over her grave for a long while, just talking to her and kind of telling her how things wound up. I hope somewhere she's getting a kick out of all this. I tried to tell her parents more about us, but it came out awkward and clumsy. I left after a few days, assuring them that I'd see them soon. But we all knew I probably never would.

I'm kind of wandering now, in the general direction of the city. In time, I'll have to get back to my apartment and my life and find some semblance of direction. For now, I'm just taking a long needed rest. I've kind of gotten to where I can sleep a little now. My dental work and my ribs are squared away. The nightmares still come, but with each passing wave, they get a little easier. I still miss Sally more than I ever thought I could miss anyone, but each day finds the ache a little less profound. Soon, I'll have to go out again, as Robert Penn Warren wrote, "into the convulsion of the world, out of history and into history and the awful responsibility of time."

It's the way of the world, I guess.

It's funny, in a way, how things turned out. The people

I was once closest to are gone now: Jimmy, Katherine, the Old Man, Sally. By some strange and perhaps perverse twist of fate and destiny that I don't even pretend to understand, I'm a survivor. I'm alive in this world.

By God, I guess it's time I started acting like it.